LET SLEEPING DUKES LIE

EMILY WINDSOR

SENARA PRESS

This is a work of fiction. All names, characters, places and incidents are products of the author's imagination. All characters are fictitious and any resemblance to real persons, living or dead, is purely coincidental.

ISBN: 978-1-9161139-1-6

ASIN: B07CYZ1VZN

This book is written using British English spelling.

THE RULES OF THE ROGUE SERIES

An Earl in Wolf's Clothing (Book 1)

Merry Christmas, my Viscount (Book 2 - Novella)

Let Sleeping Dukes Lie (Book 3)

Marquess to a Flame (Book 4)

CONTENTS

1

KINDLE NOT A FIRE THAT CANNOT BE EXTINGUISHED.

(ENGLISH PROVERB. 1584)

Lady Castlethorpe's ball. No. 15 Berkeley Square. April 1815.

Full. Chiselled. Resolute.

Those delicious lips drew near. Slow, too slow, and her heart thudded with apprehension and hope. His eyes, a deep emerald, gleamed with want in the faint lantern light.

It would be perfect.

The gentleman breathed her name, husky and low in the sombre shadows, and he leaned closer, pressing her body to the fluted column at the concealed edge of the terrace, hands rising to her shoulders with an assured touch.

Her eyes fluttered closed in anticipation as breath drifted over her skin, warm and with a hint of…

Liver?

Aideen cracked open an eye.

The viscount's boyish face appeared comically contorted

as he pursed those full lips, rather like a pug straining for a sausage. The scent of liver puffed over her once more, causing her nostrils to twitch, but this time it intermingled with citrus cologne and a faint waft of damp linen.

Memories of a more potent kiss surged before her eyes, and with it came the scent of chocolate and leather.

Clean. Darkly bitter-sweet. Male.

Aideen hurriedly pulled away. "I'm so sorry, Lord Sherburn, but I just…cannot."

Stuttering, the poor chap opened befuddled eyes, arms dropping to his sides. "No, no. I… I should not have presumed, Miss Quinlan. Your Irish beauty has quite stolen my wits."

Pretty words to be sure, but Aideen sighed nonetheless.

The best part of a year ago, she'd been the recipient of her first kiss. A kiss she couldn't seem to forget, no matter how hard she tried.

Indeed, never did she think to receive such an embrace ever again as there was always something wrong with the gentlemen she met: too short, too broad, blue eyes, fat nose and now this. Liver and damp linen.

Lord Sherburn coughed, straightening his pleated cuffs. He was such a nice boy – eager and kind.

So why did visions of that enflamed kiss invade her mind so? Especially as the benefactor had been the glowering, priggish, pompous Duke of Rakecombe.

Perhaps it was because the top-lofty man had kissed in the same way he conducted himself – fierce but controlled. Ruthless. Those teeth grazing her neck, bruising passionate lips, his strong hands tang–

"Shall we make our way to the light, Miss Quinlan?" The viscount's gentle face smiled, eyes considerate. "We have tarried but a moment, and guests will presume we've merely been promenading. I can find your chaperone, should you so wish?"

Shaking her head, Aideen twirled a curl betwixt her fingers. "I believe I'll stay in the darkness a mite longer…to compose myself. Besides, do I hear your mother calling?"

The young man's countenance creased in worry and, sketching a hasty bow, he darted towards the soft glow spilling from the French doors.

Aideen slumped against the Doric column, wishing she'd never come to this awful ball.

Except for Lord Sherburn and a scarce few others, most of the gentlemen viewed her status as lower than a strand of slimy Irish seaweed, and she'd been regarded through female quizzing glasses so many times in the candlelight that surely her dress was scorched with little burn holes.

Mama may have been an English lady, but Aideen's wild black hair and Irish lilt proclaimed her da's lineage loud and clear.

Proper English ladies, of course, didn't wander onto terraces with young viscounts either, but all the guests had been too busy either disparaging or enjoying the scandalous waltz to notice a stray nobody.

A swift movement in the sooty night caught her eye and she straightened, peering into the austere garden.

Topiary seemed to be the prevalent fashion in this abode and tortured bushes twisted and strained, casting shadows of dragons and demons fighting their eternal battles.

The cravat appeared first. Stark white and stiff.

Thereafter, a tall midnight form coalesced around that snowy immaculateness, upright and commanding. A determined cane tapped on the York stone flags.

"For shame, Miss Quinlan," a deep aristocratic male voice drawled, "I am surprised the young pup did not wag his tail and yelp goodbye as you patted his head and sent him scurrying." He raised a gloved hand to his ear. "And hark, I hear no beckoning mother."

Aideen yearned to place her twitching fingers around the throat that uttered those sardonic words.

And squeeze, tightly.

Then kiss him senseless, smothering those firm, non-liver-breathing lips with bites until he gasped – although whether that was due to the kiss or her ever-tightening hand around his throat, she hadn't quite decided.

But over the past months, her distant relative and hostess for the Season, Mrs Beckford, had been teaching her poise and patience, so garnering all her newly learned expertise, she instead stepped forward and smiled pleasantly.

"Better a devoted young Labrador than a snarling old wolfhound…Your Grace."

Perhaps not *exactly* how Mrs Beckford expected her to greet a duke, but at least she'd managed not to curse him to hell…yet.

Aideen also remained mindful that to curtsey would be appropriate, curtsey and leave, as any unchaperoned young miss would not hesitate to do, but the little red devil who squatted permanently on her left shoulder whispered that was dull. Mrs Beckford's advice was, after all, purely that.

The last time she had seen Alexander Westhide, the Duke of Rakecombe, he had been sailing off into the sunset, literally, after he'd rescued her from a nasty little kidnapping Frenchman. She had thought they'd parted amicably but since then, she'd not seen sight nor sound of him. Nigh on a year without his cold burning stare.

She had thought he might…

Alas, her cousin Sophie had mentioned his reappearance in London late last summer, but their paths had not crossed, he had not called upon her, and Aideen had left town for the long winter months in Ireland, certain he had forgotten their amorous encounter.

And, admittedly, there was the fact she'd informed him that he kissed like a wet fish, so perhaps the fault was her own.

The moon cast its opalescent glow upon them, as though it had decided a little romantic lustre was necessary, and Aideen groaned at the unfairness of her perfect memory as his face became real.

She *had* hoped his eyes couldn't possibly be as intense as she recollected, or that he wasn't so forbiddingly tall. But needless to say, he was. All that and more, the damn English bug.

If she had to quibble, she would say his nose was a fraction overlong and possibly too thin, slightly hawkish, but sensuous lips, moulded cheekbones and lush lashes more than made up for any nostril disadvantage. Besides, she liked the way they flared with a brisk inhalation when he disapproved of something – mainly her.

As far as she could tell, the lone difference from last year was a certain leanness to his cheeks, but then Napoleon had escaped Elba in the previous month, war beset England once again, and she knew the duke was up to his neck in shady foreign affairs.

Leanness simply enhanced his callous stare.

She shivered, and it wasn't through fear.

"Did you enjoy the young pup's attentions, Miss Quinlan?"

"Er…"

The Duke of Rakecombe stepped forward, jet-black cloak swirling about him. She wasn't entirely sure how to answer, or in point of fact, why he had asked at all. But then, they never seemed able to have a normal conversation. He always riled with mocking words, and with her temper, she responded with blunt antagonism.

"Do you desire his callow touch?" he pressed again.

Aideen gulped as the ominous figure circled her, cane drumming on the stone, demanding an answer. She didn't turn. Didn't so much as move a muscle.

Two months of Mrs Beckford's etiquette lessons and not one half hour had dealt with how to reply to a haughty duke leaning far too close and taunting her with impertinent questions.

Warm breath disturbed the ringlets at her nape. Had his lips brushed her skin? The scent of chocolate floated over her shoulder, and she closed her eyes, every nerve humming his proximity.

"Did the pup quieten your shrewish tongue?" the duke whispered in her ear, and Aideen's eyes snapped open.

She spun to confront him and his cravat bobbed as he swallowed heavily.

A shrewish tongue had been the only way to be heard growing up, the only protection against her da's bitter comments. He had a voice like cannon fire and if you didn't stay sharp, the constant complaints and needless rebukes rubbed until you dulled like an overused hunting knife.

"Shrewish, am I? Well, may savage dogs eat your fee–"

"You have already used that curse." His lips quirked, so fleeting that if she hadn't been so close, so aware, she would have missed it.

"I beg your pardon?" she growled.

THE DUKE OF RAKECOMBE sighed and slicked back his hair with a firm hand.

What was he doing? What was it about this woman? And why had he even made himself known from the shadows?

No one answered.

All he did know was that he wanted to delicately carve up Lord Sherburn with the sprung blade nestled inside his ebony cane.

"You used that particular curse in Vauxhall Gardens, I recall, and I do not believe they serve twice."

Her livid eyes narrowed, and he cursed his own tongue with words more vulgar than dogs eating feet.

Vauxhall Gardens was where he'd first kissed her. He hadn't meant to. The plan, such as it had been, had involved distracting Miss Quinlan from her cousin's side in order that his comrade could arrange a tryst.

But it had all gone to hell.

Miss Quinlan had tripped in the dark and he'd halted her fall, but slender fingers had clutched at his lapels, full breasts had pressed at his chest, and before he'd been able to gain control, his wayward lips had been kissing her, all rational thought upended.

Purely the clattering of his fallen cane had brought back his senses.

And then she'd had the gall to slap his face and inform him he kissed like some aquatic creature – the wretched jade.

"I'm flabbergasted, Your Gracelessness," she retorted, "that you recall anything of that night. I can only suppose you'd imbibed too much punch. Some men cannot hold their drink."

Oh, how he wanted to punish that insulting mouth. Miss Quinlan had no restraint, no decorum, no veneration for his noble title.

He ought to stay far, far away.

He should stride off now.

He leaned down, lips meeting her heated cheek. "I remember everything, sweet cherry. The scent of violets clinging to your hair, the softness of your mouth despite the flow of blasphemies from your lips, the silkiness of your skin."

"And I recall," she snapped, that silky but stubborn chin turning, "how you looked nauseated as you wiped a hand across your mouth. How you called me a capricious saucebox and told me I kissed like a shrew."

Miss Quinlan's snarled repetition of his words that night reminded him of his motive for uttering them.

There were reasons far beyond her comprehension as to why he couldn't enjoy her acquaintance, and yet his treasonous body still refused to obey, his feet snubbed the order to walk in the opposite direction, his hands trembled to touch.

But his brain...his brain he could command. He wasn't known as a staid heartless prig for nothing.

This ruthless reputation hadn't been cultivated on some whim but to protect against closeness, against temptations such as Miss Aideen Quinlan.

With his perilous activities for the Crown, provoking dislike was wisest for all concerned.

So he stiffened his spine. Forced his eyes to winter. "And I meant every word," he stated coldly.

Most women would have cowed before his insult. Mayhap their lip would have quivered, or a bright tear might've gleamed in their eye. They would have vowed never to speak to him again, presuming him a callous bastard, and his world would once again become safe.

They would become safe.

Of course, he should have known that Miss Aideen

Quinlan would do no such thing.

When kidnapped last May, she'd scratched her ire into the Frenchman's face, and Rakecombe couldn't help the surge of protectiveness and admiration that assaulted him in equal measure as he recalled her strength, her wrath, her fire.

Miss Quinlan's lips firmed, and coyly, she peeped up at him. "To answer your earlier question, Your Grace, I did enjoy Lord Sherburn's attentions. So gentle and tender. Such soft hands. He knows how to delight a lady."

Jealousy and esteem warred within as he stared at those insubordinate coal eyes. "But like a mild doe, some women require delicate handling. Spitting cats, I have found, need firmer treatment, a strong hand at their scruff."

Her eyes flared and his whole body coiled in anticipation, awaiting…

"And churlish, covetous wolfhounds need a tight leash and muzzle. Mayhap I should purchase both for any future encounter we may have. Preferably in black to match your foul moods and clothing. Good night, Your Grace."

Rakecombe watched Miss Quinlan sashay across the terrace and into the light, a saucy swing to her hips.

So, she'd seek to tame him with a leash, would she? He wanted to laugh out loud but that wasn't very ducal.

"You can come out now, Bluey," he barked instead.

A lathy man materialised from behind a topiary cockerel, a smirk on his foxy face, and Rakecombe's eyes crossed as he attempted to observe both the retreating Miss Quinlan and the emerging informant.

They had agreed to convene here as Bluey had business in the area – he wouldn't ask what – and he himself had promised to accompany his mother home from this ball.

Dear *mater* was bound to have a litany of complaints in the carriage regarding his absence from the ballroom, his unmarried state, his disappearances, but at least it was only a short ride back to Grosvenor.

But then, as fate would have it, he'd spied the tame Sherburn drooling over the wild Miss Quinlan and temptation had beckoned.

"My apologies, Bluey, for the delay."

"No worries, Guv. I would've done the same. I likes a woman with bottom. And what a bottom," he said with appreciation.

Rakecombe momentarily considered poisoning Bluey with the secondary device in his cane, but he was an inordinately useful informant for the Crown, so instead he followed the chap's gaze.

The impudent Miss Quinlan swished through Lady Castlethorpe's French doors, that silk-clad bottom lovingly etched in the candlelight.

Indeed.

2

SUCH A HULLABALOO.

"Why did Miss Gibbon faint when I asked her to pass the platter of chicken thighs? Saints and their harps, she nearly toppled the entire supper table."

In answer to her question, Aideen received an exasperated purse of the lips from her friend Cordelia and a voluble sigh from Mrs Beckford.

Tapping her chin, she asked again, "Should I have requested the footman do it? But the thighs were only at her left elbow."

Mrs Beckford peered up from her embroidery hoop with puckered brow, a perfect silk lion adorning the material. "You should have requested the services of a footman, yes, but that was not the reason."

Cordelia, who'd capably sewed a magnificent rabbit, scooted close on the pink-striped sofa. "It was because you used that word."

"Which word? Chicken?"

"No," Cordelia replied, smiling wanly, although whether it was at chickens or Aideen's embroidery efforts, she wasn't sure. "The...body part," she whispered. "Body parts are unmentionable."

Bejabbers.

Aideen had suspected that might be the reason, but really?

Stabbing the white silk with her needle, she added a lolling tongue to her Irish wolfhound, a personal joke at the Duke of Rakecombe's expense, but the wolfhound jeered at her and more likely resembled a fire-breathing dragon.

They all sat in the drawing room of the Beckford house on Conduit Street, endeavouring to while away the morning fashioning cushion covers.

Never having had the patience for sewing, however, Aideen threw her hoop to one side and watched Cordelia as she dextrously twiddled her needle to produce an elegant French knot.

Without doubt, her young friend was extremely gifted at proper ladies' accomplishments and 'twas no wonder she'd become betrothed to Viscount Oakdean so early in the Season – embroidery aside, she also sang like an angel, played pianoforte like Mozart and had a peaches and cream complexion.

The only oddity to Cordelia was her mother, who insisted on dressing her in ruffles and treating her as though she belonged in the schoolroom – but no one should be blamed for their parents' peculiarities.

Aideen ought to have detested her, but to both their surprises, they had met and enjoyed each other's conversation during a tedious musical soirée. They appeared to bring out the best in each other, or in Aideen's case, she suppressed her worst tendencies in Cordelia's proper company.

Since losing her cousin and close friend Sophie Beckford

to marriage and rustication in the countryside last year, Aideen had felt rather adrift this Season.

Despite Mrs Beckford's admirable efforts, she didn't fit within the *Beau Monde.* She struggled to control her unruly tongue, mangled dance steps and ate too many lobster patties. She was too robust, loud and forward.

"Did Miss Gibbon *really* faint though?" She prodded Cordelia as Mrs Beckford wandered out to check on luncheon preparations. "Can one really faint simply at a word?"

An uncharacteristic grimace graced her friend's fair features, and Aideen was aware Cordelia had been in the doldrums for much of the morning, although the amount of lace around her collar was enough to put anyone in an itchy mood.

"Well, no...but that is not the point."

"What is the point then?"

"There were gentlemen present, and by swooning, she displayed her delicate feminine sensibilities."

"Pfff. If she'd missed that couch, she would have displayed more than her sensibilities."

Cordelia's lips curved, but no sparkle reached her bright-blue eyes. "Aunty Bridget says society is becoming staid. The slightest indiscretion and one is...ruined."

Huffing dramatically at the absurdity of fainting over a *thigh* faux pas, Aideen thanked Jesus, Mary, Joseph, all the disciples and the Holy Lamb that no one had discovered she'd been held against her will for more than a few hours by a scurvy French knave last spring.

Now that *was* an indiscretion of ruinous proportions.

The Duke of Rakecombe should probably also be thanked, as she was sure he had suppressed – or frightened – any gossipers.

But that would be adding the trait of kindness to his lack of personality.

A loud sniffing, and one look at Cordelia's pretty but woebegone face made Aideen huddle close. "What's wrong, Cordy? You've been sad all day. Has your handsome viscount been ignoring you?"

"No...it's... Oh, Aideen, I'm ruined!"

A bundle of frilly white muslin collapsed into her arms, sobbing uncontrollably.

Patting Cordelia's back, Aideen let her wail a short while before lifting her chin. "Did you mention thighs?" She stroked her friend's hair, becoming entangled with a lacy ribbon. "Has Lord Oakdean hurt you? I'll show you how to knee him in the nutm–"

"Aideen!" Cordelia cried, clamping hands over her ears and managing a soggy chuckle. "Don't mention any more unmentionable words. But no, it's...it's..."

"Yes?"

"My piano tutor."

Frowning, Aideen's shoulders slumped. How dull. "What's he doing? Making you learn scales? Patting your knee? I can show you how to twist his–"

"No. I... This is most embarrassing." A rose flush swamped Cordelia's wan cheeks. "I haven't seen him for an age, but at sixteen, I had a slight...infatuation, and I wrote poetry to him."

Aideen lurched back. "Did you?"

"Hmm. They were awful. I portrayed myself as a lamb and bid him be my shepherd."

"Eugh."

"Precisely. The problem is, I have received a note requesting I break my betrothal or my poems will be revealed."

"No!" Aideen cried. "But would it matter? Surely they're not that bad?"

"It isn't only that, although there was one about gambolling on the heath…" Cordelia coughed delicately. "No, it's just Lord Oakdean's relatives are such sticklers for propriety, especially his grandmother, and I believe she would then disapprove of our union and forbid it."

"But Oakdean loves you. Surely he won't fash over some foolish old poems."

Cordelia scrunched her dejected face. "He hasn't actually told me he loves me. And he did request a long engagement."

"Oh."

"Hmm."

Tapping her lip, Aideen mulled. "Have you spoken to your piano tutor?"

"Yes. I sent a message asking him to meet me at Hatchards. I took my maid of course, and…and…"

"And?"

"He told me it wasn't him who'd sent the blackmail note but admitted my poems had been…sold!"

Aideen gasped. "Lawks, they must have been good then. Will they be serialised?"

"No!" Cordelia wailed. "He sold them to Viscountess Gibbon. Her daughter, the fainting one, was always the favourite choice of Oakdean's grandmother, and I'm certain she means to betroth the delicate flower to him. The beastly blackmailing…so-and-so."

There were many words Aideen might have chosen but Cordelia was ever polite.

Stroking her friend's hand in consolation, she set her mind to work. "But surely this is all a smidgeon melodramatic."

"Oh, Aideen," her friend wailed again, "have you not observed the underhand deeds at these balls?"

"Well, not when there are lobster patties to be had and if they happen to have scotch eggs too, I'm oblivio–"

"According to the gossip columns and naming no names, a certain Miss R laid a piece of string across the library at Mr O's last month, causing Lord G to trip and fall straight into her bosom. They are now engaged. And Lady U trapped Sir E in the retiring room with a pink muff."

"Are they engaged?" Aideen asked, thoroughly confused.

Cordelia frowned. "No. He's gone to the Continent. Better Napoleon than Lady U's sisters, I suppose. But that's not the point." She stared darkly. "It's a predator's lair in the ballroom."

Breath stuttered in Aideen's throat as she imagined the black-clad Duke of Rakecombe prowling some glittering event, snarling at any debutante that got in his way, swiping with clawed paw at any badgering marriage-minded mothers…or was that marriage-minded badgers.

Either way, there was always a bigger predator.

"I will have a ponder, Cordelia. Anyone who faints at thighs cannot be allowed to get away with such wickedness."

Staring at the mantelpiece in consideration, Aideen smiled. Amid the stack of correspondence, if memory served, sat an invite to Lady Gibbon's ball on Wednesday.

Coincidence or divine intervention?

Finally, some intrigue to enliven the Season.

THE DUKE OF RAKECOMBE'S stomach gurgled and he held a palm to the un-ducal noise. How dare it.

His mother had obtained a new French chef, a certain

Monsieur Pascale Dupont, for the Rakecombe residence, but something was…off. Always the sauce was over-peppered or the meat too rare – his lamb had practically bleated its displeasure from the plate last night.

"Apologies, Rakecombe, I'll be with you in a jiffy."

He surveyed the man that kept him waiting.

Busy scribbling away, Lord Rainham was one of the principal spy coordinators here at Whitehall. Honoured with the rank of viscount last year for saving a bosky duke from poisoning – not himself, obviously, but Cousin Humphrey twice removed – Rainham was a somewhat strange chap. Nevertheless, this steadfast leader commanded Rakecombe's profound respect.

His gaze wandered; the office appeared as well-ordered as ever, but even here something else was…off.

Over the past months, he'd perceived a difference in the newly ennobled Lord Rainham. He'd put it down to Napoleon, the cause of all ills, but there felt more to it, something he couldn't quite put his finger on.

Lord Rainham had more grey hairs but didn't look so tired as usual, despite the desperate situation on the Continent. In fact, he looked in fine fettle as he set the ink well to an exact angle and steepled his fingers.

Documents were perfectly aligned on his desk.

Maps covered the walls, pinned at equal distances.

Quills remained raised, ready for flight.

A single white lily stood to attention in a tall crystal vase left of the desk. What the–

"We have a traitor in our midst."

Those blunt words put paid to Rakecombe's unease over deviant blooms. "Who?"

"I don't know but two of my men have gone missing along with some valuable documents."

"How important are these documents?"

"They include a list of informants."

"Dear God," snapped Rakecombe, hitching forward. "If that falls into the wrong hands..."

"Exactly. I'm investigating how the documents were taken, but we need to locate these men, Stuart Penbury and Gabriel Stafford. Use your network to find out whatever you can. Are they alive? If so, were they coerced? Or have they turned on us?" Rainham smoothed the desk with a palm. "Both have been with me for years, recruited from the army, but this is too much of a coincidence."

"Any of their family missing?"

Rakecombe thumbed the silver filigree adorning his cane. Last year, he'd put a bullet in the whoreson who'd abducted Miss Quinlan, a putrid villain who enjoyed kidnapping the relatives of key persons in the government and military in order to extort information, but his body had never been recovered from the river estuary depths into which he'd fallen...

"Not as far as I'm aware. Penbury's roots are in the north and Stafford was raised in an orphanage. Purely on gut instinct," Rainham continued, "I believe Penbury to be the weaker. Stafford has always been blunt but dedicated. Descriptions and so forth are with my secretary."

"Very well. Anything else?"

"Yes, take Winterbourne with you. I have the perfect mission for him coming up, but some preparation would do no harm."

"Must I?" he growled, stamping his top boot in impatience. He worked better alone. Superfluous people just got in the way.

"Don't feign joy on account of my delicate feelings,

Rake*hell*," a jovial voice lobbed from the doorway. "Where have you been lurking, my dear fellow? It's been an age."

"Not long enough, I'm sure," he replied, standing to greet the Marquess of Winterbourne with a vague modicum of warmth. And *why* did the marquess always feel the need to disparage his noble title? His Viking ancestors wouldn't have put up with it. "I've been busy, as unlike some, I also tend to my estates."

The modish smiling Winterbourne was a well-known rogue, but Rakecombe had to admit a miniscule liking for the affable fellow despite his lascivious habits. Wouldn't let him know that, of course – he had a pitiless nature to uphold, after all.

Briefly, he wondered how the marquess would handle a night out in the seamier side of London... Well, they would find out soon enough. The thought of the enemy with their grubby paws on a document listing covert names brought bile to his throat and urgency to his step.

"I'll have you know I work tirelessly at my estate," Winterbourne replied, eyes twinkling.

"Seducing milkmaids is not work."

"Faugh! Never in my life have I touched an estate milkmaid. In truth, half of them are probably relations as dear departed Father was rather prolific in his youth...and later years...and middling–"

"I must leave you gentlemen now," Rainham interrupted. "I'm for home, as there is an eighty-four per cent chance of rain by the hour of six."

A little taken aback, they both glanced over as their leader gathered his greatcoat and hat.

As long as Rakecombe had known him, he'd never seen Rainham leave his office – ever. He'd thought their leader slept here, and possibly that a clerk came in every morning to wind him up like a mechanical automaton.

"Give my regards to Lily," said Winterbourne, smiling broadly, "and thank her for the advice on Tamesworth shipping. I made a cod of blunt."

Rakecombe stared in unmitigated horror as Rainham nodded and, after centring his chair beneath the desk, headed for the door with indecent haste.

Turning to Winterbourne, he met a smug expression. "Who the bloody hell is Lily?"

"Ah, sweet Lily," the chap mused. "All thanks to me… again. Thought I might change my name to Lord Cupid." The smug expression became smugger. "No one – well except me – is impervious to *amour*, even Rainham. In fact, the taller you are, the harder you fall on your arse." He raised a brow in perusal. "Have you grown loftier in my absence?"

Glowering seemed to have no effect on the irritating marquess, so fixing his hat and donning his cloak, Rakecombe opened the door. "After you…Moth."

Winterbourne's face fell to a scowl.

Their leader always assigned meticulously considered code names to his men and the unfortunate marquess had been saddled with a flying lepidopterous insect.

Mind you, Rakecombe's own wasn't much better.

As they strode from Whitehall, he nonchalantly asked the question that had been nagging him. "What do you know of a young Lord Sherburn? Any vices?"

Deliberately not catching the eye of the man matching his stride, he marched faster and city folk shot out of the way like billiard balls.

"Pleasant chap. Nothing out of the ordinary. Why?"

"No reason," he asserted coldly. That tone ended conversations without fail.

"Not a cherry-lipped Miss Quinlan reason, by any chance? He's courting her, I understand."

Rakecombe turned into busy Pall Mall. Surely that would be an end to it. A buxom matron in green shuffled across his path and he veered, causing her to totter in his wake.

"She asked after you, last year," continued the annoying bugger. "Worried about you."

What should he say to that? He'd spent the past summer in France, even missing his friend Kelmarsh's wedding, but on his return, he'd purposefully stayed away from that Irish lure, reminding himself once more of the dangers of becoming too close to others.

Miss Quinlan hadn't been the first to be hurt by his carelessness, and he would ensure it never happened again.

He ploughed directly through the middle of a group of young bucks blocking the pavement, might have trodden on someone's foot, but no one complained.

"Sherburn will suit her," Winterbourne wittered. "Nice fellow."

Would the man not shut his bloody bonebox? This wasn't some intimate tête-à-tête. "Bah," he found himself declaring. "He is a stripling."

"I agree his taste for pastel waistcoats is a dash disconcerting but–"

"And an unfledged greenhorn. Who else has shown an interest?" He twisted to see Winterbourne raise a dark brow, so he merely stared down imperiously, marching on. "I feel a certain concern after her rescue, 'tis all."

And *concern* was all he would allow – the memory of his own dear Gwen would ensure that. He would protect Miss Quinlan from himself even if it meant his misery and her loathing.

"Hmm, concern, eh?" The marquess winked. Bloody

winked. Perhaps he should just stab the rogue with his cane and give all the widows a well-earned rest.

"Who else?" he repeated.

A mother plucked her son from the pavement as it became obvious the duke's velocity was not going to slow for a meandering tot.

"Well, there's Cambourne," Winterbourne said, ticking off his fingers and avoiding a purple ostrich plume from an ornately embellished hat.

"Lecher," Rakecombe snarled.

"Wilson."

"Gambler."

"Tythmore."

"Skinflint."

"Cockfield."

"The obvious."

"You?"

St James's Street was somewhat crowded – otherwise he'd consider deploying his cane so that Winterbourne couldn't sit for a month.

"One day, Winter*bore*," he purred instead, "I shall enjoy watching a woman take you apart till you plead for mercy."

"Hmm," the vexing rogue muttered, "I never took you, the strait-laced duke, as having a thrill for voyeurism, but I can probably arrange something with my little opera dancer. Millie can–"

"I am for White's," he interrupted, not in the slightest amused. "Meet me at The Cooper's Arms on Rose Street. Friday. And wear something inconspicuous. We will be heading for the Rookery."

With a devil's gleam, Winterbourne saluted and turned, ambling towards Brooks's whilst tipping his hat at a pretty girl.

Banishing cherry-red lips from his disloyal brain, Rakecombe glowered and strolled to his club for a decent plateful of grub and some careful planning.

Before the Rookery, there was another useful source of information to tap and he would need to take the utmost care.

3

WHAT SHALL WE BE TODAY? SWEET OR TART?

"Thighs, forearms…arse." Aideen ran through all the words that might cause Miss Gibbon to faint, although at this moment, she would prefer the girl's mother, Viscountess Gibbon, to collapse in an untidy heap.

The lady was waltzing with the Duke of Rakecombe and both seemed to be having a grand time of it.

Earlier, Aideen had noted his arrival at the Gibbon's ball, but he'd barely glowered an acknowledgement from his position by the gold jardinière, chinwagged with other nobles and then guzzled all the pigeon pie – a disapproving effigy of spotless black and white.

A few ladies had attempted to talk to him, but he'd peered at them as though inspecting rodents, before nodding and turning away. Not exactly a direct cut, but definitely a light graze.

Then to everyone's surprise, he had requested a dance with their hostess, and even from across the room, Aideen had seen the mesmerised expression on Lady Gibbon's face. He might have a disagreeable reputation, but when he chose to express some charm, they fell like delicate maidens faced with a thigh.

The duke also danced superbly, elegant but without excess, and Lady Gibbon closed her eyes in apparent ecstasy every time he tugged her into a turn. The damn bug – life would've been so much easier if he'd twirled like a prancing fop.

Scowling, she crossed her arms and tapped her foot, causing a matron to frown her disapproval.

For nigh eleven months, she hadn't set eyes on the duke and now this was the second time in a sennight. She hadn't expected to find him at Lady Gibbon's ball, as it was quite a crush of colour, and he stood out like a sultry panther in a jungle of chattering parrots.

Lady Gibbon obviously had a taste for…the ornate. Gold, golden and more gold adorned the ballroom, paining the eyes and causing a judder.

"Overwhelming," Mrs Beckford had stuttered as they'd entered. "Overdone," Aideen had mumbled.

"Miss Quinlan, your ratafia." A glass appeared before her, held by a soft white hand. "I apologise for my tardiness."

Oh, why did Lord Sherburn have to be so…so…nice! And why couldn't she adore such niceness? And why didn't she like sweet ratafia? And lilac waistcoats? What was wrong with her? She must have been born with some kind of shortcoming.

Her bosom friend Sophie adored the quiet life she now led with her genial husband, but for some reason, which Aideen had never been able to quantify, she herself preferred tension, excitement and – she glared across the ballroom floor – men who wore black and hissed at you.

"Thank you, Lord Sherburn. I believe I'll re-join Mrs

Beckford." Abruptly, she cocked her head. "Is that your mother calling?"

The agreeable chap hastily agreed, bowed, and set off in the direction of a short, frowning woman in yellow.

Aideen could almost hear the Duke of Rakecombe drawl in her ear, "Dismissed like a puppy... You need a firm hand."

An uninvited shudder took her but instead of heading for Mrs Beckford, she strolled towards the ladies' retiring room, swapping the insipid glass of red sweetness for champagne along the way.

The hallways were a blessed relief. A cloying aroma lay like fog over the ballroom, and under that nebulous layer was not clean air tickling the nostrils, but a ripe stench.

She wended her way down the lantern-lit passageway, meandered straight past the ladies' retiring room and on up the marble staircase, leaving her empty glass by a rudely grinning satyr.

A day ago, she had bumped into the not-very-honourable Miss Gibbon on a jaunt to the Tower of London to view the Crown jewels. Having managed to avoid verbally expressing any body parts...or lock her away, Aideen had instead wheedled from the fake swooner the layout of the Gibbon family's townhouse.

Toadying did not come naturally to Aideen, but every time she'd gushed over the prospect of viewing their elegantly decorated gold drawing room, she'd thought of Cordelia's glum face; she had to locate those sheep poems.

After counting the doors on the left until she came to the fifth, Aideen lightly knocked, in case a maid was poodling around. No answer came from within and so with a twist of the handle, she opened the door and peered into Lady Gibbon's bedchamber.

Eugh.

She withdrew for a moment, allowing her eyes to adjust.

Blinking, she rounded the door and closed it behind her.

Draped in a plethora of gilt and red, the room was lit by a huge candelabra with winsome nymphs gaily cavorting.

Once, when young, Aideen had mistakenly visited Mrs O'Hare's brothel. She had thought it was the dressmaker, and assuredly there had been a plethora of sheer material and pretty girls to model the clothes, but the decor had been more ornate than the altar at Waterford Cathedral. This was similar...

With no time to dally, however, Aideen began to methodically snoop for Cordelia's poems, beginning with the dressing table.

Every time scruples invaded, which was often as she kept encountering frilly jonquil garters and silk stockings, she reminded herself that the woman was a blackmailing witch, and besides, tonight she'd pressed her lithesome body against the Duke of Rakecombe's like one of Mrs O'Hare's trollops.

She became engrossed in a chest of drawers that held a stack of IOUs, some of which, curiously, had her acquaintance Lord Winterbourne's name attached to them.

What on God's green earth was Jack doing wit– A sudden creak of floorboard caused her to startle.

But her retreat was too slow as a shadow of black descended, whirling her back against a man's tall shape, a rough hand thrust upon her mouth, halting the shriek.

It could not contain her teeth, however, and she bit into the palm.

A harsh curse ensued but the hand did not remove itself. Instead, she was pulled more tightly against a solid, wiry torso, and a firm band pressed against her waist: his other arm and...something else.

She twisted and bit harder, only to induce a grunt and a further hauling.

"Stop wriggling, cherry," a voice whispered. "But do keep biting, I find it rather pleasant."

With the words came chocolate. Rich and dark.

Aideen continued to wriggle but released her teeth – the arrogant tongue-pad – and pushing her hands out, she discovered the firm press against her waist was his devilish cane.

Naturally, she knew what that cane concealed as her Uncle Seamus had crafted the piece.

A snarling silver dog with green eyes sat atop the ebony weapon, guarding its secrets. She'd even polished the jade orbs herself. It was how she'd discovered the duke was a spy, as her uncle had always fashioned special pieces for the War Department. Secret commissions with detailed compartments and fiendish traps.

"Remove your poisonous cane from my waist, you foul…*duke*," she mumbled against his large palm. Really, why did he turn her insults to mush? "And why do you call me cherry all the time?"

The hand removed itself, but a finger loitered, brushing her lips.

Silence fell for a moment.

Aideen was acquainted with at least five manoeuvres that would remove his other arm from around her waist, as Uncle Seamus had taught her many essentials for life in London, but for some reason she stilled, suffering that rubbing finger and awaiting his answer.

"It was actually Winterbourne who gave you the name. My cherry itch."

Oh, that was disappointing. And made her sound like fleas on a hound.

"But it suits you," he murmured huskily as his touch outlined her lower lip. "What will you be today – sweet or tart, I wonder?"

She bit the wandering finger and thumped an elbow into his gizzards.

"Tart, then."

"What are you doing here?" Miss Quinlan huffed, and he grudgingly released her warm body.

Rakecombe could ask the same question but one shouldn't hurl stones in houses of glass and he needed to make haste, but…

Miss Quinlan looked exceptional – prickly hauteur evident, swathed in the palest of blue silks.

After their…tussle, her breath was fast, and he willed his gaze to rise.

It aided not – livid eyes, sable curls and cherry-red lips. He couldn't say which feature stood out – perhaps none, but they all contributed to a delicate yet tenacious visage.

"I expect I've better reason than you to be here," he drawled, before discerning the very moment her sharp mind deduced he'd been personally invited to the fawning Lady Gibbon's bedchamber.

He couldn't help the small jolt of pleasure as her eyes crinkled with what he would like to call hurt. Her strong fists clenched in her silk gown, lips thinning in…jealousy?

It would be nice to know he wasn't the only one besieged by a certain mocking green-eyed monster.

"I thought you'd have better taste," she snarled.

Yes, definitely jealousy and he smiled with satisfaction, causing those bottomless eyes to flash with ire. He couldn't have Aideen Quinlan, but it didn't mean he wasn't able to play a little… He'd take a leaf from Winterbourne's book for once. "Lady Gibbon, or Myrtle as I like to call her, has a fine–"

A strident female voice from the hallway snapped him from his taunts.

Damnation, he didn't have time for this as informants' lives were at risk. The Irish minx scattered his wits.

Rapidly, he scanned the room. They couldn't be found here, for many reasons, and Miss Quinlan seemed to realise the same, as she rushed to the long delicate curtains concealing the balcony French doors.

Earlier, however, he'd noted the shutters had been kept open and if they hid behind those curtains and the moon dared to cast its glow, they'd be lit up as a silhouette tableau.

"No, the wardrobe," he hissed, striding over to it.

"No," she hissed back. "In stories, they always hide in the wardrobe and always get found."

Returning an exasperated glower as the voices neared, he nevertheless opened the wardrobe but found it would plainly give no quarter. Below the array of vivid dresses sat rows and rows of small boxes, each with a letter of the alphabet.

He tapped his cane on the letter P, one task solved, but as for the other…

Quietly, he closed the door and grabbing hold of Miss Quinlan, he hauled her to a tall gilt screen painted with flying cherubs part folded in the far corner of the room.

Squashing behind the sturdy florid eyesore, they both stood silent and still as the door rattled on its hinges.

"What a disaster, Simpson," bemoaned Lady Gibbon, rustling into the room.

"Yes, my lady."

More rustling.

"Lord Stewart is a caw-handed bottle-head. Red wine all down my Prussian blue silk dress. The man is blind."

"Yes, my lady."

The sound of buttons slipping.

"And not only that, but Lord Barnett's wig fell in the punch, and Lady Blackburn nearly set light to her turban on my Ormolu gilt and marble candelabra – silly trollop."

A light choke and Rakecombe glared down at Miss Quinlan in the shadows, fist held to her mouth, eyes dancing with hilarity. Slowly he raised a finger to his lips.

She removed her hand and stuck her tongue out, the juvenile jade. If she wasn't careful, he'd–

"And as for that stiff-rumped, priggish, Duke of Restraint – did you understand my humour there, Simpson? – turning up in those tight black pantaloons and then having the effrontery to decline my invitation for a more private viewing – the hoity-toity, omnipotent hog-grubber!"

More rustling and thumping could be heard, but Rakecombe's gaze was intent on the night-haired beauty before him, whose mirth-filled eyes first wandered over those same pantaloons and then lingeringly rose.

She licked her lips and he regretted wearing the apparel. Brummel's blasted fault, and the arbiter of fashion was so deep in debt it was difficult to catch the fellow to complain. Indeed, he owed Rakecombe two hundred pounds.

"The duke asked me to dance, did you know that, Simpson?" Lady Gibbon continued.

"No, my lady."

"Well, he did. A waltz. A very intimate waltz. And it's not solely his arrogance that's large, the puffed-up nodcock. And then he just collected that stupid cane and left. Left my ball!" she shrieked in crescendo.

"Yes, my lady."

. . .

AIDEEN DIDN'T KNOW where to place her eyes.

She couldn't look down. But equally she couldn't look up because deep within, something bad was happening.

It tickled her throat and she bit her lip.

But still it welled, and finally she decided upwards was the better option. Surely a blast of Rakecombe's frigid stare would quell any amusement.

If His Grace had scowled sternly or ground his jaw in flinty castigation, all may have been well.

But he didn't.

Despite portraying a study in stillness, a faint quirk rippled his lower lip and spinach eyes sparkled, softening his severe face. And in that moment, she realised something profound.

Yes, Rakecombe was strait-laced and ruthless, but he was also sardonic and dry and could see the funny side of life, even though he chose to never show it.

In response, her own lips quivered, lacking his self-discipline, and before she knew what was happening, the merest squeak of laughter absconded.

Lady Gibbon was thankfully extolling the delights of an alternative gentleman's snug pantaloons, water splashing, and so Aideen's whimpers went unheard, but for how long?

Without warning, large hands covered her ears and she was tugged forward, firm lips descending upon hers. Unstirring, they simply swallowed all sound, all breath.

Intense warmth and inherent strength.

Shock erased the tickling in her throat, obliterated any laughter.

His lips withdrew.

Palms still shielded her ears but other senses sharpened.

The fragrance of linen – clean, masculine and…dry.

The silk of his waistcoat caressing her skin.

The clenched jaw and penetrating eyes.

Those immodestly displayed thighs in tight pantaloons pressing against her skirts.

All amusement was forgotten and her hands which had hung loosely to her side now rose to slide up his chest. And although she couldn't hear voices, there remained one sound. The thud of a heart. Rapid and deep. The thud sped as she huddled against him and buried her nose in the expensive silk, breathing his scent.

Contentment flowed through her. An unfamiliar emotion, as most of the time she seemed to veer from anger to joy, never balanced. But for now, when neither of them could bandy words or drawl insults, she felt steadied. Secure.

Rakecombe, she suspected, was feeling anything but. His fingers began to caress the curls at her ear, and his breathing, she noticed, became laboured, chest heaving.

Why did they have this attraction?

She should be so far below his notice that he could tread on her and not detect a bump to his stride.

A door slammed, a sound she heard even through his broad palms.

For a time, neither stirred, until slowly his hands slid down to cup her chin, raising her head until their gazes met.

No laughing eyes, no smirking lips. He appeared…sorrowful.

"They have gone," he said simply.

Aideen drew away – as did the feeling of contentment.

Briefly, she considered asking why he had kissed her but didn't want to hear some drawled retort about halting her tongue, wasn't willing to lose that last remnant of warmth, still tingling her skin.

In silence, they rounded the ornate screen, and she wondered at his reasons for being in this chamber.

Was Lady Gibbon a spy as well? She wondered until the moment he opened the wardrobe.

"And whose initial are *you* looking for?" he asked quietly.

She gawked at the neat boxes. "I… I don't understand."

"Lady Gibbon likes to blackmail members of the ton and anyone else beneficial. Usually for trifling reasons, like attending her dreary balls, but occasionally she turns up something useful. What does she hold over you, Miss Aideen Quinlan?"

"Not me. A friend of mine. You must promise not to–" She stopped herself. How foolish. This man was a spy for the Crown – he didn't care for the poems of a child. Abruptly, she felt small. No match for a duke of the realm. "Initial G for Greenwood. There are some poems."

Riffling through the stuffed box, he raised a brow, tilting the paper towards an alabaster nymph clutching a candle. "'I frolicked upon the heath with my beloved shepherd.'"

"Er. That does sound like them, yes. There are four in total."

His brow rose ever ceiling-wards as he handed her the scrawled papers.

She waited whilst he riffled through boxes inscribed with S and P, stuffed some papers in his coat, and then neatly placed them back in their slots, closing the wardrobe door on the sleeping secrets.

"I trust you will keep silent about tonight, Miss Quinlan?"

"Of course, Your Grace."

How polite they both were. She longed to ask what emotion he'd felt behind that screen but sensed the Duke of Restraint was back – unyielding and withdrawn.

The hideous candelabra's glow cast a lustre upon his hair,

and she realised that unlike her own cold-toned black locks, the duke's held a deep redness – warm and rich, such a dichotomy to his icy visage.

He hustled her to the door and, after checking the way was clear, instructed she turn left towards the staircase.

Nodding her compliance, she watched as he straightened his tailcoat and then strode in the opposite direction. No worded goodbye or brief smile – he just walked away.

But as the duke disappeared silently into the shadows, Aideen turned and tiptoed back into Lady Gibbon's bedchamber.

Temptation beckoned to find anything she could within the box marked R of that wardrobe of secrets, but instead she crossed the room, peered behind the elaborate screen and grabbed the ebony cane left propped there against the wall.

Perhaps she wasn't the only one feeling a little out of sorts.

4

NEVER JUDGE A ROGUE BY ITS COVER.

The Cooper's Arms heaved with brawlers, scantily clad doxies and the occasional young buck looking to lose his purse, but Rakecombe ignored them all and tucked into his rabbit pie, the best thing he'd eaten all week.

Hunger did make the best sauce.

Despite his grumbles, Mother still refused to dismiss Monsieur Dupont, asserting the chef needed to settle in, and he ruminated as to whether Dupont was in fact a devotee of Napoleon, poisoning the British aristocracy from within their own homes.

Little did those dastardly French know, however, that the men and women of this little island had cast-iron stomachs – growing up on boiled vegetables and incinerated beef.

He reached for his cane but clenched air; 'twas akin to losing a limb.

For years, he had carried a special walking cane, adapted to contain sprung blade and poison, and never, not once, had it left his side. He'd even had the tailor sew a special loop on his breeches and greatcoat to secure it.

Scowling, he quaffed his ale. It was all *her* fault.

And it wasn't even as if he could now avoid her, as the capricious saucebox had sent a violet-scented note saying she had the "*stick*", and he could collect it at Mrs Beckford's musical soirée on Monday evening.

Lady Gibbon, it seemed, wasn't the only one with a taste for blackmail – as if he'd normally attend an event on Conduit Street; he had a reputation to uphold.

A couple of patrons glanced his way, but he curled a lip and their eyes hastily shifted direction.

If only that worked on Aideen Quinlan.

He recalled her softness behind that damned screen. Hellfire, he could have simply put a hand over her mouth to halt the giggles, but no, he'd thought of a superior way.

Fool.

Consequently, he'd have to anticipate some scathing insults for the soirée. Something to raise her indignation, to cause a slap, to make her despise the very sight of him…

It had always worked on chits before but in this instance, it disheartened him. He enjoyed too much Miss Quinlan's pert words, her sparkling black eyes, those cherry lips…

"There you are, skulking in the corner."

Glancing up, he snorted. "I said appropriate attire and you choose a red waistcoat."

The Marquess of Winterbourne frowned, fingering the silk and plonking himself on the bench opposite. "*Au contraire,* Rakehell. This natty colour is coquelicot, and I'll have you know these togs are all the crack for flashy arch villains of Rum-ville. I'll blend in like a virgin at Almack's."

Rakecombe eyed the poppy waistcoat and doubted it would make it out of St Giles. He'd deal with the abomination of his title later. "We will wander the Rookery and meet with some of my contacts, but I also have the name of a house on Bainbridge Street that Penbury was frequenting. I am unsure of its…use but we'll find out soon enough."

Indeed, Lady Gibbon's blackmail notes had held little value except for that snippet.

"What about Stafford? Have you been able to establish his whereabouts?" asked Winterbourne, who without so much as a twitch of the hand or nod of the head received a jug of ale and a wink from the pretty barmaid.

"He has vanished as though a ghost, but from all accounts the fellow is forthright yet trustworthy. His forte, however, is infiltration of Bonapartist factions so I presume he's a canny sort."

Pulling on his black leather gloves, Rakecombe noted the squashed faces of two bare-knuckle combatants head to a back room. The alehouse's nickname of Bucket of Blood wasn't for nothing, but he hoped the crooked-nosed one remained standing; he'd wagered five pounds on him.

"We had better not go by titles this evening," he commanded Winterbourne. "You may call me, for one solitary night, Alex."

"Good Lord! You have a given name?" The rogue fell back, hand to brow. "I considered you born into this world a Rakecombe. Popped out with tight cravat and cane, gurgling your displeasure."

"Amusing…Jack."

"I know, but one doesn't like to sound one's own trumpet. Well," he said, straightening the red silk monstrosity adorning his chest and draining his ale, "let us rush in where angels fear to tread. I have a feeling amusement will quickly wane in St Giles."

JACK WAS CORRECT.

They cut down a side alley signed, coincidently, Angel Street – a misnomer if ever he had heard one, both for its occupants and themselves.

It constantly amazed him how one could be standing amongst the glittering houses of the ton one moment, and then, with a sideways step in the wrong direction, be walking amongst dwellings exuding filth and poverty.

Elegant London squares gave way to putrid lanes; gleaming shops became flash houses; light ebbed in the narrow alleyways; and drabs cried their wares, every sin available.

And yet despite the miasma of danger, people went about their everyday lives. Washerwomen gabbled over wet linen, grubby ragamuffins played marbles on the steps of an orphanage, and a toothy old crone sold cloth from a wagon – probably the fate of Winterbourne's waistcoat tonight.

In silence, they continued onto Long Acre, and avoiding Seven Dials, he conducted Jack via King Street, purposely taking him beyond their destination and further down Dyott Street where Rakecombe paused.

Wishing his cane wasn't in Miss Quinlan's possession, he instead stabbed out a leather-clad finger. "That abode with the red curtains is the Charity Hospital which you paid to have refurbished after the brewery flood."

Jack startled, gazing up at a drab building with a spotless entrance. "What? I don't–"

Rakecombe just smiled. "I thought you'd like to see it."

"How the devil do you know about that?"

"As patron I'm required to approve donations. Make sure you're not all mouth and no blunt. You, at least, have both in abundance."

"Patron? I..." Jack spluttered.

Pursing his lips, Rakecombe debated how much to share.

Twenty-three women currently lived there, largely prostitutes with disease or awaiting childbirth, although any woman was welcome if they wished to escape the Rookery. There were other hospitals, but this one was closest to his heart. A woman called Mary Lane ran it with a strict head and a soft soul, having experienced the worst that mankind could offer.

"Hmm," he merely said.

"I read of the incident," Jack reflected. "Buildings destroyed and eight people died, did they not? Including children. I prayed they didn't drown. People say it's a peaceful death, but…I cannot imagine it so."

Rakecombe frowned. He'd forgotten… What platitudes could he offer for Jack's drowned mother? He'd heard them all himself and although the sentiment was always well meant, it never helped. Not deep down. "Your hefty contribution to repair the hospital was much appreciated."

"I'm glad," the marquess murmured. "But I thought you hard-hearted, utterly ruthless, and now I hear of this patronage. It leaves me feeling quite upended."

"No need to fret," drawled Rakecombe, picking a piece of lint from his woollen waistcoat. "I am feeling positively pitiless tonight."

They strode on in thought for a while, dodging nefarious liquids, dogs and hogs.

"So, are you patron of other charity hospitals?" enquired Jack, as they turned left down an alley, veering to avoid two scraggy chickens. A hackney might have got them so far, but the walk to the Rookery always focused Rakecombe's mind. Would he find Penbury? What had dragged the astute fellow so low.

"A few."

"All in London?" Jack harped on.

"No, some are in Wales," he answered, distracted by a lad brushing overly close to his coat pocket.

"And when did you become patron of this hospital?"

"Eleven years ago, after Gwen's death. It was in her memory that I…" He snapped his mouth shut.

Damn and blast. What was it about Winterbourne that made one gabble so? The bugger could draw blood from a stone, so he clenched his fist to iron.

"I remember Kelmarsh mentioning Gwen. A sister who died young?"

"Yes," he replied curtly. He never spoke of beloved Gwen. How could he? The blame for her death was a burden he must carry forever. A wound that would never heal.

"It affects us," Jack said, eyes empty. "Loss. It steals a part of our soul that we can never recover."

Rakecombe nodded. He cloaked himself in a ruthless mien, but it appeared he wasn't the only one with a veil hiding inner darkness.

The two of them simply concealed it with differing tactics.

THEIR DESTINATION on Bainbridge Street did not appeal.

Squalid, with a splintered door, it gave the impression of abandonment until you peered in and noticed a few patrons sprawled over tables, glasses still held in limp fingers, possessive even when cup-shot.

So far, they'd gained little information. Rakecombe had questioned a few familiar ruffians whom he paid to keep an eye out for anything untoward – although in the Rookery that term was loose. One lad had told of seeing a chap with Penbury's description, but nothing was certain.

A surprise had been Jack. Or more to the point, himself

and Jack. They made a good – he almost choked on the word – *team*.

Whilst he himself terrified informants with threats, Jack coaxed information with good humour. Two doxies were on Rakecombe's payroll and with Jack's geniality, they'd admired that waistcoat of his and wittered on, revealing more about this bowsing ken on Bainbridge Street.

A gin shop.

He'd hoped for a brothel. Old soakers were so much more difficult to question.

Pushing the thin door that held a fist-sized hole in it, Rakecombe sauntered in. An ashen young girl scrubbed with a threadbare cloth, her stare vacant, a bruise marring one cheek.

As they seated themselves at a cobbled-together table, she hurried over.

Normally, a barmaid's eyes gleamed with avarice at the sight of him – he may wear old clothes but they recognised a man's worth solely by posture – but this young girl just gazed dully.

"Blue ruin and information," Rakecombe growled low.

She timidly looked over her shoulder to a hulking great brute slumped over the counter.

"We will pay for both," murmured Jack, smiling.

With a deft nod, she scuttled off to a back room and came back more promptly than a butler at White's, with a bottle and three glasses.

"Jim don't mind talk if yer buy us a drink. 'E'll jus' think yer after a tup." She looked up hopefully. "Are yer?"

"How old are you?" asked Jack, brow furrowing.

"None of yer bleedin' business," she said, pouring gin with a shaking hand.

Bruises dotted her pale wrists and Rakecombe felt the

usual helplessness descend whenever he came to this part of London.

Despite owning the hospital and several other places, it was never enough.

With all his titled authority, he tried to persuade government to help and although he received toadying promises, no new measures ever saw the light of day.

The powers that be blamed poverty on the war, they blamed the drink, they blamed laziness and low morals – bloody hypocrites. He'd like to stuff a couple of them down here and see how long they survived.

"Have you heard of a man called Stuart Penbury? Blond hair and grey eyes with a–"

"Talks funny?" the girl interrupted.

"He's from Manchester."

She scrunched her forehead. "Like I said, talks funny. Don't pronounce fings right."

"Indeed. Did he come here often? When was the last time you saw him?"

"First came 'ere to meet some bloke, but then 'e had the itch for Beth, the other girl." She leaned close and Rakecombe was surprised to smell fresh lavender. "Then Stuart jus' fancied the bub, like they all do."

Sitting back, she sniffed the glass, wrinkling her nose. "Dunno why. Stuff's rank. Smells o' cats. Anyhows, a couple hurled in 'elter-skelter last week and they jus' grabbed 'im. Beth screamed but the woman – a swivel-eyed flash mort – told us she were 'is sister. And that were that. I 'eard the fella say they was taking 'im up north. Poor Stuart – they 'ave to eat grass up there, yer know."

Jack took her calloused hand and placed some coins in her palm. "Hide them," he said, folding her fingers over the silver.

"Ta, but 'e always finds it." The girl jerked a thumb to the collapsed giant. "And then 'tis worse. I got thumped for 'iding a ribbon… I didn't filch it. It were in the gutter." A wistful expression transformed her pale features. "It were blue. Bit bloodstained and that…"

All at once, Rakecombe stood, but his – he hesitated to say comrade – remained sitting, staring at the bruised girl.

Rakecombe sighed. You couldn't save them all, but…

Grabbing hold of her upper arm, he roughly pulled her to standing. Jack protested but was bending to catch the gin bottle as it tumbled from the table whilst Rakecombe swiftly whispered in the girl's ear, unobserved. "If you want a way out, go to the hospital on Dyott Street. Tell them Alex sent you."

A faint nod and he pushed her away. She fell into another table with an exaggerated cry.

"Get your stench away from me, girl," he sneered. "I'd rather swive a sow." And he stalked out of the godawful place.

"WHY DO THAT?" Jack finally asked as they strode down Denmark Street, almost free from the Rookeries. "What had she done?"

Dusk had fallen, cloaking them in a leaden fog that choked one's snout and stung one's vision. The narrow lanes had quietened, people rushing for home before the encroaching malevolent dark.

The marquess had been utterly silent as they'd traversed St Giles, obviously thinking the worst of him. They always did and he usually cared little, but for once, he didn't want to endure this affable lord's disgust.

Gads, what was wrong with him? He had one friend in the Earl of Kelmarsh; he didn't need another.

One could have too many friends.

Exhaling, he halted his stride. "That slumbering goliath was twitching, not slumbering at all. No one sleeps in the Rookery without one eye open."

Jack peered at him, dumbfounded. "I thought–"

"Yes, I know you did, but when I grabbed her, I told her about the hospital. I must be careful, however, as two years ago, it was robbed by a disgruntled cock bawd. Men like that could destroy all our work if they think their women are disappearing." He stripped off his gloves and flexed his fingers.

"Lud," Jack said aghast, "all this ruthless posturing, but underneath you have a–"

"'Ello there, m'dimber coves, fancy a tumble?" A slattern in shabby green silk wangled her way between them, patting their arms.

"I prefer my women to have washed within the last decade," drawled Rakecombe as he removed the lady's wandering hands and ignored Winterbourne's smirk.

Heavy footsteps sounded from behind... More than one.

"Somefin' wrong with our women, fat culls?" a booming voice demanded.

"Lawks, Jimmy," the female octopus replied. "I were jus–" She said no more as a thickset hand wrenched her away, shoving her to the gutter.

Rakecombe heaved a sigh. Oh, for God's sake, and they were scarcely twenty yards or so from the St Giles boundary.

Turning leisurely, he observed a man looking markedly like the slumbering oaf from the gin shop emerge from the shadows, his form lit by a small lamp outside one of the houses – probably a brothel, the only ones advertising their doorways.

"You two look well fed," the oaf said, smiling and dangling what transpired to be a large cudgel. "And I know someone who pays ten quid for a decent body. Eh, lads, let's mill the bastards."

Two men, this time scrawny, appeared like wraiths.

Another time, another night, intruded before his eyes – blood, tears, Gwen's screams – but he willed the scene away.

Control.

Grasping air where his cane should be, he instead looked to his bare knuckles in faint regret – so common but needs must, and he didn't fancy his innards being clandestinely dissected on the morrow by some eager quack.

"The ladies tell me I look better *sans* clothes," jested Jack, peeling his leather gloves off.

Rakecombe slid a hand down. He didn't have his cane, but he did have...

The Jim lookalike sniggered. "I'll be having that red waistcoat off you, pretty boy."

Holding a hand to his chest, Jack gasped, although Rakecombe then saw his fingers slip inside the damn frippery. "I don't know which to be more offended by, old chap. The fact you think I'm a boy or that you don't recognise coquelicot."

Rakecombe reached into his own pocket as Jack distracted them, feeling for the solid hilt of his dagger. He'd known that bloody, red silk eyesore would cause trouble.

"Cock wot?" the oaf snarled, swinging his cudgel. "Oy, are you raggin' me?"

"No, no. Co-quel-li-co," the marquess enunciated as his fingers slid out, now with a metallic glint to them.

"Give the man your waistcoat, Jack."

"It's hand-painted silk from China! Little worms gave their lives for this cloth, and that man will have no idea how to wash it. Miggens my valet is the only one who knows how."

Deftly, Rakecombe slipped his carnelian signet ring off as it was most revolting when skin got stuck under the gold setting. "Is a waistcoat really worth your life?"

"Well, when you put it like that… Yes, it cost me nine guineas."

They attacked as one, taking the villains by surprise. The taller wraith squawked at the sight, probably too used to quivering sapskulls.

Rakecombe took on the nearest two, hoping Jack could manage the hulking Jim. He smartly smashed his fist into one villain's cheek and felt a glancing blow himself.

The second coward circled around his back and as Rakecombe punched out a further fist to the gut, the other man grasped a tight arm around his neck from behind. A stranglehold.

But using the leverage, he kicked out, catching the ballocks of the man in front who howled with agony and bent double. Rakecombe then smashed a knee to his quaking chin, heard a resounding crack, and the rat fell backwards, clonking his skull on the cobbles.

A sharp jab at Rakecombe's throat promptly caused him to still.

"Not so tough now, are you," taunted the wraith, panting breath misting the blade held to Rakecombe's skin.

"No, you are quite right, you are the toughest," he hissed. But in an instant, he elbowed the villain straight in the kidneys whilst hurling his head back, breaking the man's nose with a wet crunch. The knife dropped away and swirling, he slashed out with his own dagger, scoring the man across the chest. "But I am the deadliest."

The wound wasn't going to kill, but one never knew – he might die of infection. The rat scurried away, knowing the odds were not on his side tonight.

Muffled groans broke from a side alley and Rakecombe scrambled to the sound. He never should have left Jack alon–

With face harsh, the currently unaffable marquess bashed the huge oaf's head against the wall whilst simultaneously punching his gut with those metallic glinting knuckles.

The flailing man was no match for the sheer strength and intensity of Jack Winterbourne.

"Enjoy hitting women, do you?" growled Jack, aiming another punch.

Rakecombe winced as head encountered wall again. "The man's unconscious." He stepped forward, catching the marquess's fist. "Enough."

Wild eyes met his, and for a moment, he thought Jack might lash out, so he gripped yet tighter, both their knuckles stretched white and bloody.

Finally a nod, and the villain was released to slide down the wall in a heap, groan emerging.

Jack turned away, heaving breaths and slamming a fist to the wall.

Who would have thought the marquess had quite the temper buried deep under all that jovial *bonhomie*?

Rakecombe let him rasp some more, watched his shoulders ease, anger draining as quickly as it had arisen.

"Let us depart, Jack. I often find myself in need of a wash after St Giles…and a stiff whisky wouldn't hurt." He placed a hand on his shoulder. "We will talk tomorrow, but it appears one of us needs to pay Penbury a visit in Manchester, and since I am a duke, that would be you."

The marquess was silent for a time, until twisting his head, a half smile appearing. "Certainly. If we can discount Penbury, it will make our search easier." He ran a hand through his hair and the immaculate Brutus coiffure was restored once more. "But for tonight, I need something gentler than whisky. Lady Gibbon has blackmailed me to supper and I do so admire such cunning."

They strolled from the alleyway, Rakecombe slipping his signet ring back on. "Well take some horse blinkers if you do. Her bedchamber resembles a bawdy house."

"And how would you know what either of those look like, Rakeprude?" Jack scoffed.

He glared at the quicksilver chap. "Mission related."

"Faugh! And by the way, now we have worked together, fought together, loved together, do you think I might know your codename? 'Tis only fair."

"We have not lov…" Rakecombe hesitated. In point of fact, there was no reason why he shouldn't disclose his *nom de guerre*. Probably best to get it over with. "I'm a Dog."

"All men are at heart, old boy, no need to–"

"No. My codename."

A smirk, if he wasn't mistaken.

"I can see the comparison." Jack chortled. "Snarling, fearless, pants after Irish bones and chews–"

"I think Rainham will tell you," he barked, "it's because I am tenacious, dangerous and good at catching rats."

5

CONSCIENCE MAKES COWARDS OF US ALL.

"Do you wish to explain, Alex dear, why we are attending a musical soirée at the Beckfords'? Aren't they the same family you invited to my little rout last year?"

"No and yes."

On hearing his mother sigh, the Duke of Rakecombe fiddled with his jet cufflink, the carriage veering around a corner. No doubt, Mother would love to hear how his prized walking cane had ended up in Miss Quinlan's possession. She'd clap her hands in glee at his lack of concentration and furthermore deduce false suppositions.

His plan for tonight was simple: Eat. Snooze. Retrieve. Depart.

"Their daughter married the Earl of Kelmarsh, did she not?" Mother pestered. "And they have no other daughter, do they?"

"Yes and no."

The carriage rumbled over cobbles, causing his crumpet to throb and reminding him the ducal transport needed to be re-sprung. One of the miscreants from last night must have caught him a blow, as his eye socket had a bluish tinge and ached like the very devil.

"Hmm," his mother murmured in that way his mother always murmured when she was pondering.

He glanced across and met her thoughtful eyes, knowing his own capability for insight had not been inherited from his father's side.

"Perhaps I simply require some edible food?" he muttered. Indeed, he was so damn peckish, his gizzards felt like his throat had been cut.

She laughed lightly.

His mother, despite the past turmoil of their lives, still held a ready smile, and he wondered how she did it.

Lines creased the corners of her eyes, her blond hair slowly fading to ash, but when she smiled, she appeared years younger. The Earl of Fotherington had been courting her for three Seasons.

With cautious eyes, he watched her tap a satin-gloved finger against her mouth. "Are there any other ladies attending who hold your interest?"

Luck was with him, as the coach swayed and jolted to an abrupt halt, terminating his mother's interrogation. If she received any inkling as to the reason for tonight, the barrage of questions would be prodigious.

A footman lowered the steps and he made his escape before holding out a hand. Mother descended, graceful as ever, and stood beside him, gazing at the Beckfords' elegant but petite house on Conduit Street.

Her satin glove patted his side. "Well, I trust you implicitly, Alex dear. So, if we need to be here, then here we are."

Guilt clenched at him for a time. Why did Mother hold

such trust when he'd betrayed it so gravely in the past? "Mama–"

"I do remember meeting the Beckfords at my rout, very nice people. Didn't they have an Irish relative with them, as well? A pretty, dark-haired girl. A Miss…now what was it?"

A trap.

A deadly trap.

More fatal than a Rookery snare. And coming from Mother, not a very subtle one.

The question was whether he should fall into it or skirt the precipitous edge. He'd try the latter. "A Miss Quinlan, I vaguely recall."

She glanced up, eyes twinkling. "Why, yes, dear. Is she here also?"

The trap widened, edge falling away. "Mother, she is an Irish nobody." There, that should put paid to any flawed thoughts.

"Hmm." She tapped his arm smartly with her fan. "And I was a Welsh nobody, so don't take that attitude with me, young Alexander Westhide."

Feeling all of ten years of age, he took his mother's hand and kissed the back. "And Father could not have chosen anyone better."

She beamed up at him and clucked his chin – about the furthest she could reach. "When will you men ever learn," she said. "I chose *him*, dear."

Fountain. Hour of ten.
R.

AIDEEN GAZED AT THE NOTE, the bare words so at odds with

the curled ornate writing. The tail of the R swished across the notepaper, bold and rampant.

The demanding devil.

Smiling, she burned it in the low fire of the drawing room, recognising his tactics. Her father often used the same. Control. Even if one doesn't hold all the cards, issue commands and the control shifts, so subtle one hardly notices.

With a shrug, she turned to survey the guests. The earlier arrival of the Duchess of Rakecombe and her son had caused a rapid chirping to ripple the room.

The Beckfords were already acquainted with the duke, but never would he have graced them with his presence without a little…persuasion.

Aideen had considered many ways to return the cane: she could have merely asked him to call, but where was the fun in that? Yet easier, an errand boy could have delivered it to him with red bow attached – no need to even see his scowling face.

But Mrs Beckford had been feeling morose at not having her daughter with them this Season, and Mr Beckford had lost eight guineas at piquet again, so what better way to cheer them up?

A difference of opinion as to what the pianoforte considered to be the high note and what Miss Gibbon sang caused Aideen to wince, and she plonked herself down next to Cordelia at the back of the room.

Tapping her foot in time with the wailing, an astonishingly beribboned Cordelia nudged close. "Thank you so much for the poems. However did you recover them?"

Oh, I wickedly stole into a viscountess's room, kissed a duke and stared at thighs in tight pantaloons.

"Pfff, 'twas nothing," she replied.

Aideen snuck a glance at said duke, also lounging at the back. An array of food had been laid out before the music had begun and he'd scoffed – if a peer of such high rank could be said to scoff – the lot.

Now he sprawled replete, eyes closed. It didn't appear to be wholly boredom, but an outright weariness, not helped by his sombre clothes.

A wave of sadness engulfed her.

Had she really asked him here for the Beckfords' social benefit? Or for herself?

His demanding kiss haunted her nights, his cold green eyes her days, and yet when they met, they fought like cat and dog.

Despite being the god-daughter of the noble Waterford family back home, and despite the fact Mama had been a baronet's daughter, she was, in essence, an Irish nonentity as far as a duke was concerned.

And as such he would…could have no interest in her.

Cordelia clapped enthusiastically as the wailing ended and another young miss skipped to the pianoforte. Aideen glanced at the mantel clock. It was nearly upon the hour of ten, so she whispered to her friend of visiting the retiring room and headed off with heavy heart.

The Duke of Rakecombe strode out into the night, feeling somewhat…content.

After the over-capered sauce on his undercooked veal at home, the simple but delicious supper of the Beckfords had soothed his ire.

The claret had been damned good as well.

Now just his cane to collect, a rollicking spar of words with Miss Quinlan and all would be right with the world.

Of course, Napoleon always put a spoke in one's wheel, but Winterbourne had hoofed it up north to locate Penbury, and so Rakecombe now focused on the search for Stafford here in London, although it had proved unproductive as yet.

Earlier in the day, he had been carped at by Stafford's grizzled butler, who'd complained he'd not been paid for three weeks, that he couldn't tend the closed-up house without a maid and that the kitchens had run out of apple butter jam. Sneezing, he'd also whined there was no coal. Rakecombe had never met such a sniveller.

Tomorrow he would visit coffee houses and force himself to drink the foul beverage whilst probing for gossip – surely someone had spied Stafford in London.

Time, he felt, was running out. That list of informants must be found.

Slowing his step, it wouldn't do to seem eager, his gaze sought the small fountain at the back of the garden.

He halted in his tracks, all contentment dissipating in a moment – *Deuced woman!*

"What in the hell do you think you are doing?" He marched to Aideen, perched by a lantern on the stone plinth of the fountain.

Damn it, she'd unscrewed the finial of his cane and was prodding inside the neck.

"Arrah, no need to get your tight ducal pantaloons in a twist...Your Grace. I was simply checking the mechanism."

He snatched the cane away and held out his hand for the silver dog finial. The wench just shrugged and passed it over.

"You can tell your Uncle Seamus," he muttered, screwing it carefully back on, "that it works perfectly. I can't believe he lets you work on these."

"I loved this piece. It suits you. The adorable little puppy with jade eyes."

"You insolent baggage…" He ceased roaring as twinkling obsidian eyes laughed up at him. His shoulders relaxed. "Miss Quinlan, you shall be the death of me. Baiting a duke is, I believe, frowned upon."

"But I think you like it," she replied, standing.

The scent of violets overwhelmed him, and as always when near Miss Quinlan, he became aware of the great danger she posed. From the very first time they'd met and she'd scolded him for looming, his long-practised reserve had begun to crack.

He did like her provoking words. He enjoyed her bold humour. He adored those tart lips.

All those scathing comments he had thought up last night came to the fore. He would tell her she was an Irish upstart, that he disliked conversing with someone so low in status. He would say her lips were too sour and that she wasn't pretty. He would hiss he hated violets.

But they all dwindled to naught.

Ultimately, he was a coward who couldn't bear to see hurt in her eyes. He was a coward every which way.

Rather than insults to push her away, he should tell her the truth – that in his life there was no room for a duchess, no room for entanglement.

Unlike his friend Kelmarsh, he didn't want to relinquish his important work for the Crown; he needed it and in turn, the Crown needed him with his unique access to the upper echelons of society, but menace from the enemy or from dubious contacts stalked him always, so very close behind. A beloved could too easily step into their path.

"I'm grateful to you for retrieving my cane."

She curtsied and then held out her hand. He took it, letting his eyes wander.

Some might say she wore a grey frock, yet all he saw was flashing silver, beckoning him like stars and deciding his fate.

But he knew where his fate lay.

This would be the last time, he vowed. He'd ask Rainham for a mission far away. She'd marry a safe gentleman with soft fingers and a mild manner, who didn't brawl in St Giles on murky nights.

Miss Aideen Quinlan was not for him. Women were fragile. In public, he even kept a circumspect distance from his own mother so as not to bring danger upon her.

Bending, he lightly kissed her hand, when all he really wanted to do was pull her close, wrap his arms around her and see how long they could burn together.

But control, the cornerstone of his life since his twenty-second year, fought passion, and passion fought that control.

A perceptible quiver ran through her. He was no innocent. He knew their sparks and baits were part of something bigger – craving, desire, need. It arced between them.

But lust could be restrained.

So he prepared to step back, to end it, when all of a sudden, delicate fingers brushed his eye.

"Have you been at an Irish wedding?"

"I beg your pardon?" He gazed confused, endeavouring to shy from her touch.

"They give out black eyes instead of favours – have you not heard it?"

He shook his head, and a hand caressed the bruise, lightly, tenderly.

"You must be careful, Your Grace."

So long had it been since anyone had cared, so long since anyone had touched him with such utter gentleness. Because all he did was scare them away with harshness.

But there was no scaring away Aideen Quinlan and so with a groan and all good sense abandoned, he pulled her close, threaded his eager fingers through her hair and kissed her with irresponsible carnal possession.

AIDEEN SURRENDERED.

Determined lips smothered her own as a hand swept down her back, hauling her near.

She shouldn't be surrendering: she should be biting that marauding tongue, pulling the finger back painfully on his seeking hand or bringing her knee up as his hips pressed.

But she couldn't. Because this kiss was so all-consuming, so intoxicating.

When he had skimmed lips over her hand, he'd appeared sorrowful.

Lonely.

Father always said she had no tender feelings, that she wasn't even a proper girl, let alone the boy he'd wished for, but her heart had wept at the duke's bruised eye.

"Touch me again."

The deep words growled against her mouth and she realised her hands had fallen quiet against his chest – confused and unknowing.

As his lips nuzzled her cheek, so she cradled the side of his face anew, brushing his puffy eye with sensitive fingers.

"More," he groaned.

For once, she did as she was told, dragging her hand around and finding his nape, the hair ruthlessly short, no poetic curls for the Duke of Rakecombe. She liked it. The roughness against her fingers, and she dragged her nails along the edge.

"Aideen, you don't–"

Never did she find out exactly what she didn't, because his large hands cupped her bottom and drew her tight to his body – so tight she could feel his waistcoat buttons pressing, a light stubble grazing her neck and strong thighs pushing against her skirts.

His mouth returned, hard and seeking, tongue invading. No longer the Duke of Restraint but Recklessness.

A hand now swept up her side, so she slipped an arm within his tailcoat, smoothing his spine as much as his fitted clothing would allow. It spurred him on and he nipped at her lip, thrust those slender hips, and heaven help her, she did the same.

Fingers scrabbled at her satin-clad shoulder but then suddenly stilled, utterly motionless. He panted harshly, and she glanced down.

The flawless white of her bared shoulder contrasted against his raw-red knuckles; one had bled a little, smearing her skin.

Returning her eyes to his, she could see disgust and horror, but was unsure of the cause. Her? The blood?

"Alexander Westhide!" A female cultured voice rent the air. A voice that demanded attention.

"Oh, Aideen..." A sigh of disappointment. Familiar.

"Ohhhh!" A squealy gasp. Not a clue.

Biliousness arose in Aideen's stomach, and she wanted to bury her head in his waistcoat and *never* come out.

But Quinlans were cut from staunch cloth, and Uncle Seamus had forever said one should tell the truth and shame the devil, so as the duke drew back, she straightened her spine and faced their audience.

It was less numerous than she'd anticipated.

Three women: a saddened Mrs Beckford, a disgruntled-looking young debutante and the Duchess of Rakecombe.

Aideen had a time discerning the latter's expression – disapproving or amused, she couldn't tell.

Expecting the duke to stand away, to deny his involvement…somehow, he instead clasped a hand around her wrist.

"Mother. You wished to know my reasons for attending tonight's soirée?"

The duchess nodded, hesitant.

"It was to choose my wife."

6

'HAPPINESS IS NO LAUGHING MATTER.'

(RICHARD WHATELY, ARCHBISHOP OF DUBLIN, 1787–1863)

Surely 'twas impossible for a person to be still living if they hadn't breathed for twelve hours.

To be sure, she'd not breathed last night when bundled upstairs, or when put to bed by her maid, or whilst sleeping, and she quite definitely hadn't breathed since waking at dawn.

Whenever she tried, her throat contracted.

And another entirely new development in the life of Miss Aideen Maura Kathleen Quinlan was that she appeared to have been struck dumb.

Uncle Seamus said she'd been born to the world jabbering, tongue running twelve score to the dozen, and yet… She opened her mouth.

Nothing.

Not that she needed to say anything as Mrs Beckford was more than making up for Aideen's muteness.

At this very moment, she chattered over the breakfast

table about how well-mannered the duke was and how honoured Aideen should be.

Honoured?

Certainly, she was aware it had been a grand gesture on his part to save her reputation from ruin, although she'd an inkling it had also been to save his own pompous hide.

The duke had not suddenly developed a tendre for her, and if she'd been in any doubt, his tight lips and angry eyes on the stalk back from the fountain would have soon undoubted her.

He'd probably regretted the words as soon as they'd been uttered, but what else could a priggish duke do when confronted with such a reproachful threesome?

Well, not kiss her in the first place, of course, but the milk had already been spilt. Indeed, it had copiously flooded until they were chin-high and drowning.

Aideen scowled as Mrs Beckford babbled on about trousseaus and wedding fruit cakes. But what no one seemed to have taken into account were the very words the duke had so coldly drawled: *"It was to choose my wife."*

Conceited, puffed-up, overconfident, egotistical…

The more she thought upon it, the more incensed she became. There were so many ways he could have worded it:

"I was about to ask the beautiful Aideen to be my treasured wife." *Perfect.*

"I am hopeful Miss Quinlan would honour me by consenting to be my duchess." *Very Rakecombe but acceptable.*

"You must allow me to tell you how ardently I admire and love you." *From her favourite book, so unlikely.*

"You don't have to marry him, you realise."

Aideen frowned. An odd thought, until she realised it wasn't in her head but the astute Mr Beckford.

Peering up, she found warm brandy eyes twinkling at her

over a fork full of bacon. "Just saying, Aideen dear, you need not marry the young buck if you don't wish to. Duke or no duke."

His wife's eyebrows shot up. "What? Of cours–"

"No," Mr Beckford said mildly. "What is most important for our girls, Edwina?" He reached to twine his fingers with his wife's, their gazes meeting.

A moment of jealousy engulfed Aideen. They looked so… affectionate. Mr Beckford was rather a quiet man but over her time spent with the family, Aideen had realised he was no hen-pecked husband. He radiated silent strength.

"Happiness." Mrs Beckford sighed.

"Exactly so," responded her husband. "The duke sent a message earlier. He will be here on the hour of eleven, so I suggest you think carefully, Aideen. But no one is forcing you. We will support whatever decision you adopt. Yes, it might cause a disruption if you decide otherwise, but we are not of the higher tiers of society. We will survive and having Sophie as a countess will help."

The words brought tears to Aideen's eyes and she hastily dashed them away. Her own father would have demanded she obey, brandishing his fury with harsh curses. He'd probably have called her a harlot.

Perhaps she was. She'd hardly fought off the duke's impudence but instead relished his touch.

Pushing her unfinished breakfast to one side, she stood. "Thank you. I do not deserve your kindness after the events of last night–"

"Aideen," Mrs Beckford interrupted, holding up a palm, "you are not to blame in any way. The duke has a decade over you in both years and experience. Blame lies solely in his hands. Take a rest in the morning room and I'll bring you a cup of chocolate."

"And, Aideen," Mr Beckford added as she turned. "You are as a daughter to us in every way, so if you require me to call him out, I will. I'm a dab shot, eh, wife of mine?"

That wife of his blushed, and another time Aideen would have stayed and inveigled that *entire* story, but nodding gratefully, she wandered out.

Mrs Beckford's words had given her pause to think. Rakecombe's years did not detract but doubtless added to his appeal. Men like the young Lord Sherburn *behaved* so young, more concerned with gambling and carriage racing.

And then there was chocolate.

Some men smelled of horse, sweat or liver, but scrumptious chocolate?

Certainly not a reason to marry but one to add to the cauldron of consideration.

After plunking herself on the mahogany floral ottoman, she flicked through a tatty old copy of *La Belle Assemblée.*

Why, when one needed to think, did one's idea pot empty?

No reasoning or conclusions arose; instead, there lay a gaping hole of indecision and befuddlement.

How she wished Sophie was here for some sound advice. She could send a message for Cordelia to call, but felt her friend was also in the dark concerning men, if not more so. Lord Oakdean was markedly monosyllabic – or brooding as Aideen would label it.

An article caught her eye: "Maxims and Rules for the Conduct of Women" by Countess de Boufflers.

Idly, she studied items on the list.

1. In the exterior, decency and cleanliness.

Well, she could accomplish the second.

4. In language, truth and perspicuity.
She did sometimes fib but thought she could manage to be articulate…or long-winded, depending on how one viewed it.

5. In domestic life, rectitude and kindness, without familiarity.
Oh dear.

Her father had always bemoaned she should've been a boy and perhaps, after all, he was right. Life was certainly less formal for them, and her manners would have been better suited to a male of the species.

But damn them all – she liked being a girl, and she liked being Aideen Quinlan. She peered at the list again.

"I don't think you need that old twaddle, Aideen love," said Mrs Beckford, arriving with the promised cup of chocolate and placing it by her. "The duke seems to admire you exactly as you are from what I spied last night."

Cursing the redness which coursed beneath her pale Celtic skin, she nevertheless smiled. "I don't know. We always…argue."

Mrs Beckford crossed to sit on the dainty chaise, and Aideen wasn't quite sure what to expect after her defence of the duke at breakfast. Certainly not a furious reprimand but maybe some gentle persuasion.

"Have you *any* common ground?"

"Erm." Furiously, she thought over the time she'd known him. "We both like books. I remember him saying he was a prodigious reader."

"A most pleasant pastime for husband and wife. If you decide to marry, you have to work on what pleases you both and be patient but, Aideen…friction is not always a harmful element to marriage."

Aideen's eyes widened as redness now travelled up Mrs Beckford's neck, tinting her like a rose.

"Is it not? But we fight and bicker. Nothing like your Sophie and the Earl of Kelmarsh."

"That is their character. Those two enjoy tranquillity, but… I know you will not believe it now, but when my husband was young, he had quite the temper and I was no namby-pamby miss either." She coughed gracefully.

"Really?"

Mrs Beckford flicked open a fan, which lay on the chaise, and wafted it vigorously. "We had some skirmishes, but I knew, deep down, he was the only man for me. And the making up can be most…agreeable."

Aideen coughed *ungracefully*.

The fan snapped shut and earnest eyes shifted to her. Despite having difficulty following Mrs Beckford's etiquette guidance this Season, Aideen had great respect for her. And she so desperately needed advice.

"You have to search deep down, Aideen. Not on the superficial surface but within. Do you want this man for the rest of your life?" Mrs Beckford patted a cushion nervously. "I will not say this again as 'tis a dash indecorous, and dukes may sleep differently, but…well, do you want to see his face across your pillow every morning?"

Yes, yes, yes, Aideen's heart screamed, but so many inner concerns yelled *no, no, no.*

"I can't be a duchess," she wailed. "All the formality! I have no manners and should've been a boy like m'da always–"

"Anyone can learn manners and social graces." Mrs Beckford hastened over and jostled up on the ottoman. "What cannot be learned is kindness and humour and understanding, and you have those in abundance. As for your father... Did you know I visited Waterford before your birth?"

Aideen shook her head.

"Your mother was sure you would be a girl. So excited, she was."

"Didn't she want a boy? Like Da."

"No, she didn't. And your father couldn't have cared less at the time either – anything to make her happy. But when she died... Well, he lost himself and I'm afraid you were lost too. He turned his focus not to you, his daughter, but inwards, and anger consumed him. It still does. I thank God for your Uncle Seamus, even though he did teach you some highly inappropriate conduct."

"Oh."

"And I also doubt you know that your father was the one to name you."

"What?" She gasped.

"Hmm. Said any girl of his was bound to be fiery and stubborn."

Lips parted but Aideen was once again unable to speak.

"I shall leave you to think," said Mrs Beckford, patting her knee. "But one other matter to ponder on." She pursed her lips. "I talked of the duke being a man of years and experience. A man that should know better. So, the only reason for him to make such a grave impropriety is because you must call to him in some way. He does not appear to be a man controlled by lust. Far from it, his reputation is somewhat priggish." Mrs Beckford stood. "So, to make such a severe slip demonstrates profound...emotion."

Aideen's lips snapped shut.

Bejabbers.

7

TEMPUS FUGIT.

The Duke of Rakecombe really didn't have time for this.

After last night's little rumpus, he'd headed out for a pre-arranged meeting with his resourceful informant Bluey but not been able to uncover the merest trace of Stafford.

Bluey would continue to ferret away though, and today, he himself was supposed to be scouring coffee shops for gossip.

Instead, he was winding the lengthy way around Grosvenor Square with his grandmother's ring in his pocket.

For once, he hadn't wholly formulated a plan yet. He often did his best thinking in bed, but restless memories of that deuced kiss had occupied his thoughts.

Wandering onto South Audley Street, he decided to take the long-cut and head for Berkeley Square.

If he wished to be an utterly ruthless bastard, there were still a number of ways he could get out of this mess a bachelor.

Essentially there were only three witnesses, all bribable in differing ways – they could be made to forget that he'd ever uttered the word *"wife"*, although that debutante had most likely blathered to all and sundry.

He'd since learned from Mother that she'd been angling for the vacant position of duchess. He didn't enjoy being cold-hearted – well, actually that was a falsehood – but God forbid, she chewed her hair.

So...to his current problem.

Obviously, he could bundle Aideen off to Ireland with a quantity of money, enough for a cosy house and servants.

Or, as a duke, find a cash-strapped lesser noble to leg shackle the girl to.

Or he could, in fact, do nothing and leave the wench ruined, deny he ever mentioned marrying. Everyone would understand – she was so far beneath his station in life they should never have even met.

It might yet enhance his callous reputation.

But beneath the rational, down below the wise logic, he felt a stirring animal growl its rage.

How revoltingly primitive.

Rakecombe coughed as he realised he'd strolled twice around Berkeley Gardens and so exited the next corner, which unfortunately meant he was further away from Conduit Street than when he'd first entered the blasted square.

He really didn't have time for this.

Or, of course, he could marry...

Last night, faced with that threesome of witnesses, all he'd wanted to do was protect Aideen's reputation, and his mouth had spoken without consulting anyone.

But could he marry?

He'd vowed he never would or at least wait until he was too old to continue in his work, his reflexes too slow. But he reckoned he had at least another ten years within him.

Could he marry and yet continue with his work for the Crown?

As he wandered onto Hay Hill – was this the quickest route? – he thought of his sister Gwen. They'd been so close, shared everything, and that had been the cause of her death. So maybe if he did marry but kept his wife…at a distance, all would be well.

Indeed, if he was never seen with his wife, and surely that was how half the *haut ton* existed anyway, there would never be any trouble. He could hire guards as he did for his mother – dear Mama had never once noticed the man who'd consistently trailed her for ten years.

A faint tremor slunk down his spine, raising the issue that Aideen could never be kept at a distance, but he was a duke, and a miserable malcontented one at that. She would fall into line.

"Excuse me, good sir, do you know the way to Old Bond Street?"

Rakecombe glared at the bacon-fed fellow who'd dared to intrude.

Did the lackwit not see the hurry he held? "I no live 'ere," he scorned in his best Parisian accent, and without waiting for the fellow's fatuous answer, he ambled on.

Now which was quicker? Grafton Street or cut across South Bruton Mews? He'd try both.

Briefly, *very briefly*, he wished Winterbourne was around as he was always overflowing with hopeless advice, but then again, it would cost Rakecombe his pride, so perhaps it was best the fellow was still up north.

Looking up, he realised this was Clifford Street, and so he hummed and hawed.

How did one get to Conduit from here? Could he take a

detour and cut across another mews? He didn't have time to piddle around the streets of London.

Whilst deliberating, his legs set off down Saville Street, so he followed, wielding his cane every so often on a stray song sheet littering the ground, and adding up all the reasons to marry.

He did need an heir. The current beneficiary was cousin Matthew, who had unfortunately inherited the calamitous family trait of gambling.

Sapskull Matthew was kept on a thrifty stipend and Rakecombe had made sure that even if he did inherit, the estate and monies were bound up tighter than a strumpet's corset.

Grandfather Thomas, another with the ill-fated gambling habit, had nearly bankrupted the Rakecombe name with his reckless wagering on ducks in a wild goose race.

Fortunately, he'd been trampled by a frisky mare and Father had managed to claw back the monies, instilling in his own son the need for sobriety.

So, an heir. Useful.

A wife would also keep away any marriage-minded misses and their devious mothers. Although he'd always been successful enough on that count.

Any other reasons?

An innate sense of honour? Mayhap. Not that he minded his reputation gaining a dash more heartlessness, but he had been raised with a sense of integrity, and if he reneged on his words it was likely his mother would cause his ears to ring.

Were there any more reasons?

"Oy, watch where yer going, cork brain," a grubby little urchin yelled as Rakecombe ambled into his bundle of newspapers.

He really didn't have time for all this dilly-dallying.

Perhaps he ought to mull it over in The Coach and Horses on Burlington, but consulting his fob watch, it was nigh eleven and he was *never* late.

Putting on some haste, he wandered down Swallow Street and came to the wrong end of Conduit.

Damn.

Of course, what he kept ruthlessly suppressing was this odd…need he felt for Miss Quinlan. That aching want as she'd touched his eye last night. The overwhelming desire to have her beneath him. No doubt lust played a part, but he'd felt that before.

This appeared to be deeper, but he purposefully shied away from probing further.

There was no time.

If he married Aideen Quinlan, she would belong to him. And only him. No woolly crowned Sherburn drooling over her, soft hands pawing.

With mind made up, he strode down the street that the Beckfords inhabited, glad after all that he'd taken the time to remove his grandmother's ring from the safe this morning.

AIDEEN SIPPED the now cold chocolate and willed her heart to stop thumping so stridently.

The duke had arrived well after the appointed hour of eleven, but he'd immediately demanded to speak with Mr Beckford. She knew this was proper but couldn't help feel a tinge of resentment.

They were discussing her life, her future, and she wasn't even there. At least she could rely on Mr Beckford not to be cowed, but even so…

"Aideen? The duke has requested to speak with you privately, and I have agreed you may converse on the terrace with the door open. But Edwina or a maid can stay if you so wish?"

Pivoting, she found Mr Beckford with a looming black shadow at his heels. Devil's minions, the duke resembled the Grim Reaper some days – he need only swap his ubiquitous cane for a scythe.

"That is acceptable, sir."

"Good. Remember my words this morning, dearest."

Nodding, she led the duke through the drawing room and onto the small terrace. The birds cheerfully chirped, and an audacious russet-red squirrel ran along the oak tree, all utterly unaware of the life-defining scene about to take place.

Aideen waited for him to speak; for once, she was going to let someone else do the talking.

"I apologise for last night," he finally said.

"Which bit?"

"Excuse me?"

"Which bit are you apologising for? The kiss? For being discovered? Or for stating that you've found a wife in such a pompous way." Bah. She never could hold her tongue. – it was like trying to gag a rooster at dawn.

He stalked closer, and she had to admit to a frisson of excitement. His stride was meant to intimidate, to make a person step back, but as a child she'd loved to be pushed high on the swing, so high she'd squealed in fright and exhilaration. She might fall. She might be hurt.

The feeling was the same.

"I apologise for putting us both in this intolerable situation."

Ah, so he was regretting it.

Over the course of the morning, she had convinced herself that maybe a long engagement would be best. To see if they would suit, see if they could sit in the same room together for one whole hour without provoking or…kissing.

It was true she could retreat to Ireland, but gossip travelled faster than the four-in-hand club at full tilt, and no doubt Da would hassle some squinting squire into marrying her. One with sweaty hands and fetid breath, and in that company the duke emerged a better option, even putting aside his verdant gaze and firm thighs.

So, the duke then…but with an extended engagement.

Perchance, they could attend the theatre and take rides in Hyde Park. Talk sensibly and find what else they had in common. And when the Season ended, if they were still contrary, they could part amicably, the gossip having died down. A little.

But it seemed he had changed his mind. Well, no matter, she would weather the ruination.

"'Tis fine," she agreed. "I do not wish to marry a duke."

"I beg your pardon?" He peered with incredulous eyes. She'd always thought the colour akin to spinach, but they were lighter in the day, almost like lichen in an Irish forest. "Everybody wishes to marry a duke," he said somewhat arrogantly.

"I don't. All that prancing around and sniffing at people."

"I do not prance…ever." He took another step forward, although he glanced at the open terrace door with narrowed gaze.

"Oh, 'tis well for a duke," Aideen continued, feeling quite roused. "You prowl around and appear haughty, and all the women throw their skirts up and–"

"I have not perceived your skirts sailing skywards."

She was about to say he never would either when he took another step, leaned close and inhaled.

"I didn't mean sniffing quite so literally," she whispered.

"You drank chocolate this morning."

"Yes."

Green eyes gleamed before he began to sink downwards.

Appalled, excited and utterly bewildered, her stare followed his broad shoulders as he kneeled before her, nose practically in her gown. She could even make out the dark auburn strands in his harshly restrained hair.

"Miss Quinlan, become my wife."

"Erm. Why?"

The duke's shoulder twitched, and she realised he was laughing. With face now raised, she could see the mirth, lips curving and little lines crinkling to the side of his eyes.

He appeared younger, warmer.

He appeared suave, virile, aristocratic and awfully difficult to refuse.

"Only you would ask me that," he said. "But I believe we'd deal well together."

"We vex one another."

"Not all the time," he drawled from the ground. "Do you need me to point out the advantages? Or are you avenging yourself on my knees." He shuffled. "Aideen," he said seriously. "I am a duke, and I do not ruin young women. I am sure we can put aside our vexations and pass a pleasant life together. And we do have a certain…attraction."

Pleasant sounded most dull but he was correct about the attraction. She hesitated for the briefest of moments.

"I… Yes, I will marry you." There, it was said, and she would ask for a long engagement in just one moment.

She'd thought resignation would be the overriding expression on his handsome visage, but it was more possessive as he rose to his full height once more, looming close.

Oh, lawks, what had she done?

Would he kiss her? To seal the agreement? They'd never kissed with forethought…at least not on her part.

"Mr Beckford informed me you were raised in your mother's religion which makes the process easier. Despite your voluble curses and praises of the saints, you are not in fact Catholic. Did your father not protest?"

"It was my mother's wish, and I don't believe Da much cared."

An imperious eyebrow raised in query but she so hated explaining herself. At least they had that in common.

"My mother fell ill after my birth and never recovered. Da was too distracted."

"I hope you do not require your father to attend the wedding? You are of age, and Mr Beckford stated that he held guardianship whilst you are in England."

Aideen frowned. That was true but surely 'twas too soon to be worrying about guest lists. "I assumed a long engagement to be certain we can–"

"Three days."

"What?"

"We will be married in St George's, three days hence."

"But…but… That church will be unavailable for months. There's a waiting list." Curiously, that was the sole argument which came to mind.

"I am a duke and lists do not apply," he proclaimed.

Tapping that damnable cane and dislodging a flagstone, he continued, "Directly after this meeting, I will approach the Archbishop for a special licence. He attended dinner last month, so there should be no problem as we had a different chef then. I shall also inform Prinny this afternoon. He owes me a mint so won't kick up a storm."

Aideen's mind addled. Dining with the Archbishop. Meeting? Four days. *Prinny*! "I don't think–"

But her thoughts were ignored as her upper arms were grasped and a firm mouth pressed itself against hers.

He briefly pulled away. "I want you, my chocolate-coated cherry...and soon," he muttered, before hauling her close once more.

A polite clearing of throat made itself known from the house and she was instantly released.

"Three days," he growled and strode off without looking back – a rather bad habit of his.

Grumbling at his high-handed tyrannical manner, Aideen glared at the retreating upright spine.

She supposed she ought to be flattered he wanted her, despite her lowly status, but that wasn't why she was marrying him.

It was because she desired the damn bug as well...and soon.

Aideen sighed. No carriage rides in Hyde Park then.

8

ONLY TWO FRIENDS ARE NECESSARY.

Rakecombe poked at his dinner.

It held no resemblance to any rabbit he was aware of, and so sighing, he sprawled back and quaffed claret instead.

The dining room echoed to the clank of his crystal goblet on the polished surface, and a footman hastily refilled it before returning to his station at the wall.

Now the lone sound in the cavernous room was the ticking of the clock over the mantel. He gazed around the table that seated thirty-six and wondered why he hadn't eaten in the study.

His mother had been called away to an unwell friend in Richmond a day after the Aideen debacle, and so far, he'd dined at his club every night.

Unfortunately, he'd promised not to dis-employ the French chef while Mother was away and so tonight he was stuck. He could go out, but his wedding was on the morrow and he would require a clear head where Miss Quinlan was concerned.

Drumming fingers on the mahogany, he considered the

investigation. His informant had discovered that before Stafford's evaporation into nothingness, he'd been seen conversing with an unknown Frenchwoman. It didn't mean much, as many émigrés dotted London, but it was interesting.

But as to the chap's vanishing...

Well, nothing had been seen or heard of him, and Rakecombe had covered a lot of ground in the past few days: busy coffee houses, crowded taverns, grim backstreets and squalid lodgings. There were only so many places to hide in London. He could be dead, of course, in the Thames or on a surgeon's dissecting table, but Rakecombe just had a feeling.

Stafford's code name was Chameleon and considering their leader's propensity for choosing apt aliases, he guessed the chap was veiled from sight and living on air.

Indeed, Stafford had spent two years in France posing as a wealthy French investor, and one year in England posing as an anti-monarchist, so he was obviously excellent at what he did. Both guises had seen the disruption of several plots against the Crown.

So why? Why betray after such sterling work? The chap had no family and earned enough for a comfortable house and the odd servant.

A footman commenced lighting more candles as the room darkened but Rakecombe waved him away. It was so bloody quiet. He may as well retire abed to read.

"I know he's here," bellowed a voice from the hallway.

"His Grace has requested he not be disturbed," declared Rawlins the butler, with a tone as arrogant as Rakecombe's own.

After an "oomph", the dining room door was thrown open, an outline of black silhouetted against the light.

"There you are, sitting in the dark on your lonesome.

Come along, we are going out to celebrate…or commiserate. You can tell me all about it. I'm all agog to hear how you acted the *rake* for once."

"Winterbourne, did you damage my butler? And what did you discover in Manchester?"

Throwing himself into one of the delicate hand-carved Chippendale chairs, the marquess winked. A parrot-green waistcoat clung to his person. Mayhap coquelicot was not so bad.

"I scarcely trod on his foot. And Manchester was bloody awful. Like the girl said – couldn't understand a word. No grass for supper though and the women are luscious. Penbury's sister has an arse like a peac–"

"Was Penbury there?"

"Hmm, he's there. Looks terrible – sweating and casting up his accounts right, left and centre. Enough to make you want to give up the grog," he said, pouring himself a generous glass of claret. "We had a long chat, when he was able, but he's not our traitor, I'm afraid. So, where next?"

"Someone must have seen Stafford. We will talk to that butler again tomorrow."

Winterbourne stared aghast, glass held aloft. "Goddammit, you're getting married tomorrow!"

"It will only take the morning, if that."

He knew the impression he was giving, but to maintain his distance, and ensure Gwen's fate never befell his future duchess, it had to commence now. At the very beginning.

Since the loss of his sister, aloofness was a persona he'd become familiar with.

"Cold-hearted fellow you are, but I have no doubt the delicious Miss Quinlan will warm you through like a pan of pea soup. Now come on. We are off on a spree."

Aideen didn't warm: she seared him, and the pan of soup would be boiling over the stove, causing a bloody great mess.

"I thought to stay in," he grumbled.

"And do what? Eat…" The marquess peered closely at Rakecombe's full plate. "I say, what is that?"

"*Fricassée de lapin forestière* accompanied by *l'ail à la Bordelaise*."

"Hmm. Let's head to the Cyder Cellars in Maiden Lane for some victuals."

"No, I–"

"They do a devilishly good hashed goose with beans. Not to mention the rich red cherry tartlets."

Rakecombe gave a repressed glare but couldn't deny the hunger worm.

THE CYDER CELLARS was heaving with gentlemen and non-gentlemen alike.

Nobles, actors, singers and poets ate cheek by jowl, the wine flowed in abundance, and the goose was damn good.

Broad tables filled the room and waiters weaved their way amongst the jug-bitten clientele. Occasionally a fellow sang a ditty or enacted a sonnet or fell over – it didn't matter as all were vastly entertaining.

Much as Rakecombe hated to admit it, Winterbourne had been right. He'd spent far too much time brooding in the dark of late. He loved the theatre and song, and yet he'd immersed himself in work, even missing the masterful actor Kean's appearances.

A chap across the room broke into song. *Una's Lock,* he believed it was entitled.

"You better listen in," the marquess yelled above the

hubbub. "Might give you some ideas for your wedding night."

Grunting a reply, he sank his teeth into the cherry tartlet.

Winterbourne leaned forward, vile green waistcoat now unencumbered by jacket. "Sooo, Alex…"

Rakecombe tensed. He should have given the blasted marquess a false name as the chap now used it with impunity. No one called him Alex, except his mother and that was only in private. How would it sound from Aideen's lips in that Irish lilt – his full name – slow and lyrical.

He waited for *Jack's* interrogation.

"How did you and the delectable Miss Quinlan end up wrapped around each other like eels? Dashed unprofessional to get caught. I have a rule about that. Number three – Better to die with no clothes on than to be ensnared in a wedding coat."

"We were merely kissing," he answered coldly.

"Twaddle! Miss Parker is spreading an entirely different story. She squealed there was no gap between you."

No, there hadn't been. He'd felt every inch of Aideen's fulsome body. And he'd wanted her closer still. He wiped his brow: it was damnable hot in the Cyder Cellars.

"It matters not. We are to marry. She will produce an heir, live in the country, and we will stay far from each other's lives."

Jack's eyes narrowed. "And you think Miss Q will stand for that?"

"There's no choice. I cannot give up my work and 'tis dangerous to have her close."

"Well, best of luck, but I don't think you have a hope in hell. I also think you underestimate her gravely. She's a plucky lass with a bright mind. Remember that Frenchman last year?"

No, he didn't want to remember. Her bruised face. Her torn dress. The blood under her fingernails.

Did Winterbourne not see that was exactly why they would live their lives apart?

Disregarding the question, he was about to dig into another cherry tartlet when a slap on his back interrupted him.

He turned.

Oh yes, his other friend.

Bram Walcott, the Earl of Kelmarsh, former comrade and now happily married rusticator stood before him, beaming with bloody good health and a brown glow to his skin. He looked like a peasant.

"Bram?" he said, standing, "what are you doing here?"

Shaking hands, he noticed the change in his old friend – no shadows encircled his eyes and his lips fell to an easy smile. Was that retiring? Or marriage?

Last year, Bram had dis-attached himself from Crown work, but it hadn't been without its problems, and during the course of his troubled courtship, Rakecombe himself had met Aideen.

In fact, when you came to look upon it, his upcoming marriage was all Kelmarsh's fault.

"You didn't think we'd miss the wedding, did you? And Sophie *is* Aideen's cousin. I worried you'd be drinking claret in some shadowy corner of that mausoleum of yours and reading dreary poetry, but the butler told me you were here with this rogue."

"I was more worried," the rogue drawled, filling Bram a glass, "that Rakeprude might need some instruction before his wedding night. We could provide him with pictorial explanation."

Rakecombe couldn't prevent his lips from vaguely twitching. Winterbourne did amuse from time to time.

ANOTHER PATRON CLAMBERED onto the adjoining table and took a deep breath.

"Poets praise Chloe's shape, her complexion, her air,
Coral lips, pearly teeth, and fine eyes;
A fig for them all, they can never compare
To my charmer's elastic white thighs."

"Chap's bawdy song reminds me of that widow at Oxford. Remember Mrs Chloe Russell?" Bram lolled in his chair, looking content after four jugs of claret, three glasses of port, two brandies and a cheroot. He also looked stewed to the gills, thought Rakecombe, speculating on his own external status.

"Lud," replied Jack. "Fine figure of a woman and the instigator of many a cub's dreams."

"Was it you?" Bram pointed a finger at the rogue. "I always believed you won that bet."

Rakecombe sprawled back, frowning. He knew the bet they talked of. Mrs Russell had been the widow of a former professor. Pretty and vivacious, there had been a wager as to who could bed her first with the claimant having to describe her garters as proof. Sometime later, the absurd wager had been collected, but neither description nor name of the victor had been made public.

"Nope, too young." Jack held his palms up. "You forget I'm a fresh pup compared to you two, and I was just finding my feet in those days. Wish I had though; she had bosoms like–"

"Winterbourne," snapped Rakecombe, "Mrs Russell is a respectable lady."

"*Alex*, my fine fellow, you *have* to loosen up. 'Tis only in jest. I advise some brandy before tomorrow morning…and tomorrow night."

"I can only hope," Bram slurred, elbows now on the table, "my mother-in-law hasn't had time to speak to your betrothed about the wedding night."

"Why?" asked Rakecombe, intrigued and worried in equal measure.

"'Cos she fed Sophie some cock and bull story about stamens, stigmas and pollination."

Silence met this pronouncement.

"Gads," muttered Jack, "no wonder debutantes look so petrified. Still, I'm sure you have a vague idea of what to do, Alex, and you can always send for me if you have trouble. I can call instructions from behind a screen. Or you could blindfold me. Millie has a–"

"Enough." Rakecombe rose, listing slightly, glad Jack had dragged him out but now wanting to thrash the bugger. "I am for bed," he pronounced, "as one is getting married on the morrow."

After unsteadily gathering cane and jacket, he veered past the strewn tables, toppled bodies and scattered empty chairs, before glancing over his shoulder. "And by the way, Mrs Russell's garters were Pomona green with white lace trim."

Winterbourne and Kelmarsh could be forgiven for their stupefaction, as he wasn't the rake of his name in any literal sense, but in his youth, before his world had ended, he'd dallied on occasion.

The ladies had liked his discretion, but he doubted Mrs Russell cared any longer. He'd seen her on the street once, married again with five children and another on the way.

He staggered up the stairs and out the door, nearly falling in a puddle – damn claret – when an arm slipped under his right shoulder.

"Rakecombe, you old dog," said Bram, chuckling.

Another arm slipped beneath his left. "An unmitigated cur, I'd say," Jack added, eyes moist with mirth.

With his friends supporting him, or each other he wasn't sure, they lumbered along whilst Bram and Jack quibbled over the parallels between botany and sexual congress. He winced and hoped to God that someone with more modern notions than Mrs Beckford had spoken to Aideen tonight.

They meandered through Covent Garden, circumventing its various ladies of the night, and gradually quietened in their own thoughts.

He could guess Bram's – thinking of Sophie, no doubt, but peering at the marquess, he noted a slightly glum expression now the night was nearly over. Perhaps he'd invite him home for a nightcap. Winterbourne hid emotions not many saw.

But then so did he.

When he'd spoken of his impending marriage, he'd thought panic would be the main emotion flooding him, but instead a deep satisfaction had threaded its way down his spine.

Thrilling, rousing but dangerous nevertheless.

No more arguments from those sweet cherry lips. No more provoking insults or baiting words.

The hoyden would obey him and be his forever.

AIDEEN HOPED the duke didn't expect her to obey his every word once they were married.

Some men, she had noted, became most dictatorial once in the parson's mousetrap, and indeed Mrs McNally from Ballyduff had her pin money deducted if she queried her husband in public.

With thoughts akin to a lump of wet turf, Aideen lay like a corpse on the bed.

Earlier, Mr and Mrs Beckford, Cordelia and herself had enjoyed a genial dinner to *celebrate* her marriage on the morrow, and although she had hoped Cordelia might join her for a late-night prittle-prattle, Mrs Beckford had sent them off to bed with a severe warning about wedding day wrinkles caused by lack of sleep.

But sleep was not forthcoming; instead, a hundred different notions assailed her and now she'd be a crinkled sultana for the ceremony.

Saints in their halos, tomorrow she'd become a duchess. Married to the pompous Duke of Rakecombe. His mother hadn't even been to call, citing an unwell friend, but Aideen knew what that meant – she disapproved.

Not only that but there was the wedding night. She hardly knew the man and yet…

She would be naked.

He would be naked.

They would be naked.

Together.

Then again, she had heard some odd specifics about the English aristocracy and their nocturnal arrangements, so maybe not.

A soft knock on the door halted her musings, and she prayed it wasn't Mrs Beckford with more botanical advice for tomorrow night. She pretended to sleep.

"Aideen?"

Recognising the voice, she flung herself from the bed and threw open the door. "Sophie!"

Hugs and tears were exchanged as she greeted her cousin with abandon. Cordelia stood behind, wielding a bottle of champagne in each hand.

AIDEEN DUMPED the last vestiges into her glass as her friends lounged about the bed in various states of inebriation.

"Has Mrs Beckford advised you about the wedding night?" asked Cordelia, scrunching her nose and chewing a ribbon. "I asked Mother, but she told me I shouldn't worry about little things like that."

Sophie snorted, spilling precious champagne.

"She did try," replied Aideen, "but I told her I'd seen the kitchen maid and the footman in the stables when I was sixteen."

"You told my mother that?" Sophie screeched, hands held to her cheeks.

"I had to. I couldn't bear it. She had illustrations from Sowerby's botany book."

"I didn't get illustrations," Sophie groused whilst Cordelia's head twisted from side to side in tandem with the conversation, huge innocent blue eyes avid with curiosity.

"After your debacle, she probably felt it necessary."

Sophie sighed. "I do hope the duke will treat you gently. I like him tremendously, but he can be more than a little…"

Aideen's head nodded but her thoughts disagreed. She didn't want the duke gentle. She wanted his hard, demanding body and searching rough hands, his raw knuckles skimmi–

"Erm," interrupted Cordelia, "if I could just ask, but… would anyone care to enlighten me?"

Aideen and Sophie stared at one another, then to their champagne glasses.

"Does it have anything to do with nightcaps?" prompted Cordelia desperately. "I've noticed my father wears a nightcap if he wishes to join my mother in her bedchamber."

Opening her mouth, Sophie then closed it again.

"Or curtain tie-backs? I know all about those," Cordelia tried again, face frantic. "My aunt told me that matching curtain colours to their tie-backs is a pleasant subject to dwell upon when a husband visits you."

Opening her mouth, Aideen instead glugged champagne.

Sophie stepped bravely into the breach. "I don't believe I can imagine your Lord Oakdean in a nightcap. And that's a good thing," she reassured Cordelia, patting her hand. "You'll just have to trust him and not listen to anything your mother or aunt says. At all. In any way. Ever."

"But...but..."

"Have you not seen animals?" asked Aideen. "In the fields?" Surely her friend had noticed some strange behaviour in spring.

Cordelia's brow furrowed. "Playing?"

Saint Ninnidh help her.

"More...jumping on each other."

"Oh!" Her eyes widened to their limits but then lowered, shoulders easing. "You're always teasing, Aideen. Honestly, a sip of champagne and you come out with the most ridiculous ideas."

Aideen smiled. She loved Cordelia immensely, but her friend's mother had instilled a strange incorruptibility about her.

"Well," said Sophie, raising the remnants of her champagne. "I say we toast Aideen's marriage. May it forever endure without nightcaps or curtain ties."

9

WRTH GICIO A BRATHU, MAE CARIAD YN MAGU.

WHILST KICKING AND BITING, LOVE DEVELOPS. (WELSH PROVERB)

The one downside to Rakecombe's wedding day morning was the sight of a sotted marquess and snoring earl in his normally immaculate study. The loiter-sacks slobbered over his furniture and had noticeably scuffed the silk.

Had the twosome really been so deeply cut that they couldn't find the guest chambers?

He himself had awoken snug in bed, but perhaps Rawlins had lent a hand, in part earning his exorbitant wage.

Considering the quantity of hashed goose, claret and brandy he'd consumed, Rakecombe felt rather well. No doubt, skipping chef's breakfast had aided his agreeable constitution. A selection of pastries had been sent up but they'd wept with butter and he'd pushed them to one side.

He shook Winterbourne's shoulders as the chap drooled over his chaise, feet bare.

"Gerroff, darling," the rogue slurred. "Maybe later."

"Get your hairy arse, *darling,* off my furniture. You have one hour to return home, scrub yourself clean and attend my wedding."

Blood-shot eyes opened. "It's a nightmare." They closed again.

Slightly easier to awaken was Kelmarsh, who guiltily realised he'd sent no message to his wife about the impromptu nightcap.

The two wastrels sluggishly gathered their thoughts and strewn waistcoats, and Rakecombe bustled them with indecent haste to the hall, denying them breakfast – in truth doing them a favour.

Upon arrival at the main door, where his efficient butler stood with their coats, he promptly twisted to Kelmarsh as a thought had been preying on his mind this morning.

"Should anything happen to me…in the future. Look after Aideen, won't you? I need to know she'll be protected." His friend nodded, eyes grave and knowing. "And you also, Winterbourne. For some reason, she favours your acquaintance."

"Of course, old fellow," he replied, clapping a hand to his shoulder. "But no more *tristus canis* today. We live for the moment as the future is forever just that. Now," he said, running fingers through his immaculate hair despite a night on the chaise – how did he do that? "Have you anything other than black for your wedding? Or else the mourners… I'm sorry, *guests* may get the wrong idea."

Rakecombe thought for a moment. "I have an off-black waistcoat with charcoal thread running through it."

"Hmm. I'll send something over. No need to thank me."

AIDEEN SAT. Twitched. Fiddled with her lilac wedding gown. Even her toes jiggled in the silk slippers.

Everyone had abandoned her, citing the absurd notion that she needed some time to herself this morning before the *big event.* Time to gather her thoughts and to rest.

She didn't.

Only when reading did she ever have restful thoughts, the story transporting her to another place, but she could hardly bury herself in a book now: the words would be a hodgepodge.

Furtively, she gazed over at a purple box deposited on the side table.

Sophie had brought it earlier as an additional wedding gift, but she'd made Aideen promise on her lucky clover not to open it until tonight. What Sophie didn't know, however, was that her lucky clover had never performed as wished and she'd given up on the dratted thing a year ago.

The wedding gown rustled as she stood and meandered in a roundabout way to the box as though someone was watching her through a crack in the door. She skirted a chair and peered at the many flowers on the mantel – from everyone except her spouse-to-be.

Well, if the entire family were going to leave her alone, what was she supposed to do?

Covertly, she skimmed a finger under the box lid. There was something silky, something–

"Miss Quinlan?"

"I didn't do it. It wasn't me," she shrieked, turning and knocking the box to the floor.

A lady, and there was no doubt this *was* a lady, stood in the doorway. The Duchess of Rakecombe – soon to be addressed as Dowager.

Oh heavens.

With spine straight and head high, the duchess perused Aideen from mauve slippers to the violets in her hair. The lady herself wore an exquisite deep navy gown with matching pelisse – a fashion plate of sophistication, and even though Aideen was taller than the older female, she felt lower than a snake.

"Miss Aideen Quinlan," the duchess repeated, her tone all hauteur.

Was that a question or a statement or a command?

"Yes, Your Grace." She gave her best curtsey, kicking the box under the table.

"Hmm. An unusual given name. It means *little fire*." A fierce glare followed that question. "Are you?"

Aideen considered a clanker, but they were to be related and she would only be able to hide her true nature for so long.

"Yes. I have been known to be on occasion."

Her Grace's eyes began to fill with tears and her lip quivered.

Fiddlesticks, as Mrs Beckford would say.

The small woman dashed towards her and Aideen flinched, but then…

Uncle Seamus was good at hugs, hearty and strong; they smelled of smoke and wood. Mrs Beckford's were appreciated, but always at a distance as they creased one's gown. Sophie's were mad and tangled.

This lady's was enthusiastic and heartfelt, arms surrounding Aideen's waist, tight and sincere; she smelled of expensive silk and orange blossom.

"I'm so glad." The duchess pulled back, face wreathed in smiles, satin hands cupping Aideen's cheeks. "I worried he'd marry some milksop miss and that isn't what the boy needs at all."

Boy? "Erm, thank you."

"You're perfect, my dear. I can tell. And us Celts must stick together."

"Celts?" Aideen stared at her imminent mother-in-law's face as intelligent faded green eyes rolled in disgust. She was pretty, not in a handsome way but soft, like a peach, and age looked well on her.

The lady elegantly seated herself on the settee and patted the silk cushion next to her. "Has Alex not told you anything about our family?"

Aideen perched on the edge. "We've not had many…conversations."

"Oh, the naughty whelp."

"I didn't mean–"

She laughed, a delicate trill. "I was delighted when I saw him kissing you so ardently. I'd almost despaired of him, you understand. He needs to…unstiffen a little."

Aideen couldn't contain a snort. "You are not what I expected, Your Grace."

"Pish, call me Meghan. I know he likes to act the priggish proper duke, but he conveniently forgets that his father and I eloped to Gretna Green."

"What?" Aideen gawped.

"My, he hasn't told you anything, has he? Are you sure you want him? We could travel to Egypt instead. I've always wanted to go and am seeking a suitable companion. We will get on famously, I can tell."

Aideen was used to Uncle Seamus talking at tangents, but she did enjoy Meghan's thought process.

Did Aideen *want* the Duke of Rakecombe?

Unfortunately…yes.

"Why did you go to Gretna Green? Did the then duke disapprove?"

"Oh, gracious no, dear." She leaned in. "My own father did! Isn't that wonderful? I grew up in a tiny harbour village in north Wales. Gentlefolk, yes, but no title, and years in England has erased the accent. Anyhow, my Matthew, Alex's father, was in Wales for the air – he always suffered from delicate lungs – and we met whilst I was sketching the castle. It was love at first sight." The lady sighed.

Egad, and Aideen thought she talked a lot. "So why–"

"I had more money in my reticule than his family had in their vaults. His father, Alex's grandfather, was an absolute gambling wastrel – lost everything. Of course, he had the entailed estate but it was not well-tended and so gave no income. My father thus considered Matthew of the same ilk, so we eloped, dear. Fortuitously, well, not to speak ill of the dead, but Alex's grandfather died suddenly, and we spent years rebuilding the monies and estate – such happy times. Along came Alex and then Gwen. But my Matthew died of those weak lungs and then...we lost Gwen also." She took an immaculate handkerchief from her reticule and dabbed at rounded cheeks.

Without hesitation, Aideen clasped the duchess's hand in hers. "I'm so sorry about your husband; you must miss him greatly. And I apologise for my ignorance, but who is Gwen?"

"Oh!" She scowled. "I'll have Alex's guts for garters. Gwen was his sister, my daughter, born four years after Alex. She was taken from us at eighteen years."

Aideen hugged the now sorrowful woman. The word "taken" allowed for so many interpretations, none of them good.

"How truly awful. I'm so very sorry for your loss."

"'Twas long ago, my dear. At the time, it hurt like a mortal wound and though it still aches, I can breathe easier now. My Matthew used to say life is not life without bitterness, for how can we appreciate the sweetness. I am not sure Alex has learned this yet."

Meghan stood but not before another forceful hug. "I am so glad he is to marry you. And if you are concerned about society, as I was at your age, do not worry a jot, for we will be a twosome to be reckoned with. As for Alex… He needs someone to challenge him, to interest him, but even more, to love him. He is not the easiest of men, but I know he would be worth it. I know he could give so much, if he would only allow himself. So I hope you will come to love him, Aideen. See you in church."

A buss to the cheek and the scent of orange blossom departed.

Aideen sat, her thoughts a mumble-jumble.

The duchess's words had struck deep, but the question was not perhaps *could* she come to love him, but whether she already did.

10

WHITHER-GO-YE.

A WIFE: WIVES BEING SOMETIMES APT TO QUESTION THEIR HUSBANDS WHITHER THEY ARE GOING. (GROSE 1811)

The aisle loomed ahead, an elongated path of fraught unease and enormity.

And at the end of it stood her spouse-to-be. Or rather the back of him, as although guests had twisted for a glimpse of her, Rakecombe remained unperturbed.

How typical.

Mr Beckford patted her arm and cast a questioning glance, to which she responded with a smile. She herself had agreed to this wedding and a Quinlan never backed down, so grasping his hand firmly, too firmly judging by his grimace, the two of them meandered down the aisle as though they'd all the time in the world.

Amongst the guests, Sophie fluttered her fingers from a pew to the left and Jack winked from the right. Mrs Beckford cast a watery grin and Meghan positively beamed.

Rakecombe still remained unperturbed.

Finally, as her skirts rustled against his leg and Kelmarsh

nudged him with an elbow, he tipped his head in her direction.

It would almost have been a disappointment if he had smiled, a cliché. Firm lips held their place, cool eyes inspected and nostrils flared, so she merely raised a brow and then faced the man of God about to marry them.

For the duration of the ceremony, the Duke of Restraint reigned supreme, his bearing officious and unbending as though a blade prodded his spine, skin like ice when their hands were joined in holy matrimony.

And no warmth entered his eyes when he held out his arm for them to depart the church as husband and wife, although his gaze did pause to linger on the violets in her hair.

A part of her wished he'd show some slight contentment at marrying her, but then again, his solemn countenance had in truth given credence to this life-binding ceremony and she'd felt a certain comfort in his firm avowals to care for her always, in sickness and in health.

But the fact remained, he'd resembled an icicle.

Indeed, an icicle might have been preferable – at least they melted in spring.

"I AM GOING out and will not return for dinner."

The stern voice, not requiring of reply, interrupted her thoughts, and she eyed her husband of barely one hour across the celebratory wedding table, guests and family chatting around her with inebriated enthusiasm.

He hadn't melted during the carriage ride to the Rakecombe residence. Instead, he'd grown yet more tense, more aloof, and the only saving grace to all this starchiness were his clothes. A bottle-green tailcoat, an emerald waistcoat, black breeches, and an amethyst stickpin which matched her dress.

The damn bug looked utterly splendid, but had he attempted to brighten up his attire for her benefit or–

"Glad to see my togs fit you, Rakehell," boomed Lord Winterbourne as he plonked himself on the seat next to her husband.

That would be a no, then. Jack had persuaded him.

How very...disenchanting. And now he was going out. On their wedding day.

Yes, their marriage had been forced, but surely he liked her well enough to spend a few hours with her?

But perhaps he didn't. Perhaps a certain desire was all he felt, and the surly shabbaroon had tired of their banter already.

She looked away, not wishing him to see the hurt, but ended up clashing eyes with Jack – who saw all too well, she realised.

"You look divine, Aideen. Perfect," the rogue flattered. "Has Rakeshame also told you that? Or is he being coy?"

Abruptly, she straightened her spine. She was a Quinlan...and now a Rakecombe. The combination appeared heady. "No, Jack, he hasn't. To be sure, he has been most solemn and inaudible. One would think he is not happy with *his* choice."

"Perhaps, Your Gracefulness," Jack declared, "he just needs a little encouragement. What say you, Rakeshame, how do you find your bride?"

The full aristocratic gaze speared her way and she steadily glared back. His eyes wandered over her ringlets, paused on her face, narrowed on her lips. Lower, his perusal caught on her bosom, caressing her waist, until finally it landed at the table.

"I cannot wait for supper," he drawled.

Jack choked on his wine, and Aideen scowled. The arrogant jackanapes. "Perhaps, Your Grace, I will also be *out* and not return for supper."

His nostrils flared, eyes livening to a verdant forest, and he leaned forward. She did the same.

"Hellcat," he hissed.

"Hellhound," she answered.

They were inches apart. The green in his eyes became absorbed by black and that dilated gaze dropped to her lips.

"I think this conversation should continue tonight," murmured Jack, slanting into their midst. "Such sweet love play does not belong at the wedding breakfast table."

WITH FOOD still heaped upon the serving platters and guests still making merry, Aideen watched her husband depart the festivities with Jack. She knew the marquess also worked for the Crown and so supposed they must be off on spy business.

If there was some reason behind his hasty departure, she wouldn't mind being abandoned quite so much.

Napoleon and his minions didn't care that he'd married today, and enemies of the state hadn't sat down for a cup of tea and put their feet up solely because Miss Aideen Quinlan had acquired a husband.

In actuality, she and Uncle Seamus had worked all hours on occasion too, crafting some urgent piece for the fellows at Whitehall. Fiendish snuff boxes with hidden space for papers, pistols that fitted in a beaver hat and waistcoats that guarded guineas. All for the freedom of these islands and the Continent.

So how could she begrudge an afternoon?

Contemplating the grand room, she felt pleased the duke had suggested hosting the breakfast at his Grosvenor abode as the Beckfords' would have been too small. She had attended here once as a guest but living in this austere house would be a different matter.

Tall ceilings and cold marble caused the place to feel unloved, and sound echoed eerily in the substantial rooms. The servants had stood at the steps to greet her – all thirty-two of them, not including those from the stable mews – but they'd acted welcoming enough.

Family and close friends still filled the room, with Meghan chatting to Sophie and Cordelia, whilst the Earl of Kelmarsh sat with a certain Viscount Rainham.

She tapped a finger against her mouth and scrutinised Lord Rainham.

A shrewd face. Intelligent and wise. She'd noticed him talking quietly with Rakecombe earlier and assumed he must be something to do with Crown affairs.

At that moment, he glanced up as though hearing her thoughts. Both men stood and made their way to her.

"Aideen, you look beautiful." Kelmarsh grinned. "May I introduce the Viscount Rainham." She held out her hand. "And Lord Rainham, may I present, Her Grace, the new Duchess of Rakecombe."

The gentleman kissed said hand. "Delighted, Your Grace. And such a pretty given name, means litt–"

"Yes. I'm afraid I am," she responded before he could ask.

Lord Rainham smiled, displaying straight white teeth. "Then you are perfect."

"And you're the third to say that today. It could all go to a girl's head but thank you, I don't know why."

"The duke needs a robust companion." He paused, looking thoughtful. "Are you aware of my connection with your husband?"

"I believe I can guess, my lord."

His brow lifted, and his gaze inspected her again. Finally, he nodded. "Come meet Lily Mereworth, my wife-to-be. She asked me to marry her last week."

Lord Rainham hustled an open-mouthed Aideen to the delicate blonde she'd seen at his side earlier, and she was once again envious of a loving couple as introductions were made.

Although there was no overt physical show of affection, Lord Rainham's hazel eyes softened as he beheld Lily and the lady's smile in return was equally tender.

In an instant, she recalled Rakecombe and herself spitting words over the wedding table. Would they mellow with time? Was she normal to enjoy the baiting? The taunting?

"I must speak with Mr Beckford," said Lord Rainham. "He wants to know why he keeps losing at piquet." He bowed to Aideen. "Give my regards to your Uncle Seamus when you write to him." And with a subtle wink he turned, leaving Aideen open-mouthed...again.

"Congratulations, Your Grace," said Lily Mereworth, and Aideen wondered who she was talking to.

"Oh, that's me," she gasped. "Please, call me Aideen... It's too strange."

The lady laughed, a broad warm chuckle which she felt impulsively drawn to.

"You are reminiscent of my betrothed." Lily's eyes flitted to the deep-blue tailcoat of Lord Rainham. "He has recently been made viscount but still looks around for one when thus addressed."

"Did you really ask him to marry you?" Aideen blurted before raising a hand to her runaway mouth. "Oh, I'm so sorry, that was most rude."

But the lady just giggled again. "I did. Although I didn't lower to one knee. That would have been frightfully improper."

Aideen laughed with her and felt…content. She gazed around the room, at the loving Beckfords, at Sophie and Cordelia, at Meghan, staring wistfully at the wedding cake, and at this sweet lady that she felt would become a good friend.

This was her family now, she realised. Not always of blood, but of friendship and mutual care. And she was enfolded within it.

RAKECOMBE STOOD NAKED beneath his bathing contraption and pulled the rope, letting the freezing cold water sluice his body.

It cleared his head but did not halt the raging lust that had beset him all afternoon. He angrily pumped the handle again, venting his frustration on the device. Water shot up the pipes and he pulled the release rope once more, dispensing the contents directly onto his face.

Once in a while, he requested heated water be put into the storage vessel of this newfangled apparatus, and if he was lucky, it would still be warm when he crept in. But tonight he needed some ice-cold clarity.

It was a half after nine and he'd been informed that following the wedding breakfast, Aideen had toured the house, dined with his mother and then retired abed, ordering that no supper was required for him.

The minx.

Fortunately, his valet Thorn knew his master's habits well and had laid out cold meat and bread. Most of the servants had been given the night off as part of the celebrations, his valet included, but he often asked for the bathing device to be filled and food to be left on the dresser.

If a night's investigation had ended badly or without result, he didn't want to be fussed over by Thorn. He wanted to be left well alone.

Towelling himself as he stepped out, he pondered on what to wear. A bronze-coloured banyan had been laid out but that felt presumptuous, so he strode over to the wardrobe and gathered shirt and breeches.

Not that this afternoon's investigations had concluded negatively.

Winterbourne had suggested taking Stafford's carping butler to an ale-house to loosen him up.

He'd loosened aplenty – boasting of his conquests, complaining of how cold the house was and bemoaning his master's lack of manners. Apparently, he considered Stafford an uncouth thug and lamented the shortage of decent families to butler for.

Perhaps he had sought employment and if the grizzled fellow had been a chef, Rakecombe might have been interested.

After that, he'd departed the ale-house in order to sort out a guard for Aideen. Someone reliable and quiet. A veritable shadow that she would never see.

It had taken longer than expected as he'd been obliged to interview sixteen candidates but eventually an unassuming but suitably brawny chap had been selected.

Now dressed, Rakecombe slugged a brandy.

Would his wife's door be barred to him? He had, after all, left Aideen alone at their wedding breakfast, and what had seemed such a good idea yesterday evening now seemed utterly despicable in the cold light of day.

He'd abandoned his beautiful bride with unknown guests in a strange house.

He'd called her a hellcat.

Swiping a hand over his face, he wondered if he should even attempt to enter her quarters at all, as 'twas probable he'd get a chamber pot in the physog. And he wouldn't blame her.

But surely as soon as they'd burned through this lust, they could live their lives peacefully...and separately. His gut seared in torment, and he wasn't sure it was the brandy.

Snatching up the decanter and two glasses, he headed to the adjoining door and knocked. No light shone beneath, but a candle near the bed would cast only shade.

His insides twisted, and the decanter wobbled in his grasp.

God, was he...nervous?

"Yes," a soft Irish voice answered, and he grasped the handle whilst juggling the glassware. Thus, he must have projected the quintessential befuddled bridegroom as he lurched into the room.

He stopped dead.

The duchess's bedchamber had remained unoccupied for aeons. His mother had vacated it when Father had died, citing too many memories, and even that hadn't been enough as she'd then moved into one of his smaller townhouses. She still used their family abode for soirées and came to dinner once too often, but he wondered if she was to thank for the fresh decor.

Immaculate silks festooned the bed in a deep rust and new furniture adorned the room: an elegant writing desk, a dressing table with huge mirror and a comfortable striped silk chaise. In the far wall, a new fireplace glowed to counter the damp of London spring.

The lone item he did recognise was the walnut wardrobe, but the probable reason it hadn't been removed was because it was the size of Piccadilly.

Aideen lay in the middle of the huge bed, reading a book by candlelight, wild black curls cascading around her. She wore a night robe, a frilly white concoction that obliterated any sight of her body, fastened tight to the neck.

She put the book aside and clasped her hands, lace now obliterating any view of even that skin. "Your Grace. I hope you had a successful afternoon?"

Was that sarcasm or genuine interest?

It annoyed him that he didn't know, that he didn't know *her* well enough to discern the truth. But then he wasn't here for polite chit-chat.

His lust told him not to waste time. It ached to rip that frilly item from her, devour her whole.

But that wasn't very ducal.

Tonight, he needed his control in more ways than one.

In order to keep his future distance, he would need to maintain calm and full awareness of his body's reactions and emotions. It would be all too easy to become carried away with the duchess. To utter words that should remain unsaid.

"Very," he finally answered, rather stiffly even to his own ears. With care, he deposited the decanter and glasses on the writing desk. "Can I pour you a drink?"

Aideen nodded, although she also pointed to the bedside table and he noticed a cup of something.

"Tea?" he queried.

"Chocolate with brandy. Warms the cockles. But a glass undiluted would be...relaxing." She licked her lips.

If she was trying to bring him to his knees then she was succeeding, so to curb the threat, he turned and decanted two glasses.

From the corner of his eye, he saw her push the coverlet back and swing her legs to the floor. The frilly robe enveloped her in a mass of ribbons and lace and frills and– It was hideous.

"Where did you get that robe?" he asked solicitously as she walked towards him. He'd never seen her in anything so horrific – normally her taste was impeccable, tight silks in colours that lit her skin and eyes.

Their fingers brushed as he handed her the glass.

Damnation, the merest touch set him afire. What would happen if they were skin to skin?

"Mrs Beckford's bridal present."

A deterrent? He took a sip of liquor.

"But," she said, twisting a ribbon at the neck, "perhaps you might prefer Sophie's wedding gift?" The ribbon parted, and the ridiculous frilly item slid from her shoulders.

He couldn't splutter his brandy – perhaps because his mouth had dried. Everything had headed south at the sight of Aideen.

A deep ocean-blue night-rail draped her body with alternate bands of gossamer and plain silk, begging his fingers to discover the secrets beneath. A low bodice framed pale skin and material clung sensuously to her curves, trailing her slender waist and full hips.

The curve of her breast was shielded by silk, but only sheer material swathed her legs.

"Beautiful, Aideen." There was no point denying such a blatant truth.

“Thank you,” she whispered, “the colour is a little dark for me, but–”

“I am not talking of the night-rail.”

A red flush caught her cheeks and he wanted to lave that heat from her skin. “I am most apologetic for calling you a hellcat. It was…impolite for a bridegroom.”

“Are you?” she asked with a sideways glance, sipping and then slowly licking the brandy from her ripe cherry lips.

“No,” he admitted. “You are beyond doubt a hellcat. My very own exquisite hellcat.”

Her rook-black eyes flared at his possessive tone and he silently cursed.

There was only one way to occupy his insolent tongue and so he put the glass down.

She did the same.

11

DISTANCE IS RELATIVE.

Tender or urgent?

Rakecombe knew which his body demanded but Aideen was a maiden despite her brazen tongue. He pressed a single finger to those red lips and they trembled beneath his touch.

For all her boldness, his hellcat was nervous. He caressed downwards with that one finger, across her neck as it arched, and along the edge of the material, until he met the ribbon at her breast.

Hooking a finger in the sheer silk, he pulled her closer, and their bodies brushed. He cupped that resolute chin and lowered his mouth.

Soft satin and warm temptation.

The kiss began leisurely.

Never before had he taken the time to savour Aideen but oh, how he did now.

Brandy, chocolate and violets engulfed his senses and he wished he hadn't been such a stubborn fool to abandon her this afternoon.

He could have picked the flowers from her hair, seen it

fall loose, slipped that lilac wedding gown from her body with tender appreciation.

Not that the blue night-rail hadn't turned his brain to pudding, and he slid a hand down her back, the material a teasing barrier to his desires.

Finally, his searching fingers found that stunning derriere and he palmed it, before pulling her tight to his body, mouth never leaving hers, breath forgotten as the storm built and their tongues tangled.

His wife gasped as their bodies fitted seamlessly. She must be able to feel his desire, his want, but she didn't pull back, and that gasp hadn't been maidenly shock either.

None the less, to ensure she knew exactly what was happening, he ground his pelvis against her softness whilst nuzzling her ear.

No protest came; instead, a low moan greeted his impudence, and he repeated the action – this time to assuage his own aching groin.

Never had he been so aroused, so heavy with need than at this moment. Nigh on a year had passed since he'd first met Aideen Quinlan and in that time, she'd oft disturbed his thoughts both by day and by night.

Their mouths met again, but restlessness replaced leisure and hands no longer caressed with ease but with potent fervour. His kiss grew rougher, but it was he that groaned as she nipped his lip and drew away.

Sooty eyes stared, glazed with passion, lips swollen, and he walked her backwards until she met the wall, the Cranford-red paper hangings a luscious backdrop to her midnight-clad form.

He envied that mask of silk clinging to her breast and thus yanked at the material until her pert nipple offered itself behind the gossamer band of the night-rail.

Vaguely, his brain implored him to be more circumspect with his innocent wife, that he lay her down and handle her with restraint, but this was Aideen.

His bold, mischievous, passionate Aideen.

And so, holding her gaze, he lowered his head and flicked a tongue over the veiling material. She jolted…and then moaned. So he did it again and fingers clenched in his hair, pulling him close.

Her hips bucked as he sucked silk and skin into his mouth, and gasping pants escaped her. Aideen's long fingers explored his shirted chest, pulling at the material and creeping into the open neck. The scads of material must have frustrated her because she stole around to his sensitive spine and as her fingers scratched along it, control slipped away; he grunted, tugging her strap down, desperate for naked skin.

So white as to be virtually translucent, that skin heaved, and he slid a palm gently over her breast, not wanting to mark her.

Yet it seemed Aideen desired firmer, thrusting herself into his touch.

Alas, his hands were calloused from fights and so forth, but she didn't seem to mind; in truth, the wilder he caressed her skin with rough fingers, the louder she moaned.

Fervently, he shoved the silk down, over her hips, heard something tear, and paused.

Control.

Maintain control.

But Aideen took that moment to explore, her fingers sliding past the band of his breeches.

A guttural groan absconded as she brushed his groin, a tender skim, but then she returned, firmer, bolder, moulding her palm to his rigid length.

Rakecombe's hands shot down to capture her wrists.

"Bed. Now."

IT MUST BE the first time their thoughts had ever concurred, thought Aideen, as the harsh command was growled out.

What he didn't seem to consider was that she was backed up against the wall and he was gripping her wrists. She couldn't stir.

Not that she minded her entrapment.

In fact, two hours ago, she'd thought she would be spending her wedding night with the fictional Corsair, as she had done quite a few nights since meeting the duke. A good substitute, she'd thought at the time, but now, gazing at her husband's handsome face, she much preferred the corporeal.

He'd bathed somehow as she'd heard peculiar sloshings from the master bedchamber next door and his hair was damp. It wasn't sleeked back as usual and now she could see why he brutally suppressed it, as a dark curl dangled over his forehead.

Curls and the Duke of Rakecombe dare not mix.

His breath panted, and his features appeared harsh and unforgiving, but his eyes… They gleamed with want and a wildness that both frightened and excited her.

"I cannot move, Your Grace," she whispered. He stood fully clothed, and she should have felt intimidated or nervous but instead the sensation of linen against her breast and his breeches rubbing at her thighs caused an awfully strange rumpus within.

He leaned close to her ear, still clutching her wrists, hot breath causing a squirm. "Say my name."

"The Duke of Rakecombe."

His lips minutely quirked. "Say it." And he bit her lobe.

"Alex."

"My full name... Please."

"Alexander."

"Again."

"Alexand–"

She was grasped from standing, twirled in sturdy arms and plonked on the soft bed. A tenacious body followed, bracing itself on forearms, before even more tenacious lips claimed any additional words with swirling possession.

The feel of his weight was ravishing. She'd landed with legs a dash splayed and he took full advantage, easing them apart with his feet and thrusting his hips.

That hard, male length she'd tried to explore surged at her core, seeking entry even through the barrier of his silk breeches.

His eternal restraint seemed to have snapped.

Alexander had begun the evening with controlled kisses but now the ferocity that she sometimes glimpsed beneath his meticulous exterior had been unchained...and she loved it.

Aideen pulled at his shirt, endeavouring to haul it over his head, but he took command, throwing it to the floor in a most un-ducal manner.

She ogled his body: slender but not skinny, firm muscles flexed in arm and chest, a smattering of hair covered his torso, and on his left shoulder, a nasty scar covered with a...

"Is that a tattoo?"

"Hmm," he growled, as his hand swept over her stomach and hip.

"Of an initial D?" She *was* trying not to ruin the moment, but really? The erstwhile stuffy duke – although he wasn't currently being very stuffy – had a tattoo.

She gasped as that hand encroached between her legs, brushing with feathered strokes, then firmer.

"D for Duke?" she enquired, stifling a moan as his fingers caressed in pulsing need.

No answer was forthcoming, and he continued to rouse, the sweet pleasure building within. His mouth moved to her breast again, laving and sucking with ruthless resolve.

"Demanding?" she queried with a cry. Her hips ground in tandem with his hand, body writhing until she could stand the tautness no longer. Too much. Not enough. "Desperate?"

Alex's gaze pierced her, those fully lashed green eyes steadfast on her face, his fingers pushing, rubbing. Lips brushed her neck, tasted her skin.

"Darkness," he whispered. "Destructive darkness." And he nipped at her neck.

The tightness exploded, gushing through her body. Limbs seized and back arched and all she could hear was his voice.

"Desolate. Dangerous," he growled, still grinding his hand. "Yes, Aideen. My little fire…Aideen."

She melted into the rust coverlet, body pliant yet shuddering.

Divine.

Lifting hazy eyes, she expected to see a smug expression on his face but instead saw a man possessed as he ripped at the fall on his breeches.

He didn't remove them, just shoved the clothing down and nudged her legs wide. She'd felt lax and fulfilled but with his movements, his obvious and overwhelming need, her desire pulsed once more.

Bruising kisses and an abrading thumb at her breast caused her to arch yet again and with a satisfied grunt, he pressed forward, his arousal blunt and solid and thick, surging against her core – not tentative but persistent and adamant and not to be denied.

Gasping, she shoved hips against his, encircling his neck with eager arms, kissing his throat. He strained and she cried out at the sensation.

Unyielding. Stretched.

He reared, sank, took her mouth in a kiss once more and thrust. Deep and hard.

Lips stole her cry, a harsh pinch, but then…

"It's so…tight," she whispered against his mouth.

Rigidly shut eyes lifted and he groaned. "Hell, yes."

"That's not a good thing," she stated, but Alex gently rocked his body back and forth, forth and back, face turning.

Clasping her leg, he pulled her thigh about his slender hip, so she did the same with the other and a growl rumbled from him as he slipped deeper, the fit eased, and he brushed something deliciously pleasurable.

"Alexander," she murmured, and he twisted, eyes meeting hers.

His features were a mask, severe and cruel in the candlelight, but his lips were tender, his hands supple as they stroked over her skin.

And then he thrust in earnest.

Steadied on forearms, he began a rugged heavy rhythm. It obliterated all thought, all speech, as searing aching need spread throughout.

She scratched that need into his back and he bucked under her touch, acceding to her wishes and pounding with unrelenting pace.

Pleasure engulfed her once more, but this time ecstasy rippled in long waves, endless as he continued his raw act of possession. She cried his name, sensation hurtling through bone, blood and skin, feeling turned inside out.

A kiss took her, a rough ferocity, but no sooner was her mouth captured, it ended and fierce eyes stared down, his movements wild and relentless.

"Yes, my Aideen, I so need..."

His jaw gritted, and cursing, he buried his face in her neck, hips now driving in savage short jabs. A guttural roar echoed the room as he convulsed, body heaving and slick. Aideen scraped her fingers down over his buttocks and another low moan left his throat.

She wished she'd been able to see his face as he'd found his pleasure but would be content with his shaking body and coarse whispers of passion.

Her own body felt so wonderfully malleable and floppy beneath his, as though made of dough, and when he finally rolled, she made no fuss as he hauled her close, stroking her hair.

Alexander's chest heaved, and she drew a finger down the line of hair, delighting in the tremor it produced.

Closing her eyes, she wondered how she would feel seeing his face across the pillows tomorrow morning?

Tenderness? Contentment... Love?

But her exhausted body didn't care for such fanciful sentiment and her thoughts drifted away as she fell into slumber.

THE LEADEN DAWN AWOKE RAKECOMBE, and he peered at the shutterless window with annoyance.

Where the blazes–

A soft breathing stirred the air and he realised his shoulder was numb. Not unusual as his old wound still gave him gyp, but this time, the cause was a dark-haired siren of a wife.

He swiped a hand over his face. Hell, and he thought himself a master of control. All had been well until he'd heard his name on her lips.

The slow lilt had sent desire streaking throughout, including the portion of his brain responsible for restraint, and if she ever found out what that lilt did to him, it didn't bear thinking about. She'd have him twisted around her little finger.

Murmuring from the corridor distracted him: the maids beginning their duties. He had to leave. If he stayed, he would take her again.

It had happened once more in the night. He'd awoken to soft buttocks brushing his groin, his hand on her breast, her breathing fast, and he hadn't been able to resist. Caresses had become secondary as he'd plunged his body into hers, and she'd been so ready…

But that was yesterday.

Today, he had to implement the plan and although they would be required to meet for the procreation of an heir, it would be better to keep some distance for a while, to let the blood cool. One night was all he would allow himself for a period of time.

And without doubt, he did need to double his efforts to find this traitor. Informants' lives depended on it.

Aideen Quinl– Or rather the Duchess of Rakecombe was a distraction he must avoid – for everyone's safety.

Briefly, he wondered what his sister would have made of his new wife. He had a feeling she would have approved, would have liked Aideen's boldness and total disdain for his arrogant ways.

But his sister wasn't here. Her joy silenced forever. And whose fault was that?

No one's but his.

Honesty, he'd decided all those years ago, was the better option with his family, so they could be aware and alert to the dangers which followed men such as himself. He'd thought additional guards for the house, vigilance with strangers and caution in speech would keep everyone safe. But he hadn't counted on Gwen's–

Aideen snuffled, and he gently shifted her from his shoulder, denying the possessive thrill as he noticed ruby marks on the curve of her neck and breast. She mumbled into the pillow, something about thighs, but he thinned his lips, forcing the smile away.

Warmth evaporated as he wrenched himself to stand.

Strewn on the floor were his breeches but his shirt had disappeared, and nude, he walked to their adjoining door.

Fleetingly, he recollected that moment of heady carnality when they'd been merged so very deeply. He'd lost his wits, groaned her name, and said he so needed…

Needed what exactly?

Stepping through to his bedchamber, he closed the door behind him.

And turned the key.

12

WHAT CAN ONE EXPECT FROM A PIG BUT A GRUNT.

"Is everything to your satisfaction, dear? I hope you're not unhappy?"

Aideen stabbed her liver-tinged sausage and wrinkled her nose.

Unhappy.

That was the understatement of 1815. No, she wasn't unhappy. She was utterly fuming.

Five days ago, she may have answered Meghan differently. Indeed, she may have even simpered that she was stupendously ecstatic. Now she didn't have enough fingers and toes to count the wrongdoings of her husband; she severed her stringy bacon ruthlessly.

But for starters…

He never dined with her.

He was always out.

He'd spoken to her solely once.

Bleary-eyed, she had awoken after the wedding night to a stern dictate about bolting her shutters at dusk.

Not being her sharpest at first light, she'd had no witty retorts or scowling reproofs. She'd simply gawked at him, as he'd stood there, all tidily dressed for the day in deepest black, with eyes as aloof and unblinking as a lizard's.

She recognised such tactics – use dictates to undermine one's foe. Or wife.

Onto other misconducts…

He'd not visited her bed again.

Deuced man, he'd even locked their adjoining door. A trifling endeavour, of course, as Uncle Seamus had gifted her a lock-picking device, but it was the intention that mattered.

He ignored her.

And even if they did happen to pass in a hallway, he treated her as if an inanimate object. She'd tried to speak but he'd hurried on, feigned deafness or glared – sometimes all three. She had no wish to live in his pocket, but a "Good Morning, my duchess" might be appreciated once in a while.

He had a man following her.

"Meghan, have you noticed a young, well-built chap lurking about?"

Her mother-in-law helped herself to an extremely runny egg – even the white dashed around.

"Oh, you'll get used to that. Alex has had a guard trailing me for years. I pretend not to notice the poor fellow, but I often wish to invite him in for tea, especially when it's raining."

Aideen harrumphed. She didn't actually mind the guard – a useful precaution with her husband's work, but he hadn't even asked.

Narrowing her eyes, she glared at a portrait of the duke high on the wall, which equally returned her scowl to the breakfast table.

Each night, she'd heard him enter his room extremely late, and then there had followed all that sloshing noise. It wasn't a bath – wrong splash – and it wasn't merely some ewer and basin. It sounded as though he had a personal raincloud in his chambers.

But he never came near her door.

How could she speak to him if he was never there? Ask him if they could possibly attend an event together? Or dine together? Or read? Anything really.

Of course, she knew he was busy spying on people and dealing with matters for the Crown, and that had consoled her until she'd learned from Jack that her husband had attended Lady Rowe's ball on Tuesday…alone.

Why hadn't he invited her?

And where were all the other society invites? Post seemed to disappear before she arose.

Was he ashamed of being seen with an Irish upstart?

The duke had also informed the butler to refuse all house calls until "the duchess had settled in." But she didn't feel the need to settle in. The Quinlan household in Ireland was on the large size and she'd been organising that well enough since she'd been old enough to give orders – so around eight years of age, she recalled. And in any case, the dowager duchess had been a wonder, calling in for breakfast and chatting about duties and so forth.

Boredom was not the problem as Meghan also had a surprising amount of charities which she patronised, and Aideen was only too happy to help, especially as they focused on hospitals in deprived areas rather than ladies sewing blankets.

No, she was…lonely, used to a busy home full of Uncle's hounds and relations popping in for home-distilled whisky.

The one caller had been Jack, whom she'd seen more than her husband in the last week. He'd been for tea, for a sherry and accompanied her to Gunter's.

She glowered. Perhaps a duchess's married life was supposed to be like this.

Separate. Cold. Unaffectionate. Lonely.

"Meghan? Did you and your late husband spend much time together?"

"Gracious, yes. He was quite modern and liked to involve me in the accounts and so forth. And we always dined together. And walked together. And rode together. And then the evenings…"

Oh.

A caring sage-green gaze drifted her way. "He's acting a bacon-brained buffoon, isn't he?"

Spluttering coffee, she nodded.

"Hmm. Plunkett, his man of affairs, will be arriving for their meeting at five today – happens every Thursday. Alex then has a brandy to recover. I suggest you corner him then, when he's mellowed."

"But…" Aideen hesitated.

Beneath the fuming was a deep sadness. Now he'd sated his lust, he wanted nothing to do with her. Bored with his wife after one night – it didn't say much for her attractions.

Maybe her father was right: her unladylike conduct gave a disgust, her boldness a repellence.

Meghan stood, sauntered over and then leaned on the table in a very un-duchess-like manner. "Aideen, you are beautiful, warm-hearted and such delightful company. It's Alex who is the dullard. And if it is any consolation, he is being a monster to all and sundry. I heard tell he even lost his temper with Lord Winterbourne at Lady Rowe's ball. He also cut Lady Lucas in the street for waving at him, and apparently his response to Lord Studland when the poor man queried after his welfare in White's was most ill-mannered. It's all the gossip."

Aideen frowned. Yes, Rakecombe had a reputation for being a bit callous, but all this did sound a smidgeon more ill-tempered than usual.

"You are under his skin, Aideen, scratching away." Meghan leaned closer. "Keep scratching, dear. Dig deep. Or…" She drew back. "…pish to the lot of them and we'll go to Egypt together. I do so like donkeys and can quite imagine us traversing the sands with some handsome Ottoman Sultan as guide."

RAKECOMBE QUAFFED his brandy and scratched his jaw.

Plunkett had left a half hour earlier with his tail between his legs, and Rakecombe knew he'd have to apologise for his foul mood. But dammit, nothing felt…right.

It was the search for Stafford, of course. It caused him sleepless nights and hence his discipline to wither.

This morning, he'd also met with Rainham, and since there appeared to be no leaking of the list of informants, it was now being presumed that Stafford and the documents were no longer of this earth.

Winterbourne and himself had been assigned other tasks, but something stirred maggots in his brain. A niggling doubt.

Via Bluey, he'd discovered that Stafford had been involved with a woman whilst undercover in Paris. Had she persuaded him to become a turncoat? Betray his country? Was a woman his downfall?

Sighing, he clonked his head against the high-backed chair, exhaustion probably accounting for his bad humour.

God forbid, he'd even had to act contrite with Winterbourne, which had been akin to peeling his fingernails back. The marquess had behaved irksome, asking why Aideen wasn't with him at the Rowe's ball, and he'd vented his lack of sleep on the fellow who'd solely smirked and mumbled about cherry itches.

Of course, he should have extended the long-standing invite to his wife, but it was too soon.

He knew he couldn't look at her without…needing.

Not that she was the reason he couldn't sleep, obviously, but when he did manage a few hours, his dreams ranged from downright erotic to strangely deviant: Aideen tracing the D on his shoulder with her tongue whilst her slender fingers pleasured him; Aideen tied to the four-poster covered in cherries…

Lust alone could explain those dreams but the one about her modestly reading to him in bed was downright perverse.

If he kept away long enough, the lust would dissipate. One night ought to have been enough, surely.

A knock on the door and he bade them enter – probably Rawlins as he'd asked for some fruit, the only item edible in this house.

Briefly he speculated if his duchess had noted the dire cuisine. Now his mother was no longer head of the household, maybe Aideen would give that chef his marching orders.

It wasn't Rawlins.

His wife entered before closing the door behind her. April was a sparse month for fresh produce, but some stored apples filled the fruit bowl she held.

Had Eve come to tempt him?

"Duchess," he acknowledged. Keep it formal and all would be well.

"Alexander."

He swallowed. Did she have to call him that? Did she

know what it did to him? He gulped brandy, drinking in her presence after successfully avoiding her for five days.

A sweet peach dress swathed her body, with a bronze-coloured shawl draped about her shoulders. That coal-black hair was fixed in a loose coil and a few ringlets framed her face and cascaded over her bosom. Pretty as a bloody picture.

Three years ago, a French spy aptly named The Red Temptress had tried to seduce him for information, but she'd left without success, concluding that he was a joyless, phlegmatic, bloodless, English stone and coincidently…not a spy.

The woman had been outstandingly beautiful and skilled in flirtation, but she had nothing on Aideen.

Beyond doubt, his wife could have him leaking secrets like a rusty bucket if he wasn't careful.

With swinging hips, she placed the bowl on the table and twirled a ringlet. He slitted his eyes – what was the minx up to?

"I should like to attend the Miltons' masquerade ball two nights hence."

"No."

That ball skirted the very edge of propriety. A fair few guests were Cyprians, and most could have been, they behaved so badly. The rest weren't much better, even if they were from the scions of high nobility, and in addition… Well, he himself was due to attend that ball in order to rendezvous with a certain Sir Phineas as he'd served in France with Stafford and might have information on this Frenchwoman.

Being a priggish duke and all that, it was not an event he would normally grace with his presence, but needs must. Sir Phineas had wanted to meet somewhere he wouldn't be recognised – where better than a masquerade?

"No?" his wife queried, black eyebrow raised in blatant haughtiness. That was his trick, but she did it very well.

"No. Rakecombe stock do not attend such scurrilous events. It's not respectable, my little leprechaun."

Ire flashed in her eyes. So, she didn't like that appellation; he must use it more often.

"Why are you English obsessed with leprechauns? And I'm not little."

"Compared to me you are. Little and delicate." And fragile. So breakable. So precious.

She stalked over, and he forced his lips to steel, limbs motionless, even his eyelashes stilled.

What if his life was different? What if she'd come to simply talk about the day? He'd tug her to his lap and hold her tight. Share an apple.

But no temptation was worth a life.

"I wish to attend a ball and dance."

"Go shopping instead."

"I have already been shopping."

Yes, Plunkett had mentioned that – to his account book's detriment. "The theatre then," he said in his best dismissive tone.

"Who with? We have been married five days and didn't even have a honeymoon. It would seem a little odd if I attended events on my own. They'll say…"

Yes, he knew. They'd say the duke was bored already. That they would live their lives like half the ton did. That his marriage was no more than a forced farce to a nobody. "And would they be wrong?"

A gasp escaped her whilst guilt and self-hatred gathered low in his belly.

He very nearly stood, very nearly pulled her to him, but he forced his mind to Gwen, her green eyes shocked in death. He imagined Aideen, all fire extinguished in the quick draw of a cold blade.

"Ask Winterbourne to attend you," he drawled, closing his eyes to the torment within. "You enjoy his company and I keep tripping over the wretched man wending his way here to pant at your feet."

"May the devil make a ladder from your spine," she snarled, and he inwardly smiled. He adored her curses and hadn't heard one for a while. All felt tranquil as she hissed her anger – his little hellcat would never cower beneath his snubs.

Oh, how he needed…

He shook his head. "Indeed," he continued, "why not assign him the green bedchamber since he's here so often."

Aideen leaned over the desk, and he waited for the adroit retort but it seemed she had decided on a differing tactic.

Fingers brushed his jaw where it had been itching earlier, and he willed the hairs on his arms not to rise.

She licked her lips and he hooded his eyes to prevent her from seeing his reaction.

It couldn't have been successful as she did it again.

"I think, Alexander," she purred, twiddling another ringlet, "I'll assign him the master suite, for all the time you spend in it." The hand removed itself from his jaw and she plonked an apple on his desk. "After all, 'tis easy to rob an orchard when no one's guarding the apples."

She sashayed from the room, still clutching the bowl of fruit, and slammed the door behind her.

He glared at the solitary apple. It was mouldy and had holes in it.

Eve had taken her revenge on mankind.

13

EVERYBODY WANTS TO BE A CAT...

The tail was coming along nicely but the whiskers were proving rather difficult. Thank heavens for Cordelia and her sewing prowess.

"I wish I was to attend such a glittering occasion," her friend said wistfully, and Aideen patted the slumped lacy-white shoulder, getting her fingers caught in a ribbon of seed pearls.

Blithely taking no notice of Rakecombe's contrary edict concerning the Milton masquerade, she had requested that Lord Winterbourne escort her.

A dash of blackmail had not gone amiss concerning his IOUs with Lady Gibbon, although he'd merely looked amused and muttered about having already settled them in kind.

Without doubt, she would not have gone if Rakecombe had said yes, or given his reasoning, but the imperious "No" had stiffened her resolve in a trice.

So here they were, sewing a tail for her skirts, a pair of gloves with claws and a mask complete with whiskers.

Cordelia sighed again, and Aideen considered fulfilling

her role as duchess and having words with her friend's betrothed. Weren't all duchesses supposed to be matronly gobermouches?

"You haven't written any more shepherd and sheep poems, have you?"

"Goodness, no. It's just…" The tail was put to one side. "Lord Oakdean is attending the Miltons' ball as well."

Aideen's eyebrow shot up. All the ton was aware of the Miltons' masquerades. They managed to stay the right side of respectable only because of their host's huge influence, but everyone knew they were a smidgeon risqué – not suitable for newly engaged viscounts or young ladies – which was why Aideen wanted to go.

The duke may not be attending, but for once in her life she'd be most intrigued to view the high society goings-on, masks only serving to reveal their true selves.

And besides, she'd heard the Miltons served superb lobster patties.

"How do you know he'll be there?"

Fiddling with the velvet tail, Cordy's entire demeanour spoke of guilt. "I was awaiting Oakdean in his drawing room and started sifting through the post – purely as something to do."

"Of course," agreed Aideen, jostling up on the settee and not believing her for a moment.

"Well, the Miltons' invite always has elaborate gold lettering. My brother used to go so I recognise its style."

"It doesn't necessarily mean he's attending."

"I spoke to my maid who is sweet with the footman at Oakdean's, who in turn is cousin to his valet and therefore had it confirmed."

"Oh."

"Hmm."

"You could always..." The idea was scandalous, and a duchess should shy from scandal, but... "come along?"

Blue eyes widened like Wedgwood cake plates. "No! I couldn't... Could I? No... Well. No. Although..."

"Lord Winterbourne will chaperone us. And you would be in disguise." She tapped a finger to her lip. "But no, you are right, it's a bad idea. I'm such a bad influence and a terrible frie–"

"It's a fabulous idea," Cordelia gushed.

"It is?" Oh lawks.

"Yes," her friend assured, a fevered light entering her eye. "I have been coddled and sheltered and hidden for nearly twenty years and sometimes I feel as though I will marry Oakdean and nothing will change." Aideen gawped as Cordelia stood and paced the rug, ribbons struggling to keep up. "Sometimes I feel he is only marrying me because I am the diamond of the Season, and when we marry, he'll place me on the mantelpiece, admire me for an hour and then put me away in a cupboard again."

"I didn't know you felt that way."

"No, because it is selfish and wicked. How can I complain when on my weekly visits to the orphanage I see such poverty? But I feel so...stifled." She flopped back on the settee in a very un-Cordelia-like manner.

"But how will attending the ball help?"

"I want to be free for one night. Not an ornament or a proper miss but a person. My own person. Do you know my mother makes me practise laughing to sound young and girlish?"

Aideen shook her head.

"Well she does – closes her eyes, listens, and tells me if it's too loud or deep. Then I have to do it again and again until it has the correct balance. I'm not allowed supper otherwise."

Unsure what to say, and glad she was half-Irish, Aideen gave her friend a hug: the English were a peculiar lot.

"But, Cordy," argued Aideen, aiming for some propriety, "what if you are seen? You'll be ruined. You spoke of Oakdean's grandmother–"

"I've been reconsidering, and I never should have succumbed to that blackmail. If Oakdean loved me, he wouldn't care about lamb poems sent by a foolish child." Cordelia twisted, face defiant. "I am taking a leaf from your book, my dearest friend."

Oh, Beelzebub, thought Aideen, please no. "Erm, that might not be wise."

But Cordelia shook her head, ringlets bouncing with enthusiasm. "I saw how your husband gazed at you on your wedding day. As though you were cake, but Oakdean is always so…polite. He kissed my forehead when we became engaged – my forehead! – as though I was but twelve years," she ranted.

Never having seen this side of Cordelia, Aideen was both impressed and worried. "But what happens if you are recognised? Your pristine reputation will be in tatters."

"No one shall recognise me as my costume will be superb, and I shall tell Mother I am staying the evening with you. But if I am identified and Oakdean is disgusted, then I shall voyage to Egypt as companion to your mother-in-law."

"Oh. Has she asked you as well?"

"Actually, she said we could all go together. I've always wanted to see the pyramids."

Cordelia picked up the tail and continued to stitch, humming to herself.

And that was that, it seemed.

THE MANTEL CLOCK chimed eight as Aideen nervously pulled her satin black gloves tight. She and Cordelia had torn apart an old fan, using the bone sticks to create wicked claws sewn onto the fingers, and Aideen had to admit they did look grand.

Not only that, but any gentleman that dared to take liberties would find a claw in their neck…or indeed any appendage that presumed to stray too close. Perhaps she ought to draw a picture for Uncle Seamus and he could incorporate claws in his fiendish designs.

She meandered to the long mirror and perused her form.

A midnight-black silk dress sheathed her, colourless except for her pale skin. She twisted and smiled at the long tail emerging from the rear in a sensuous curl.

The ebony mask was also a wonder. Cordelia had proved a dab hand at painting silver scrolls around the eyes and a glittering nose. Long whiskers, crafted from the shafts of feathers, had been affixed and they danced and bobbed with any slight movement.

Lastly a small pair of pointed velvet ears sat atop her head. They were a little skewwhiff as Aideen had sewn them as an afterthought when Cordelia had departed to organise her own costume.

Aideen laughed at the sight in the mirror, but her tone was forced, and she knew that if she dwelled upon her thoughts, the black attire suited her mood.

When she'd married, she had presumptuously assumed that Rakecombe did essentially like her. That they would spend time together. At the very least breakfast. But for the past two days, he'd continued to avoid her as though she'd the plague.

Barely one week married and already they lived separate existences.

And absence did not make the heart grow fonder. She could feel hers freezing over like Father Thames last February.

She tried to remember the day he'd proposed, the words he'd used. Rakecombe had proclaimed want, may even have starved after her like cake as Cordelia had suggested, but it appeared he'd now eaten it whole and didn't want seconds.

So, damn them all.

Dancing. Champagne. Lobster patties. The important things in life.

"Aideen?"

The voice quivered from the doorway and she spun.

Saints in their stockings. A sheep.

In stark contrast to Aideen's black, Cordelia was clad entirely in pure white. She had hoped they'd be able to enter the masquerade unseen, but she now suspected they'd be...noticed.

A white wig complete with huge floppy ears – better formed than her own – covered her friend's usual honey-blond curls. The mask was also white except for black smudges around the eyes and a button nose. Woolly stuff had been attached to the décolletage, the waist and hem. An exceedingly long tail was draped across her arm.

Surely sheep were less well endowed in the tail area?

Spying the anxious eyes behind the mask, Aideen dashed over. "You look delightful, Cordy. Like a...lamb let out in a spring meadow for the first time."

"Oh, good. That is the effect I was after. I didn't want to appear like mutton."

"Gracious no, you look beautiful. Now Lord Winterbourne is–"

"Here I am, my loveys. I understand I've two beauties to escort."

They both whirled and stared open-mouthed at the stunning gentleman before them.

Of course, she had always known Lord Winterbourne was a handsome man, and tonight, she had to acknowledge they would be the envy of every female as they entered the ballroom together.

Byronesque black curls fell perfectly to broad shoulders, and nestled in his artful hair was a pair of red horns – still better made than her own. A black-and-red mask obscured his features with leering demons painted upon it. Flashing white teeth as usual – heaven knows the powder he used – above an immaculate cravat and black jacket. But the waistcoat was a poppy red, devilish and bright.

In his hand he held a rather dangerous pitchfork.

"That is a beautiful coquelicot waistcoat, Jack," she sighed, wishing she could wear such a colour. Alas, it caused her complexion to resemble an old rag.

"Ah," he said, rushing forth to kiss her hand. "Why did we not marry, Aideen? You appreciate the prevailing fashion like no one else. Instead you married His Colourlessness."

Cordelia giggled, and Jack sketched a bow. "And who do we have here? But an innocent lamb with flesh so very… succulent." Her friend tittered yet more and Aideen whacked his arm with a claw.

"Tonight, we are Lady Hellcat and…" She turned to Cordelia.

"Erm, Lady C. Lamb?"

"Oh no, lovey," said Jack, "that's already taken by the scandalous Caroline and one is more than enough, I assure… ewe." He perused her from foot to ear. "You shall be Miss Peep."

All agreed, Cordelia sprang for the door, but Jack grabbed hold of Aideen's arm, dragging her to one side.

"Why the bloody hell is Miss Cordelia Greenwood, the ton's darling and absolute innocent, going to the Miltons'? I'll be hung, drawn and fleeced of my favourite waistcoat if anyone finds out, especially Oakdean."

"She wants a night of freedom. Before the tedium of marriage."

Jack peered carefully into her mask. "Rakecombe's hurting you, isn't he?"

"Nonsense, I just–"

"As I thought, you're in need of my assistance." He patted her arm in an avuncular manner, so at odds with his physical aspect. "My rules are normally for the gentlemen, but I don't suppose women are much different, especially you, Aideen."

She wasn't sure whether to be flattered or affronted. "What rules?" she nevertheless asked, intrigued.

A wide grin split his face, a devilish twinkle to the fallen angel's eye. She peered down for the cloven hoof.

"Why, the rules of the rogue, my dear Aideen. And we will start at number one. A little jealousy never goes amiss."

14

LAMBS TO THE SLAUGHTER.

Caligula's hand slid to Aideen's bottom, so she stuck a claw in the despotic emperor's stomach and with a guilty grin, it withdrew.

So far, the masquerade had been splendid – sublime dancing, highest-quality champagne and superb lobster patties. The ballroom echoed to the sound of merriment as Caligula waltzed her across the floor. She'd already twirled with lions, wolves, a Zeus and if she wasn't mistaken the Prince Regent – the real one.

The palatial townhouse resembled a Roman villa, Bacchus' feast being the theme: fountains dripped with wine, statues disrobed in the corners and guests reclined on low couches, devouring grapes and figs with their fingers.

But as the night wore on, she realised how apt that word was. Because the ball was wearing. Wearing and false.

Caligula bowed as their waltz came to a welcome end and then toddled off, probably to find a lady not averse to bottom patting…or his beloved horse, and Aideen took herself to lean against a mighty statue of a semi-clad Venus.

Gazing out at the multitude, she recognised the wife of an

earl disappearing into the gardens with a younger man, their gaze intimate.

No one made blatant overtures at this ball, but silk fans were whipped around in a frenzy of hidden messages, eyes flitted to the alcoves and notes were passed from hand to hand.

An undercurrent rippled the room, an insincerity that stole her own enjoyment.

Without love, was this her future?

Dark, dangerous, but desolate.

The very words her husband had growled now defined the masquerade for Aideen.

Jack, of course, was in his element, their entrance having caused quite a stir. Currently he was waltzing with Cordelia, and they made a striking couple, causing many an envious female eye to follow from behind an elegant mask.

To give the devil his due, he had chaperoned her friend most judiciously thus far, and Aideen herself was more than capable of detracting unwanted advances. The claws gave a nasty scratch, but her uncle had also gifted her a small bejewelled knife which she'd affixed to her garter.

A tatty pirate approached for a dance but she shook her head. Sadly, the one man she wanted didn't feel likewise.

Perhaps she should retire to the duke's principal country estate. Meghan had described the place as wonderful, a sprawling castle in the Derbyshire countryside. She'd feel at home amongst the green hills and wild flowers, not this bleak landscape of pretence and deceit.

A grinning Jack swiftly appeared, breathless and with arms wide.

"Aideen, lovey," he said, leaning improperly near – was he foxed? "Smile and caress my lapel."

She gawked at him dumbfounded. Surely, he didn't

think–

Drawing yet closer, he whispered in her ear, "Rule number one."

Without thought, she reached up to smooth the velvet, a pit of sorrow filling her belly.

Her husband must be here. The only explanation for Jack's attentions. Was that why the duke hadn't wished her to attend? Was his priggish reputation no more than a guise? Did he seek the hidden pleasures of this ball? Was his wife too dull and innocent?

Surreptitiously, Aideen scanned the throng of masked guests for a figure in black but saw no sign. "I'm sure he won't recognise me."

"And I'm sure he will," replied Jack. "Now laugh, Your Grace."

She followed the command, always having been able to feign cheer in the face of her da's bitterness, and serenely, she brushed a hand over Jack's waistcoat, purring her delight at the beautiful red silk.

"Steady on though," he muttered, "I've seen what your husband has in that cane of his and I might have a use for my tallywags later in life."

That produced a more honest laugh. "Did you know he was here? Why didn't you tell me? I never would have come if I'd known." She smiled through the question and gazed adoringly.

"Well, I might have helped choose his apparel…" Jack winked before sheepishly glancing over one shoulder. "He's gone, but I'm convinced he recognised you as his demeanour was stiffer than usual. He didn't appear happy."

No. The Duke of Rakecombe would not like his orders disobeyed, but then he himself had suggested Jack attend her, so there was no need to be such a dog in a manger.

"Where's Cordelia?"

"Don't worry, she's at the–" Jack peered across the heaving room. "Bugger and blast, our lamb has frolicked off. I'll be back in two shakes."

Bidding him find their lost sheep – he needed a crook not a pitchfork – Aideen instead meandered to the gardens.

RAKECOMBE DIDN'T STRIVE to tamp down the fury and envy. He let it rage.

Images battered his skull. Some foppish hand on his wife's voluptuous black-clad arse. Her cherry lips smiling at some toga-cladded imbecile. Licking the champagne from her lips as a Greek god leered at her breasts.

Aideen may consider her disguise sufficient, but he'd recognise that lush backside anywhere, and her clover pendant had been a final confirmation.

Clenching his fists, he stared into the depths of night and forced his breathing to slow.

It was his own fault, of course. He knew that. To say no to Aideen was to decree the exact opposite. Winterbourne he would send home in a box, and what the blazes was innocent of the Season, Miss Cordelia Greenwood, doing here?

Damn, how he detested these parties – full of brash young bucks and greedy ladybirds, but this was where Phineas had suggested, and he agreed it was certainly clandestine.

Perhaps he was a dull old dog, as Aideen had seemed to be enjoying herself, but he ached to be alone…with her.

Spying for the Crown got his blood pumping, but how pleasant it would be to return to Aideen at the end of a night. To speak of what he was able, to rest his head and have that Irish whisper calm his mind.

With their temperaments of course, they would always… debate, but they'd settle their differences betwixt the sheets.

Over the last seven lonely days, he'd wondered if it could be possible, but always Gwen haunted his thoughts and suppressed his hope.

Closeness meant danger in his vocation. And it wasn't some imagined reaction, some misconceived idea of what *may* happen – he'd felt the slipperiness of his sister's blood seep through his fingers, heard her last gasp. And it hurt so bloody much.

He'd leave this ball once Phineas showed. Leave Aideen to her own life.

A rustle of silk disturbed him, and he swivelled, about to snarl his displeasure at some Cyprian, but brushing past and then on down the steps to the garden was his wife, her disguise no barrier to his gaze.

Was she meeting someone? Wrath burned within.

As usual where Aideen was concerned, his feet flouted his latest resolution to leave her be and lightly followed her into the dark.

An archway of fresh-leaved roses stood at the end of the garden with lanterns swaying overhead – a perfect place to tryst, and he watched as she ambled the grass path, stopping beneath the arch to caress the small buds that awaited more warmth than England was currently prepared to give.

Certainly, she presented no rush.

Aideen turned to lean against one of the ornate posts, her head bent, and it took a while to discern her expression.

Sadness.

Never had he seen his fiery girl sad before. Angry and upset, yes, but not this muted wretchedness.

It tortured him.

Had someone hurt her? Had *he* hurt her? She always

absorbed his taunts and fired back with verve, but words could slice deep and leave wounds the eye couldn't see.

Or was she sad her tryst had not come to fruition? Was he being presumptuous in assuming it had anything to do with him?

Lust may certainly sear between them, but did Aideen actually like him? After all, he hadn't created a very likable creature.

Sedately, he slipped around the arch to approach from behind, his tread silent on the path.

"A beautiful woman need not be alone." He wasn't quite sure why he disguised his aristocratic tenor with a strong Welsh accent. Only that he didn't want to reveal his presence at this ball, a ball he'd forbidden her to attend. Or was it that he wondered for whom she waited.

His wife spun and he tensed, even though there was no reason why she would recognise him.

A tricorn hat, complete with dangling ostrich feather, covered his hair, in turn covered by a powdered white wig. His mask, in summer's day blue, obscured all but his mouth, and his clothes mirrored a gentleman of some hundred years past: pale-blue silk frockcoat with matching breeches, white stockings and heeled shoes with square jewelled buckles. A froth of white lace tumbled from his throat, choking him if truth be known, and it itched like the very devil.

The single highlight to this disguise was the excuse to wear a dress sword.

"It appears I am alone no longer." And she turned her back upon him.

He stepped near, undeterred. "Do you await a lover? Should I leave for fear of rousing his ire?" The Welsh cadence slid over that last word, prolonging it.

"No lover," she said softly, and satisfaction flared in his gut.

"A pity." He bent close but she didn't stir. Tonight, the violets had closed their petals and her perfume was darker, smelling of night jasmine and passion. "Would you care for one, *fy cariad aur*?"

Still she declined to turn, so he brushed a finger against her neck, a pale column of contradiction to her dress and hair. She gasped but he couldn't discern the cause – shock or pleasure?

He adored touching her in this moonlit paradise, the air redolent with spring blooms, and he couldn't cease, didn't want to cease, despite the travesty of this scene.

"Perhaps I have a jealous husband?" she whispered. "Are you not worried?"

"If I were your husband, I would not allow you to attend this ball of decadence as my envy would outdo Othello's."

"But then we would not have met."

Leisurely, he slanted and pressed his mouth to the nape of her neck. She startled but didn't pull away, and envy did assuredly seethe within.

Aideen arched her neck as he mouthed kisses along the warm flesh until reaching her lobe. He bit lightly. "Perhaps that would have been for the best. For both of us," he said.

A low moan greeted his words and he slid an arm around her waist, tugging her back against his body. The silks rubbed and he felt something firm brush his groin, not entirely unpleasant, and he realised it was her tail.

"My enchanting black cat," he rasped and pulled the sleeve from her shoulder, revealing satin skin. He laved, nipped, aware this dark game was becoming too twisted, but his aching body refused to end its play.

"Accept the things to which fate binds you," she

murmured.

Pushing a hand into her hair, he brought her face around for a kiss. Her lips were as he'd yearned for these past days, lush and warm, but the angle was strained, their masks clashed, and although he craved to turn her, he was more than aware of the danger.

And yet his fingers slipped down, caressed the silk of her skirts, rucking the material. Aideen curved into him, and he couldn't help but push back, letting her feel his arousal. Perhaps he should continue. She was his wife after all, but self-disgust and hurt held him back.

A mysterious contour at her thigh halted his touch. "What have we here?" he drawled.

"A knife," she answered. "To halt unworthy intruders."

Why, he didn't know, but the notion of his wife with a blade in her garter nearly unmanned him. What a remarkable woman, and faintly, the idea that Aideen wasn't nearly as fragile or artless as Gwen wafted into his thoughts, but then she raked something sharp against the back of his hand.

"Are you unworthy?" she whispered, and he realised she'd branded him with light scratches.

He groaned and pulled her tight before abruptly letting her go. He'd speak the truth.

"Yes," he answered, "I am indeed unworthy."

AIDEEN STUMBLED AND SPUN, but he'd already vanished, like a ghost of the gentleman he portrayed.

Foolish man.

Did he really think she wouldn't know her own husband?

Admittedly, the costume had suited him. On some men it may have appeared foppish but not so the duke. It contrasted with his masculinity, his rangy height and straight spine. She'd had to turn, to prevent herself from pouncing lustfully upon him.

The deep timbre of the accent had further roused her. But why had he played such a game? To ascertain if she was an innocent Desdemona? Or to punish for her presence at the Miltons' ball?

Wandering back through the garden, she heard a tapering whistle so peered across the lawn into the far dark.

The statue of a beleaguered Atlas glowered back and behind the marble, a flash of pale-blue silk and an ostrich feather in a tricorn hat caused her heart to falter.

Had her husband a tryst of his own?

But then a Roman centurion veered towards those same shadows, leather sandals causing no sound upon the gravel path.

Or was he engaged on a mission? That might explain the utter dichotomy of his clothing, his appearance so at odds with his nature.

But for all the goats in Gorey, why didn't he say so? "Please do not attend, Aideen, I will be there on business." That was all it required.

Memories of a night working with Uncle Seamus to finish a special commission intruded. He'd warned her in a hushed tone of the men that bought his wares. "These people bring danger and death to your door, so keep your distance."

Was that what Rakecombe was doing? Keeping *his* distance. She'd already been kidnapped due to their association last year so was he staying away for her own protection?

How thoughtful…and infuriating.

Then again, mayhap this was all her fevered and optimistic imagination.

With a shrug, she dashed up the steps, aware she had abandoned Cordelia for too long with a pack of salivating wolves.

Miss Cordelia Greenwood, diamond of the first water, all-round proper miss, and innocent debutante, was petrified.

The hallway leading to what she'd hoped was the retiring room lay empty except for the formidable figure standing in front of her.

A highwayman to all intents and purposes, dressed entirely in black. He wore a covering mask in soft silk, a tricorn hat, and a cloak shrouded his frame. Cordelia stepped to the left, eyes lowered, but he followed suit, blocking her path.

She darted to the right but he was sleight of hand and broad of shoulder and only needed to shift an arm to thwart her route.

Oh, goodness.

Why had she come here? Although the dancing had been enjoyable, Cordelia had soon realised she didn't belong, not understanding the secret signals or whispered words; one gentleman had asked if she bleated when tupped, whatever that meant.

"Might I pass, sir?" She was ashamed of the quiver to her voice. Aideen wouldn't act like a frightened mouse, but she lacked her friend's spirited manner.

Cordelia's eyes widened as the man shook his head and began to unravel his black cravat.

A muscular throat revealed itself. Her mouth dried at the sight, skin oddly tingling, but that was beside the point, and she spun to flee.

Almost at the stairs, an ungloved, and hence *entirely bare,* hand encircled her waist.

Quaking, she recoiled from the touch but thudded straight into a dense male body. She may have squeaked, but it definitely became a shriek when cloth was banded over her mask and across her eyes.

The world darkened.

"Please," she begged. "Let me go."

But the highwayman remained silent and the next thing she knew, she was hauled up into muscular arms. He swung her around, kicked a door, and then she could hear male jeers and applause. Pulling her into his chest, he held her tight. A warmer room and a low female moan reached her ears – where was he taking her? What was happening?

She struggled, his arms iron in their grip, but he did smell very pleasant – musky.

Finally, cool air and she heard a door slam shut. His arms suddenly released her and she yelped as she fell, landing on something soft and creaky.

Scrabbling the cloth from her eyes, she peered blearily around.

A bed. A bedchamber.

Gosh.

The abducting scoundrel had his back to her and was filling a glass with amber liquid. He'd shrugged off his cloak and did have a very nice posterior and strong thighs, she noted…which, of course, was unimportant at this moment.

Escape.

Gingerly, she edged a foot to the side of the bed, but her sheep's tail got tangled around her legs.

The highwayman spun. He'd removed his sinister mask and his eyes glittered, jaw tight.

"Oh," she moaned pitifully. "Good evening, Lord Oakdean. Wh-what a coincidence."

15

THRICE THE ADVICE, THRICE THE CLAPTRAP.

"Stafford married a Frenchwoman in secret."

Rakecombe pushed the papers over the desk towards Lord Rainham, and watched his brow knit in consternation.

"Confound it," Rainham snapped, flicking through the certificates. "I never predicted that. Not of Stafford."

"Love, as Winterbourne would say, makes fools of us all." He thought of last night's masquerade and dismissed the absurd idea that he was one of those fools.

"I see this marriage took place in France years ago. Where is she now? Was she a French spy?"

"Phineas claims he knows little, but he owes Stafford his life so he's fairly tight-lipped. The woman was a merchant's daughter, but her family were well-known Bonapartists."

Indeed, the masquerade had been most revealing. The only downside was that Phineas had mentioned Stafford's aptitude for disguise. Apparently, he could be peddling you a horse or flirting with your wife and you wouldn't even know it.

Lord Rainham stood and paced, features taut with

frustration and hurt. "I'll send messages to France, see if we can establish any more. In the meantime, well done. You were right not to give up. I just…" He sat and rubbed at the back of his neck. "I liked and trusted Stafford," he said, somewhat despairingly.

"We still don't know if he is the traitor," Rakecombe comforted. "Why hasn't the stolen information been used as yet? And Stafford has been in England for how long now? Four years or so? Where was his wife in that time? I've asked Bluey to continue snooping."

"More questions than answers, as is usual in our work," said Rainham, gathering the papers and bundling them into a folder. "Onto lighter matters, how is that delightful wife of yours? Lily very much enjoyed her company."

"She's…" He thought of her arched neck last night, arching for another man's kiss, and yearned to punch something. "…content."

"Good. You must dine with us when all this has settled. Actually, it might have to wait till Napoleon's been put away again. The summer in all likelihood."

A mite stunned, Rakecombe gathered his gloves and cane. He'd worked with Rainham for years and never once had he been invited to dine – must be his new lady's influence. "When did you meet your Mrs Mereworth?"

"Over Christmas. You remember Major Lucas Mainwaring, don't you?"

He nodded. A stalwart chap who had been horrifically burned in France, and when he'd last seen him three years ago, rather a wreck.

"Well, he's happily married now, a keen-eyed lass, and Lily's a distant relative of his wife's."

Was everyone blissfully wedded, he inwardly griped.

Thank God for Winterbourne – at least that rogue could be relied upon.

He stood, having had enough of matrimonial chit-chat. It gave him a headache. "I'll keep you informed."

"Very well. And Rakecombe," his leader called as he'd almost escaped the door, "don't let work interfere with your marriage, hmm. They can co-exist. With safeguards, yes, but your wife is an intelligent woman. I'd lay strong odds that she has concealed talents."

Barely managing a farewell, he stomped out, ramming his cane to the floor. Everyone was full of damn advice, but where had they been twelve years ago? Had they witnessed a beloved sister die from their own stupidity? He doubted it.

Advice could go to the very devil.

"If you want my advice…"

Aideen didn't.

Jack's rules, as far as she could tell, only worked for Jack, the advice a dab biased towards the interests of the rogue and not the married lady.

"I don't," she grumbled from the window seat, but the marquess cast her a wounded expression and sipped his tea whilst perched on the striped blue sofa. Better soften her tone, so she smiled. "Your rules probably don't work for ladies, 'tis all."

"Oh, but they do," Jack argued. "I've analysed all thirty-two of them and a mere three do not signify because you have different…apparatus."

Not daring to ask, Aideen sipped her own lukewarm beverage and pondered. Should she tell her husband she'd known it had been him at the masquerade? Or let him braise in his own juices over the fact she'd allowed a lace-clad Welsh scoundrel to kiss her?

Yes. Definitely the second.

"And how's Miss Greenwood?" asked Jack, poking a fleur-de-lys shaped biscuit with suspicion. "Oakdean thanked me for looking after her at the ball but said if I as much as sneezed in her direction again, he would… Well, a possessive chap with an inventive mind. I've never thought about squirrels in that fashion."

"I allowed Lord Oakdean to escort her back here from the masquerade, but she left this morning before I awoke. There was a note in the hall to say she would call later today with all her news."

Sighing, she nibbled her own unpatriotic biscuit, possibly the lone edible item in the ducal residence.

This week, she really must visit the kitchens and have a word. So far, she had felt it a little soon to interfere with the workings of the household, but they'd starve before too long.

It all converged to make her most miserable this morning. The blue devils had come to call, wandered in uninvited, sat down and were making themselves at home in her brainbox. Possibly even deciding on curtain colours.

"Not to worry about your advice, Jack. I think my husband is immune to jealousy. After all, he was the one to suggest you escort me to events, so–"

"No!" Jack slammed the teacup down, mouth aghast and eyes wide, cup rattling in its saucer. "You never told me that."

"Well, does it matter?"

"Does it matt… Oh hell… I can't breathe." He gasped as though choking and she wondered about the biscuit but it still lay untouched at the side of his cup. "I… Oh devil take it, I've realised something about His Rakelessness." The marquess pulled at his cravat as though suffering an apoplexy, ruining the exquisite l'orientale contour.

"What?" she asked alarmed, leaning forward.

"I can't say... Oh no. It cannot be..." He thrust agitated fingers through his hair, sucking in gulps of air. "Rakecombe wouldn't? No, surely not. He'd never..."

Alarm now led to anxious panic. "What about him?" she yelled, but Jack simply fell back against the sofa, a perfect expression of silent dismay and shock etched across his brow – even his curls bore distress.

"I cannot..." he uttered miserably.

A horrible thought formed in her mind. "Has...has he a mistress? Is that why he doesn't care for me? Has he been with her every night?"

Jack gurgled, hand to his chest. "Worse. Much, much worse."

Enough was enough, and Aideen flew across the room, kneeled on the sofa beside him and grabbed hold of Jack's tailcoat lapels.

She shook him rather violently. "If you don't tell me, I'll curse you with pissmires and spiders in your marriage bed."

"Pissmires?" he enquired, brow raised.

"Ants," she screamed. Nose to nose.

"Oh. Well then... He...he..."

"What? Tell me!"

Jack fell limp in her arms with a sigh. "He trusts me," he lamented, chin lowering to his chest. "The priggish, strait-laced Duke of Rakecombe trusts me. Me! Infamous rogue and renowned seducer. He *trusts* me with the well-being and all-round chastity of his wife. I'm being punished for my sins. I know I am. I mean, I'll never be able to stalk a ballroom again."

Baring teeth but laughing, she slammed the red cushion into his perfect coiffure. "You swine! I thought..."

"I know," he said, narrowly avoiding a drubbing in the potato trap and chuckling wholeheartedly. "But it cheered you up and dragged you from the doldrums, didn't it?"

It had, and she opened her mouth to say so when a polite cough interrupted.

The Duke of Rakecombe stood in the doorway, expression formidable, and all of a sudden, she was eminently aware of their indelicate montage.

One knee pressed against Jack's thigh, her skirts hoisted to reveal a fair amount of stockinged leg, gown crumpled, ringlets loose, an unbecoming flush to her cheeks.

Jack didn't fare much better: hair now dishevelled, jacket undone, cravat loose and his firm ungloved hand on her shoulder to defend the cushion bashing.

Oh, Saint Patrick's bones.

Yesterday compromised by a Welsh scoundrel, today an English rogue, tomorrow she'd better be wary of any lurking Scotsmen or she'd complete the trinity.

"Winterbourne," her husband merely drawled. "Rainham wishes to see you on the hour of five." And with a curt nod, he skulked off.

They both gawked at the empty doorway.

"See," hissed Jack. "He trusts me. We'll have to come up with another strategy since my reputation is in tatters. My fellow rascal, Lord MacDougall, will help us."

Aideen frowned.

The rules of the rogue, she was beginning to think, were just a load of beastly tarradiddle.

"I NEED YOUR ADVICE."

Aideen groaned. Not that she didn't want to help Cordelia, but her own life was in rather a pucker, let alone providing advice to anyone else – especially if it concerned matters of the heart.

They lounged on a snug couch in the Rakecombe library, a room which held an ample selection of fine books. And not only of the cultivated bigwig type either, but novels, poetry, and Gothic horror – everything from Swift to Walpole.

She wondered when her husband got the time to read any of them, as she hadn't noticed him lolling about with book in hand very often.

"Cordy," she said as she pulled her feet up and yanked a blanket over them. "I'm not sure I'm the best person. My last suggestion was the Miltons' ball and then we all got into a fine bit of trouble."

Pursing her lips, Cordelia also slipped her feet onto the couch and decorously placed some blanket over her stockinged toes. "But I've no one else to talk with. Whenever I ask Mother about Oakdean, she just mutters mysteriously about a gentleman's needs and then changes the subject to the square footage of his country house."

Poor Cordy. At least Aideen always had her uncle to advise her when growing up – a wise old owl. "I'll try my best. What happened last night?"

"Well, like I told you, he trapped me in that room."

"Yes, yes, but then what?"

"He said he'd recognised my ears from across the ballroom, so my disguise was hopeless. And then...he prowled over. Honestly he did, and it made me feel so peculiar in the belly area, and he was nearly nude, in no more than shirt and breeches, and I've always admired his well-developed form but…" She fanned fingers in front of her face. "Then, he leaned over the bed…"

"Yes?" Aideen propped herself on her fists – this was better than any novel.

"I… His lips came near…"

"Yes?"

"I could smell his cologne. Sandalwood and cigars. Musky and…"

"Yes?" she almost screamed.

"Then he… I think I parted my lips and he…"

"Cordelia! What did he do?" she shrieked.

"He told me I was a hen-witted, totty-headed girl and scolded me like a child."

Aideen's jaw dropped, and she leaned forward to pull Cordelia into her arms as her friend bawled like the child that Oakdean had accused her of being.

"Well, a high and windy gallows to him," she cursed, covering them both with the blanket until Cordelia's sobs eased. "But I find it strange," she mused. "Lord Winterbourne said your betrothed was most possessive, and it sounds like he was about to kiss you and yet for some reason held back. Why?"

"I don't think he wants me at all, only my bloodlines. I'll be nothing but a broodmare. But…" Cordelia peered up, large eyes moist. "I want *passion*."

A polite cough from the doorway.

The Duke of Rakecombe stood there, his gaze uniquely riveted on the two of them clutched together on the couch.

Oh, Saint Patrick's bones…again.

"I believe you will find an invite in the hall for the Duke of Buckland's soirée tomorrow night. I cannot escort you, but I will be there later in the evening." He nodded, tapped his ebony cane against the marble floor and stalked off, but not before another repressed glance at them both.

"Lord Oakdean is also attending," Cordelia muttered menacingly. "And I've had enough of being treated as a child."

"Er. Don't do anything rash, Cordy," she warned. "That's how I ended up married to a duke."

But Cordelia tightened her lips in mutiny. "Thank you for the advice, Aideen, but I believe it's time I took matters into my own hands."

16

GRASPED GENTLY, A NETTLE WILL STING.

A writhing darkness unfurled within Rakecombe's chest.

It wasn't the darkness of a summer's eve, fragrant and warm, but the ugly mean darkness of winter. The type that froze men in their steps and caused one to spill blood just to keep warm.

His wife *giggled* as the infamous Lord MacDougall whispered in her ear, and he wondered how the rascal would like another scar to complement the one which marred his toadying mug.

Not that females cared about the facial blemish. The broad-shouldered Scot had never revealed the cause of his disfigurement but many a lady shivered in delight at the whispered tales of a duel or acts of piracy.

Rakecombe had a feeling he'd simply fallen in a ditch when foxed and slashed his cheek on brambles.

Nevertheless, the anger that had seeded itself at the masquerade continued to grow at this soirée. He could sense it, erasing all control and authority.

Admittedly, he had no right to be jealous as this was what

he'd wanted. Separate lives. But what he hadn't been prepared for was the violent awakening within.

He'd thought it would be possible to command this hideous feeling, to ignore it or bludgeon it into submission, but it kept rearing its snarling jealous head.

Some pallid chit encroached upon him, and he was about to tell her to remove her objectionable person when Aideen glanced over. So instead he smiled at the unsuspecting pigeon.

Two could play at this game…

Rakecombe supposed his lips must have held a hint of cruelty as the chit visibly shuddered, but instead of walking in the opposite direction, as her instincts were surely screaming, she tentatively smiled back whilst fidgeting with a curl.

The motion reminded him of Aideen and his expression chilled.

Jealousy was a fool's game with no winners.

The pigeon flew away and he didn't even notice.

"I say, Rakeshame, you look like you've pissed on a nettle."

He turned that chill on Winterbourne, who'd arrived at his side to survey the horde crowding Buckland's drawing room. "'Tis purely this Stafford issue. I have to meet an informant in Seven Dials at a half after midnight and I am fatigued."

"Of course, of course. Never said it wasn't. Do you need me?" The marquess rocked on his heels, claret in hand.

Rakecombe shook his head. Bluey wouldn't show if he observed an unfamiliar face.

Despite knowing Winterbourne would never attempt to seduce his wife, Rakecombe's thoughts still churned at the intimate scene he'd witnessed on the sofa. And it wasn't that the rogue's fingers had been on his wife's shoulder, although that did bring a dull ache, and it wasn't even that she'd been displaying a long luscious leg.

No, it was that she'd been laughing, her sooty eyes wrinkling in joy.

When was the last time he'd brought his wife joy? When she'd lain beneath him in their marriage bed? But that was a different joy, not the carefree type he'd observed yesterday.

When had he ever made Aideen laugh?

He'd even been jealous of Miss Greenwood after he'd suppressed his male appreciation of two beautiful women cuddled together. Aideen was so caring and affectionate. He remembered the touch of her hand on his bruised eye, and God how he yearned to feel it again.

"*Alex*, would you like some advice?"

No, he bloody wouldn't. People had been full of it lately. But he had a feeling he was going to hear some gormless drivel anyhow. He waited for Winterbourne to drag out some trite rule or ridiculous plan.

"Life is short. It can even be brutal in this day and age." The marquess tipped his glass to a glowing Aideen. "So when some happiness comes into your life, don't deny it."

"You don't understa–"

"Yes, I think I probably do." Dark, flat eyes hollowed into him without mirth. "To deny happiness is to deny life, and we insult the dead by doing so. Don't forsake the present for past mistakes."

AIDEEN'S NAILS curled into her palm as she watched some alluring trollop smile at her husband. Uncle Seamus had once created a lady's fan with poisonous tips…

When Rakecombe had finally made his entrance at the

Buckland's soirée, he'd merely nodded his acknowledgement across the room, as though his wife was a serving maid.

Supercilious blaggard.

Forgoing Jack's rule number one – on balance it didn't appear to be effective – she made her excuses and quitted Lord MacDougall's company, to find Cordelia surrounded by an array of young bucks vying for her attentions.

Not a great surprise considering.

Apparently, Mrs Greenwood was under the weather, and so Cordelia was chaperoned this evening by her Aunty Bridget – a chaperone that not only had a voracious appetite for the card table but must also be exceedingly short-sighted.

It could be the only rationale for Cordelia's attire.

A wave of shock had rippled through the room when she'd first arrived. The diamond of the Season wearing… peony red. It was bright and shiny and decidedly *not* white, shocking to the ninth degree. Matrons tutted about the decorum of debutantes whilst those same debutantes giggled – surely she would be cut?

But the Duke and Duchess of Buckland had complimented her on the colour, which matched their paper hangings, and so with the full weight of their approval behind her, Cordelia had set the room alight. Gentlemen strived for her attention, ladies now envied and Lord Oakdean glowered from the corner.

"Cordelia?" The males parted – one of the advantages of being a duchess. Aideen had found that although the ton may stare in prejudice from behind their fluttering fans at an Irish upstart, not one of them dare make comment about the ruthless duke's wife. "You look stunning."

"Thank you, Your Grace." Her friend smiled, accepting another glass of champagne from a besotted swain. "I decided to no longer be a sheep, and I have even laughed loudly…twice."

"Er, wonderful. Has Oakdean spoken to you yet?"

"No." She frowned and took a large gulp. "I no longer think he cares."

Aideen wasn't so sure. A blaze roared in Oakdean's eyes that looked far from uncaring, but she nodded and left Cordy to her admirers.

Wandering the edges, she caught a glimpse of her husband's ebony tailcoat disappearing towards the mirrored hallway – where was he going? Another mission?

She really shouldn't. He had made it patently clear that his concerns were his own, but the anger and dissatisfaction which had marked her days caused her feet to follow nevertheless.

If a soirée was the only place to catch him alone, then the fault was his.

The hallway presented a splendid affair as supposedly inspiration had come from Versailles – albeit on a smaller scale. Mirrored in sections from floor to ceiling, it reflected the light from the chandeliers to a flickering crescendo, and tens of Rakecombes strode down it, all of them handsome and lean, the damn bugs.

Silently, she watched as he halted and scrutinised his attire, flicking a non-existent piece of lint from his jacket. He swiped a hand over his eyes, as she'd often seen him do – a sign of weariness, she'd learned.

Why wouldn't he allow her affection? He was so deuced stubborn.

Having talked – well, interrogated – his mother, she had a feeling it had something to do with his sister, but Meghan had become tight-lipped and said it was Alex's story to tell – and didn't that say it all.

But how could she ask him anything when he was never at home. 'Twas like living with a ghost – the lingering scent of chocolate in the breakfast room, the infrequent hat left on the table, the occasional footstep and sloshing noise from his bedchamber...

Another couple entered the hallway and she observed Rakecombe slip through a door to the left. Was he *working* or just hiding?

The couple took some while admiring the mirrors, and themselves, but finally departed, and she snuck over to the same door, twisted the handle and stepped through.

He glanced up as she closed the door behind her, surprise etched on his hawkish features.

Instead of discovering him on the pry, however, he stood with a glass of brandy in one hand and a book in the other.

The room appeared to be a small library with comfy sofas and decanters to hand. His jacket had been discarded over a desk, his upright form slender and fine-looking. How like him to make himself at home in someone else's mansion.

Unsure what to say or do, she wandered over. "What are you reading?"

With a careless shrug, he showed her the book. William Blake poetry. Rather depressing, she had always thought, and an engraving within depicted a dying red rose.

He surveyed her with hard eyes and tight lips, and she felt as if she didn't know this man, had never traded barbs with him, never felt his body inside hers, his fingers trailing her skin with tender reverence.

A distant stranger.

"Your Grace," she purred, drawing close, "I would like to be clear about our marriage." Those lips of his constricted yet more, and her heart stuttered. "You said we would deal well together but it seems we do not deal at all."

"You are free to do as you please," he replied, turning his back to place the book on the table. "In fact, you probably already have."

Aideen narrowed her eyes. He was baiting her, and she would usually bite without hesitation, but for once, she tamped down her ire. "Why don't you dine with me? Or talk to me? Do you dislike me so very much?"

His head snapped around. "I do not dislike you, Aideen. But I never wanted to be married. No to you or anyone."

"And yet you proposed." He didn't twitch a muscle as she circled him, gown grazing his breeches. "I've no doubt you could have bundled me off somewhere if you'd so wished." Aideen leaned up on her toes to whisper in his ear. "So why did you propose, Alexander?"

He swallowed, although no brandy had passed his lips.

"The begetting of an heir," he finally answered. "So, it didn't matter who. You were convenient."

His answer caused a clench in her chest, but something wasn't quite right. "Well," she replied, "locking our adjoining door tends to prevent any begetting."

A mocking smirk covered his lips. "I have an aversion to faithless women."

Ah, so the Miltons' masquerade was the bone of contention. She smiled, widening her eyes in innocence. "Jack says you trust him, so it cannot be he that you so grossly accuse." She put a finger to her lips. "Lord MacDougall, I have only met tonight." She leaned close, smelled leather and Alexander. "That only leaves...*fy cariad aur*."

His posture could not have become more rigid, and she raised his hand to her lips. The faint claw graze adorned his knuckles still and she brushed it with her mouth. "If you play with cats, Your Grace, you must expect to be scratched."

"You recognised it was I, yet never said a word?" he growled.

All her anger came flooding forth in one massive gush. "Do you think me so stupid, so fickle, so damn daft not to know my own husband as soon as he opens his bog mouth?" With a derisive snort, she flung her arms about. "Pretending to be a Welsh lover. Of all the ridiculous–"

"I told you not to go and you disobeyed. Did you enjoy provoking me, Aideen?" The cords of his throat strained, eyes dark. "Did you think to toy with me like a mouse? Well, I'm afraid I am not that type of man."

He yanked her into his arms, lips slanting upon hers, crushing, and she wondered how she'd so lost control of the conversation. *She* was the one supposed to be irate for his deception but instead an intense rage seemed to have erupted within him.

But despite his mood, she also sensed a desperation as his hands roved her buttocks, dragging her close as though he would never release her. She responded. How could she not? But as an equal, pulling his hair and clashing their mouths together.

This passion they shared wasn't reticent or gentle but powerful. Ferocious.

Distantly, she heard a clock strike the midnight hour and with a sudden groan, he tore away.

"I can't..." he whispered, turning on his heel and before she could utter another word, he'd gone.

HUMMING TO HERSELF, Cordelia Greenwood, now slightly blunted diamond but thoroughly pleased with herself debutante, wandered down the mirrored hallway, admiring the many pretty reflections of her peony red dress in the candlelight.

A man blocked her path – or lots of men, depending on one's view.

Not again.

But this time, she felt more confident, buoyed by her success this evening. "I wish to pass, Lord Oakdean."

Lazily, he folded his arms and leaned against the wall of mirrors. "What did your mother say about that dress, Miss Greenwood?"

She glared with her best Aideen glare. "I am old enough to choose my own clothes." And she caressed a hand down the lovely silk.

Lord Oakdean's eyes slitted, following the movement. His nonchalant posture unfolded, and he strolled towards her. "Are you?"

"Yes." No stutter, and of that she was proud.

"So, you know what a dress like that does to a man, do you?"

"Indeed. It causes them to bring you champagne and ply you with compliments," she replied honestly.

He stalked close and that muskiness overwhelmed her. "I said *man*," he whispered in her ear, "not boys."

Oh. She gulped and then almost shrieked as he spun her, spine meeting his solid chest.

They both stared at their reflection, his face over her shoulder. A bare hand toyed with the ribbon under her breast and her breathing shallowed. He was so large, smothering her delicate frame with…largeness.

"A woman who wears such a dress must have her wits about her. Must realise the effect she has. Then she can take appropriate action should the need arise."

"Should what need arise?"

His grey eyes flashed in the mirror as he smiled languidly, and she gulped again as that bare hand came up and cupped…yes, *cupped* her breast.

She couldn't breathe.

"I have been very patient, Cordelia."

"Have you?" she whispered, trying not to moan as his fingers brushed the tip. His hand looked so very broad there – darker than her own skin with blunt fingers and neat nails. It all conspired to do something exceedingly fluttery to her insides.

"Your mother told me you were guileless, unworldly, but I still wanted you. She warned me away. Said I was too…hot-blooded for her naive little girl. But money talks and your father listened. However, I promised myself I wouldn't frighten you."

Cordelia wished her mother would stop interfering with her life. Unworldly? No wonder she was a bit of a goosecap at times, being brought up by someone who wanted to preserve her at twelve years old.

Thank goodness Father had always been a greedy gut.

"I think… I think you should have talked to me and not my mother," she muttered, feeling curious tingles catapult through her – was that normal?

They both watched his hand meander to her other breast. "Does this frighten you?" he asked.

"No. I like it," she told his reflection and his eyes flickered, a storm brewing in the depths. But a question plagued… "Why were you at the Miltons' ball, Lord Oakdean? Were you with a woman?"

"No. Of course not. Pilkington's leaving spree. He's off to the Continent and we decided to combine the two."

"The jeers and clapping?"

He nodded, hand still caressing. Oakdean appeared to be

watching her face for any traces of displeasure – he wouldn't find any. She was having a delightful time.

"And the female I heard in some form of distress?" she asked.

His cheekbones flushed. "No idea. I was trying to find an empty room, but I knew we might stumble upon…activities, hence the covering for your eyes." He pulled her tight. "Cordelia, I have not looked at another woman since you ambled into the Landowns' ball dressed in godawful white frills and what looked to be a chicken in your hair."

"Dove. But you kissed my forehead when we became engaged. I hardly felt wanted."

"I was trying not to frighten you. Your mother said–"

"My mother is a bit odd, in case you hadn't noticed." She spun in his arms, hands on his broad chest. He felt so very solid – like a stone wall, but they were cold and lumpy and Oakdean was anything but lumpy…although. No, it couldn't be. Impossible. "I wrote poems about being a sheep to my music tutor's shepherd when I was sixteen, do you mind?"

"Did he touch you?"

"No. It was all somewhat metaphorical."

"Then I don't give a bloody damn. I also don't want a three-month engagement."

Cordelia stared into her betrothed's eyes and saw that same burning expression she'd noticed in the duke's every time he observed Aideen.

"Why?"

He pulled her all the more closer and she felt every flex of his powerful body.

"Because I love you, Cordelia Greenwood, and I don't want to wait a moment longer to begin my life with you."

Goodness.

"What would you suggest?" she purred. No really, she did, and linked her arms about his neck. Positively wanton.

"We could go to Gretna Green or get a licence?" His face remained serious and fierce.

"A kiss might help me decide."

Achingly tender, his lips brushed hers, bestowing light touches, and then he drew away. She pulled the hair at his nape. "Kiss me properly," she implored.

So he did. A slow, deep kiss that rolled the senses and made her ache in a truly unladylike way. She returned his kiss, copying his movements, heard his moan.

"I love you, James," she breathed against his mouth, feeling his arms tense. "I don't care where we go, as long as it's together."

17

MIRROR, MIRROR ON THE WALL…

Queen Street was no place to hasten in daylight hours, let alone the dead of night.

A few swaggering bucks wandered the streets, looking for trouble, but he ignored their drunken hoots, aware he was late for his assignation with Bluey.

The night had grown cold, keeping even the fog at bay, yet a damp still choked the lungs if one breathed too deeply.

Rakecombe buttoned his old greatcoat before plunging one gloved hand into the large pocket, the other maintaining a tight hold on his cane.

Anger still crawled in his belly and yet if someone had asked him why, he was aware he had no answer.

It felt as though he'd been angry forever but had sought to quash it, only keeping it hidden under a mien of self-control: a kindling of flames that had never really been doused, solely awaiting favourable conditions. A gust of soft Irish wind from the west and now the conflagration had grown beyond its confines.

Anger at Lord White for steering him to espionage whilst at Oxford.

Anger at Gwen for being so bold and thoughtless.

Anger at himself for being so bloody green as a youth.

Anger at the monster who'd spilt his family's blood…

The only person he didn't feel anger for was Aideen.

She'd known it was him at the Miltons' masquerade. Of course she'd damn well known. No one would ever fool his wife; it was one of the reasons he adored her so.

Scowling, he picked up speed as a bitter gust chilled his skin.

Perhaps he should visit her bed again. Unsated lust still burned within and her toying with him at the Miltons' and the kiss tonight had simply made it worse. The fact his desires weren't uniquely for her body, but also her tender voice and caring nature, he refused to consider; those desires would take what he could give and be content.

The corner of Queen Street came into view and he narrowed his eyes.

His wife also needed to learn he wasn't some callow stripling to be taunted. Playing with a raging inferno got you bur–

A harsh cry from the street ahead and he broke into a run.

The night was murky and shadowed but a few doorways held dim lanterns, and in the distance a man lay on the ground, surrounded by another two kicking him in the guts.

Harrowing grunts echoed around the narrow dwellings, but no faces peered from the windows or called for the night watch.

"Hey," he shouted, rushing on.

In an instant, he'd yanked the pistol from his greatcoat and aimed as one of the men drew a knife, arm hauling back for the throw, but the wielder fell with the slam of his bullet, the sound ricocheting, smoke curling, and the rat clutched at his bloodied shoulder, scrabbling desperately in the gutter for his fallen weapon.

Dropping the pistol and shoving his cane to the loop on his greatcoat, Rakecombe drew his own blade hidden beneath his many layers.

The other lowlife had a dagger and flipped it from hand to hand as villains were wont to do in a display of pitiful bravado.

Black hair flopped over the pug-nosed man's forehead, and Rakecombe noted that although his clothes were down at heel, they were not the common ruffian variety either.

Groaning came from the filthy cobbles, but he concentrated on the dagger in front of him which flashed then hid as a lantern shuddered in the breeze, casting dark shade and flickering light.

He waited.

The villain struck, impatient as they always were, and Rakecombe veered, slicing out before swirling, readied in a curved stance.

"Fils de pute," pug nose spat, and dread snaked in his stomach. It could be no coincidence that a Frenchman stalked this same street this night.

Now it was Rakecombe who'd little patience, and diving forward, he deftly grabbed the man's thin wrist whilst striking him fully in the face with the hilt of his dagger. He needed this Frenchman alive.

A tinge of pain grazed his own arm but ignoring it, he slammed in another clout and twisted pug nose's wrist until he shrieked, knife clattering to the cobbles, and Rakecombe was forced to release him.

"Morceau de merde," the whoreson cried defiantly, kicking out before scuttling away, tugging his accomplice with him.

Another chilling groan prevented Rakecombe from

giving chase, the agonised voice recognisable, and he kneeled in the grime to tend to the fallen man.

"Bluey?" With desperation, he grabbed his collar. "Can you hear me? Where are you hurt?"

"Stomach… Can't…"

Rakecombe cursed, not able to see the wound in this dimly lit street, but well able to feel the warm liquid seeping over his fingers. Depending on where the knife had entered, a gut wound could be fatal, and he unwound his cravat, stuffing it in wherever he could feel and then binding it tight around the midriff.

"Take me to…" Bluey reached out a bloodied hand and pulled Rakecombe's head near, whispering, "Charles Street… Drury Lane. Six…find Harry–"

Nothing could be done here, so he hauled him over his shoulder as gently as possible. Bluey grunted in pain nevertheless before falling as a dead-weight – probably for the best as Drury Lane was a fair distance over someone's shoulder with a wound to the gizzards.

He strode briskly, feeling wary eyes upon him from cramped doorways and squalid windows. Some scraggy harlot shot out of his way, her dull gaze having seen it all before.

A night long past invaded his thoughts, when the body in his arms hadn't been a wounded man but his lifeless sister.

He shook his head. A whimper from Bluey.

Dwelling on long-ago errors did little except bring forth more anger, more sorrow. He set his mind to work, questions burning.

How had they found out about the assignation? What information did Bluey have? Was this Stafford's doing?

Finally, he turned down Charles Street and number six

emerged. Not a hovel but a clean-looking place with large shutters and a solid entrance.

The abode was so tightly bolted that no light glimmered around the edges of its wooden protection, and he hammered on the door for what seemed an eternity until a slat drew back. Candlelight momentarily blinded him before an eye peered out.

"What d'yer want?" a harsh voice snapped.

"Bluey's hurt. He asked for this house." The eye didn't blink or move. "We're looking for Harry?"

With that, the slat thumped shut and then came the sound of a dozen or so bolts being pulled. He was dragged into the house and the door slammed behind him.

In front stood…

A pretty woman, slender, with a long blond plait falling over one shoulder, clothed in a white gown and wrap, the lantern light casting an angelic glow. Distress and terror lit her eyes before she straightened her shoulders and bustled them into another room.

He laid Bluey on the ample couch whilst the woman dashed to a cupboard and collected a bunch of white linens.

Blood drenched Bluey's jacket and Rakecombe threw off his own coat, pulling his knife out. The woman halted in her step but rushed once more as he began divesting Bluey of his clothes, slitting the material in one swoop.

Pushing aside the shirt, he closed his eyes to thank the heavens. Lengthy but not deep, the wound missed, as far as he could tell, any vital organs.

The woman's shuddering relief echoed his own, and he glanced around to moist eyes. "I can look after him now," she said, shaking her head. "You can leave. If no infection sets in, he'll be fine."

"Have you money for a doctor?"

"Aye, but I've nursed before, so I know what I'm doing. I'll stitch him better than most of those drunken leeches," she muttered.

Rakecombe stared as the competent woman uncorked a brandy bottle with her teeth and sloshed liquor around the wound before packing a wodge of clean cloth against it.

Unsure of her status and how much to tell her, he shifted on his heels. He wanted to be kept aware of Bluey's condition, but should he confide in this unknown woman?

"And you are, miss?" He raised an eyebrow, to which she raised hers. Higher than his own, in truth.

"I'm Harriet, Bluey's wife…Your Grace."

Two blows in one sentence.

"Ah. I wasn't aware he was married."

"We keep it quiet. Don't want his work brought home every night."

No, indeed. No one would.

"You know where to find me then? I will return tomorrow to check on him."

"Very well but come around the back and don't bring your carriage." Her face focused on her husband, stroking his cheek with tender care.

He nodded and was about to leave when fierce fingers gripped his wrist. Spinning, he beheld Bluey's eyes, narrow but open. "A warehouse… French…"

But a foul cough caught him, the grip loosened, and pain took Bluey under once again.

"I'll let you know if he says anything more," Harriet declared, before waving him out, the door thumping shut behind him and the abundant bolts thundering their protection.

The bitter wind had grown in hostility whilst he'd been

inside. It tore through the streets and into his blood-soaked coat to batter his soul.

With mood foul, Rakecombe sliced through it, eager for home, a cold drenching and a stiff drink.

THE LOCK SIGNALLED its submission with a soft click, and Aideen unhurriedly opened the adjoining door into the ducal bedchamber.

Once Alex had left the Bucklands' soirée, it had held little interest, and so she'd ordered the carriage for home, but sleep had been elusive and what with all that noise...

Nigh on an hour ago, she'd heard a chamber door slam, quite a bit of rustling and then that strange sloshing sound again.

After a short while, it had then appeared Alex had more pressing business than sleep as he'd stomped back down the stairs.

She'd lain there for possibly a quarter hour more, twitching and considering, before curiosity had got the better of her, and so using her uncle's handy lock-picking device, she had decided to explore. After all, it was impossible during the day due to that damn valet's never-ending vigilance of the master chamber – it was more closely guarded than an Irish girl's virtue.

The bed looked to be normal, with heavy dark-green drapes. A chest of drawers sat to one side and a desk on the other. Quite a dull room, all told, with few ornaments or pictures to brighten – very Rakecombe. She meandered toward the chest to peruse his nightly reading, but a miniature of a pretty, blond girl caught her eye.

She huffed and tiptoed to a narrower door on the left,

finding his dressing room; shirts and cravats folded so perfectly, she felt scared to breathe.

Pondering, she backed out. The larger door obviously led to the corridor, so she headed for the only other door in the room.

Aha, success.

In front, looming high, was a curious-looking contraption. A normal copper bath tub lay at the bottom, but four tubes, around ten feet tall, rose at each corner and seemed to collect in another smaller basin at the top. A rope was attached, and Aideen could only wonder that the nightly sloshing sound was water being sluiced from the upper basin – how unusual.

And how cold.

She placed her candle on the dresser and was about to inspect anew when a low groan from the corridor startled her. Quickly, she gathered her candle once more and crept to the main bedchamber door. It opened without a creak, and she gazed into the murkiness.

Nothing stirred but she'd heard something for certain, and so with a silent tread, she stepped out, glad she still had her lock-picking device to hand because it also contained a sprung knife. Uncle Seamus said you could never be sure what you'd find when breaking and entering – how true.

Her candle barely managed to light a few feet ahead, and Aideen shivered. The dark didn't generally worry her unless it was a stormy night in Ireland with Uncle telling tales of the dreaded *Dobhar-chú*.

With heart pounding like a herd of angry cows, she placed the candle on the side table and palmed her lock-picker ready to spring its blade. She peered down the staircase, but suddenly her body was hauled around and propelled against the wall.

All she could see was black, all she could feel was a press against her chest, all she could smell was…

"Alex?"

"Wife."

The suffocating black pulled back a little, but he declined to let go, and she realised the press was his cane. It kept her prisoner against the wall, a band above her breast, jailing her upper arms.

Candlelight played shadows on his face, revealing a rigid expression and damp hair, that sleek curl seeking freedom in the nocturnal hours.

An ebony silk banyan swathed his torso, but he also wore loose breeches and she could feel the silk pressing against her night-rail-covered legs.

"Why are you wandering this night, Aideen?"

"Er." Honesty, she'd learned, was not *always* the best policy. "A glass of water?"

He shook his head, face grim.

"A book?" she squeaked, feeling that cane meander downwards.

Thankfully, she wasn't wearing her wedding night-rail although this one didn't have much more to it. Low at the front, it was fashioned of emerald silk, with satin ribbons edging the bodice.

He leaned close. "You have half the library by your bedside, my little liar."

Unable to deny such a scurrilous but true accusation, she did what she always did when unsure, intimidated and backed into a corner…or up against a wall.

"Why are you coming home so late, Alexander?" she attacked. "Spying on people? Or holed up in some brothel as all you men are wont to do?"

That sounded remarkably like jealousy and she bit her lip.

Damn.

Alex's gaze wandered her body and her heart thudded. He didn't reply but slowly, so slowly, he began to drag the cane lower. The pierced silver decoration entangled with the ribbons at her bodice and the night-rail stretched. Aideen's breath froze as he revealed the slope of her pale breasts to the candlelight, felt the tautness of the gauzy fabric against her skin.

A muscle flickered in his jaw, but he didn't cease, eyes transfixed. She moaned as the material grazed her nipples, couldn't halt the sound. And then, so leisurely she wanted to scream, he lowered his head and licked at the tender flesh revealed.

Imprisoned, all she could do was gasp her pleasure and push her hips forward, arms bent at the elbow, fingers dropping her lock-picker, grasping forth, merely to find slippery silk.

The cane clattered to the floorboards.

Rough hands now yanked at the material, wrenching it down to his demanding mouth as he lavished kisses and bites to her skin.

Aideen hauled him near, grabbing hold of his arm, but a pained gasp escaped his lips and he surged away, panting.

"Go, Aideen," he bit out. "My mood is foul. Go."

"And if I don't wish to?" she questioned. He didn't frighten her – quite the opposite. She craved his forceful passion, knowing he would never hurt her.

Alex straightened. "Run," he snarled. "You will only have the one chance."

If only he knew. She'd never been able to run from the Duke of Rakecombe. He bound her to him in ways she couldn't comprehend, and seeing his taut jaw and heaving chest, she knew she had a similar effect.

"I've never run from you, Alex," she whispered. "In fact, it has been yourself who runs–"

She was wrenched into his arms and vehement lips covered hers, smothering all retorts. He'd been right – his mood was foul and his touch unrefined, but then she was equally enraged: at being disregarded, at being tested, at his deuced control.

Scratching at his shoulders, she hauled his banyan down, revealing his damp chest and that strange tattoo covering a nasty scar. She kissed it and he grunted in torment.

Against the opposite wall hid a delicate rosewood table and she was unceremoniously swirled and sat upon it, a porcelain angel crashing to the floor as hands rummaged at her rail, yanking the material high, shoving, parting her legs.

Deft fingers found her core, caressed and pushed, and Aideen moaned, scrabbling at the fall of his breeches.

It seemed an age since they'd been entwined, and impatience tore at her. Aideen was sure she'd be alarmed if she cared to look down – at the size and ferocity of his need – but she didn't, instead lifting her chin and jerking his mouth to hers, kissing with fierceness.

Alex responded, cursing, his lips moving to her neck and grazing the skin whilst he pushed her fumbling hands away and ripped at his breeches. Hauling her forward on the polished wood, she circled her legs around his slender hips. Felt his arousal press.

A thrust. One determined thrust and he was deep inside.

Having only experienced the wedding night, she felt so stretched, so filled, and she groaned, legs thrashing for leverage. Strong hands grabbed her thighs, held her whilst his body bucked with frenzy, the table shuddering under the force.

Sinking, surging so quickly, the rapture. The days of

taunts and silences alike had stripped her emotions bare and all sensation collided: the cloth of his breeches abrading her thigh, his chest against her breast and those bucking hips.

His face buried itself in her neck and she opened her eyes over his shoulder.

What she saw tipped her over the precipice of pleasure.

She cried out as savage bliss ripped through her, curling her toes and causing her nails to scratch into his nape.

Alex's thrusts became frantic, one palm removing itself to the wall for more power, until he too growled his release to the empty corridor, hand fisting on the flock paper.

His body jolted, face dropping deeper into her neck, breath rasping as he ran fingers through her hair.

Despite the abused table now listing somewhat, and her legs aching with cramp, she had no wish to stir, no wish to move a muscle. If they moved, all the problems of the day would return.

But gradually he did, and she now noticed his right forearm had a cloth tied around it, blood spotting the pristine white. "You're hurt?" she whispered, legs lowering to the ground. "I can get som–"

"It's nothing. A scratch."

It didn't look to be a scratch, but she knew that tone – manly pride and all that balderdash.

Instead, she raised a gentle hand and stroked his ruddy cheek.

For a while, he accepted her caress, even shifted further toward her touch, but then he opened his eyes, glanced down, and a kind of horror shone in those green orbs as he took in her dishevelled state.

He backed away.

"I used you ill, Aideen," he murmured, buttoning his

breeches with an unsteady hand yet sounding as though he'd just stepped on her dress.

She remained silent, feeling anything but ill-used, but he closed his eyes, seemingly fighting some inner torment, jaw clenched, until turning his face from her sight.

"Leave me be," he whispered harshly into the dark. "I do not want you." And he walked down the hallway without so much as a backwards glance, softly closing his bedchamber door behind him.

Such callous words and Aideen knew she should be fuming. Hurt beyond measure. Hate him for his curt denial of their passion when moments ago, he'd made such desperate love to his wife.

But she felt none of those emotions, none of that hate, because the very sight that had crested her pleasure had been the same that now prevented her from despising her husband.

The giltwood mirror opposite with its carved panels portraying dance and music had reflected all.

His smooth back, his taut buttocks, but after their ardent clash, the sheer look of desolation and distress as he'd uttered those cold words. That look had betrayed him – it had hurt Alex to say those words as much as it had hurt Aideen to hear them.

Such agony and wretchedness had been displayed in those eyes, such self-loathing.

She didn't need to despise Alexander; he was doing that more than enough for them both.

The mirror continued its silent scrutiny as she allowed the hitched night-rail to fall back down about her legs and pulled the sleeves up, the friction delicious on her sensitive, love-touched skin.

Straightening the table as best she could, she placed the

damaged angel upon it, gathered her lock pick from the floor and meandered along the hallway to her own bedchamber, humming.

Humming and scheming.

RAKECOMBE DROPPED WEARILY onto the edge of his bed and slugged a full brandy to wash away the bitter taste of lies.

"I had to say it, Gwen," he whispered to the miniature by his bedside, "to keep my Aideen safe."

His sister's green eyes glared back, disapproving.

But he had done the right thing...had he not?

18

IF FOOD BE THE MUSIC OF LOVE…EAT ON.

Cosseting a duke proved more than a little difficult when he was absent.

Aideen knew perfectly well that after last night he'd be anticipating her fury, so of course she would do the exact opposite. She chewed her toast thoughtfully.

Purposely hurting others with nasty words was a cowardly action, but it was the "why" that interested Aideen.

Beastliness always had a reason.

One might not agree with it or even understand it, but it was still there, defining actions and clouding existences.

As such, she ruminated on how to overwhelm her husband with undue amiability and charm. Because this morning that is what she planned. She would bamboozle, confuse and generally befuddle him with syrupiness until he disgorged his past to her, revealed his emotions and told her why he felt the need to distance himself quite so completely.

But the bug had left the house at a quarter after six and however much she wanted to plague her husband, her own mood was not often amiable at daybreak, so she'd stayed in bed.

Perhaps she ought to search out his man of affairs and make an appointment to meet with the duke or leave a note by his bathing device requesting his esteemed appearance at dinner.

Dinner.

Without doubt, another possible reason for him eating at his club every night could be the cuisine in this household, as to be sure, the way to a man's heart was not through deflated soufflé.

Aideen had quizzed the dowager duchess about Monsieur Pascale Dupont, but she'd looked coy and said the chef was highly trained, had seven children and needed the employment after fleeing his home country.

Stirring the watery jam, she wondered why the servants hadn't complained. Normally the butler or footmen were the first to grumble if the food downstairs was inedible. She thought about meeting with Mrs Booth, the starchy housekeeper, but the woman had been very defensive about the kitchens.

Hmm.

Aideen stood, leaving her limp French toast, and marched to the servants' stairs. If she couldn't solve her marital problems today, the least she could do was eat well.

A maid dashed out of her way with a horrified expression, but she paid no heed. Duchesses, she expected, didn't visit kitchens very often. But Irish ones did.

Halfway down the second set of narrow stairs to the basement, Aideen paused.

The scent of yeast and dried currants teased her nostrils to seventh heaven.

Without knocking, she opened the kitchen door a crack.

A maid stood by the large range, stirring a wholesome smelling vat of stew whilst a man sat at the scored table perusing a stained book. His head turned to the maid. "Those potatoes can go in now, Maisie."

He buried his nose in the creased pages, muttering to himself and scribbling notes in the margins.

The chef's hand, for who else could he be, swiped out to grab a chunk of…*proper* bread which sat on a plate to his side, and she heard a whisper of a curse as he followed the words with his finger.

"*Dia dhuit*," Aideen said loudly, narrowing her glare as she entered.

"*Dia is Muire dhuit*," the chap replied, before twisting his head, eyes flaring in horror.

She recognised him from the day she'd married, as all the servants had been gathered at the hallway in welcome: deepest black curly hair tumbled over a handsome forehead, whilst pale-blue eyes flickered in worry within an extremely pale face.

If he was a French chef then she was Queen Maeve of Connacht.

"Where are you from?"

Obviously realising there was no talking his way out of this – even if he was Irish – the chef bowed his head. "Wicklow, Ya Grace."

"Hmm." She stalked over, eyes flicking to the gawping maids. "Let us continue this conversation outside…and bring that bread."

The sun shone weakly as they climbed the steps to the gardens, a haze preventing its full warmth, and the not-so-exotic chef desolately followed three feet behind.

"So," she began, pausing under an apple tree, "why the pretence?"

"I…" He peered at the heavens as though expecting divine help from the saints above.

"No yarns. The truth."

He scrutinised the ground as though the aid of the inhabitants below might be more useful in this situation. "I trained in Dublin, in the best houses, Ya Grace. But I married an English lass, and she was so homesick for London. I tried to find work here but everyone wants a fancy French chef."

"So you thought to be one?"

"Had to. Otherwise I was treated like dirt, told I was a thieving bogtrotter, that I'd snaffle the silver and cook their children." He tugged at his thick hair. "A few would have taken me on but at half the wage, and we've four babes with another on the way."

"The dowager duchess said you had seven children."

His eyes shifted. "Four. Seven...hard to keep tally, Ya Grace."

Having been prone to exaggeration herself on more than one occasion, she could hardly admonish. "And does she know you are not in any way French?"

"I dunno to be truthful. I knew a French fella once, a footman, so I'm grand *fait* with the accent. I gave it lots of zhats and zizes and it seemed to work. Even threw in a few *zut alors*."

Aideen doubted the astute Meghan had been fooled for a moment but it was obviously her soft heart which had been touched by the...seven children. "But the food? You say you've worked in the best houses but it's...it's..." She trailed off.

"I know how to cook the finest English and Irish dishes, but I was employed as a French chef, so I've been cooking French fare." His gaze flickered. "I've a book, but it's all in foreign so I've had a few problems, and I can't afford to buy one in English. But I've made friends with a Frenchie in the ale-house and he gave me a few hints."

"Such as?"

"Lots of herbs and pepper. Don't overcook the meat. Cut everything up really small and splash around the salt."

Aideen was sure Jacquiers at The Clarendon would be spitting bile at this summation of French cooking. "Why haven't the servants said anything?"

"Everything was grand." He shrugged. "I cook French fer upstairs and no one's complained, but I cook Irish or English fer downstairs." He handed her a piece of the bread, wrapped in a serviette.

Biting into it, she was transported home. To evenings by the fire with Seamus, slathering butter on warm bread until it ran down your fingers.

She missed home, she realised. The hills so verdant it burned the eyes, the freshness of a spring morning, the lichen-covered forests. She missed the laughing people, the cuddles from Uncle and the harsh coastal wind blowing her hair free and wild.

Not everything there was perfect, but London was all stern propriety and icy stares. Indeed, her own stern duke needing warming with some hot Irish stew and a soft caress.

Looking up, she noticed the man fiddling with a thread on his worn jacket.

"Your French dishes are awful… I'm sorry."

His face fell bleak. "Well, that's it then. I'll gather m'things. Forgive me, Ya Grace, fer–"

She held up a palm. "But your bread and the aroma of that stew are divine. So, present your finest meal tonight – nothing French – and we will talk again tomorrow."

Aideen watched the chef's eyes lighten. She knew hundreds from the Emerald Isle had come over, thinking the London streets were paved in gold. But the reality was equally grim. Blood and sweat lined these streets too – of strife and poverty and the hardship of war.

"Ta, Ya Grace. I'll cook ya a fine bit o' home, I will."

"Wonderful. And one other issue…Monsieur Pascale Dupont."

He coughed, eyes twinkling. "Er. It's Padraig Duffy, at ya service." And he bowed.

"Hmm. Please send up a light luncheon of that bread and then I'll starve my stomach until tonight. We will also see about a book on French cuisine. No harm in adding another string to your fiddle, so to speak."

The chef nodded and with a jaunty wink, headed back.

"And by the way," Aideen called, "there are only three children, are there not? Or is it two, Padraig?"

A waggish grin crossed his handsome face. "Depends if ya include the one in the oven, Ya Grace."

Evidently her fellow countryman didn't need to kiss anything to talk blarney.

RAKECOMBE FELT…UNSETTLED, odd and a dab nauseous.

And it wasn't the food either. A perfect lamb roast had been presented tonight: tender cuts of meat – not bleating – with a fresh minty sauce, fluffy perfectly cooked potatoes and reassuringly normal-shaped carrots.

Vaguely, he wondered if Aideen had dismissed the French chef but didn't ask. Couldn't speak. Every word he thought to utter felt trite and banal after last night's bestial act. So he quaffed more claret instead.

He hadn't intended to dine at home as he'd wanted to visit Bluey, but the chap's wife had sent a message saying he was insensible due to laudanum and to call on the morrow, so he'd been at a loose end.

When he'd returned from a meeting with Rainham, a note had been pinned to his bathing device, requesting his attendance at dinner. It wasn't the words that had intrigued him, however, but how the hell that note had got there in the first place.

His chambers were always locked or Thorn was present. After all, he did occasionally have sensitive information in the safe. So how had Aideen managed to enter?

Stealing a glance, he then wished he hadn't. She looked so very lovely.

Perhaps dining at home hadn't solely been curiosity about the note's placement, but a need to make sure she was well, that her eyes were not sad or hurt by his utterly uncivilised behaviour.

But she was obviously quite well. In fact, fairly stupendous and currently wittering on about replacing his study chair as it was far too old and uncomfortable for him to sit in.

Where was the anger he'd expected? The profanities and flashing ire? He'd anticipated nettle patch curses and furious obsidian eyes, but she was so cheerful it made his teeth ache.

A cerulean gown had been poured over her tonight, the silk tight and revealing, and although the majority of her hair was swept back, two fat coils were draped over her décolletage, ocean black against the luminosity of her skin.

The current unsettled feeling had arisen when he'd noticed the dark smudges on her neck as she'd bent to pour the mint sauce. Smudges he'd caused with his lips and teeth.

He'd taken his wife like a whore and the thought nearly brought up his lamb. Aideen deserved better than him, better than a foul, angry wreck that in turn shouted, ignored and then swived her in a bloody corridor as though she was his next breath.

Goddamn, she'd looked so sublime last night after his evening of blood and pain, and the past days of intense want had crashed over him.

Need, possession and all the sentiments he'd vowed never to feel for Aideen had surged as she'd stood her ground before him, wilfully declining to return to her bedchamber.

All this time, he'd tried so hard to stay away. To stand firm for her own safety, to live their lives apart, but one look from those coal eyes and all his vows had fled.

But throughout this self-admonishment, a part of him – located south of his belly but north of his knees – affirmed how very good it had been. How tight and eager her body had felt. How he himself hadn't escaped unmarked as his neck still tingled from those sharp nails.

That was no excuse, however. His lie of not wanting her especially had no excuse.

"Can we acquire a puppy?"

Aideen's eyes were wide with artlessness as he shook his noggin to clear it. What?

"I want a puppy. Please, husband of mine. Uncle Seamus has forever kept dogs and I miss them. Their wiggly tails and cute snuffle wuffs and–"

"I beg your pardon?" he spluttered. He never spluttered. Spluttering was for callow youths and men without teeth. But then it wasn't every day your *little fire* of a wife, who ought to be spitting venom, requested a puppy and waffled on about...snuffle wuffs?

"I'd like one. I thought you may have friends with some pups." She smiled, face open, and he felt instantly on guard. What was she up to?

"I do not have any friends." He didn't mean that. Well, he did but he didn't mean to say it.

"I see you talking to people at balls."

"They are acquaintances. Aideen–"

"Well, can you ask them?" she pleaded. "I think a puppy would enliven this echoing place a little. Have you tried the mint sauce, by the way? It's divine, so fresh. And I know you like cherry tarts, so–"

"Aideen. I apologise."

Hellfire. Over the past year, he'd made more apologies than in his entire life, even filched one from his wife's favourite book last spring. Considering the circumstances, he could hardly use that Mr Darcy's again – he'd be cast out for plagiarism.

She stared, eyes wide, a morsel of lamb held to her lips.

Gritting his teeth, he continued, "I'd had an awful night, but it was no excuse to..." He tried to think of a word but none were suitable in delicate company.

"Ravish me?" she supplied. Thankfully she'd dispensed with the servants whilst they ate. "Make passionate love?" she suggested, chewing thoughtfully. "Oh, this lamb is divine. You can almost taste the sweet spring grass, and the potatoes are so flavoursome. Don't you agree, Your Grace?"

He didn't know what Aideen schemed, but she was tangling him in knots.

Was this her revenge? Talk him to death with superficial chit-chat about food and puppies. Had she been taking advice from Winterbourne? That was his tactic.

"I was not gentle," he continued, "and–"

"Alex," she interrupted firmly.

Peering up from his flavoursome potato, he paused, anticipating the worst. He wished she'd just cosh him over the head with her goblet or curse him to the seven dirges of Hades or press her fingers into the knife wound on his arm. Then he'd feel better.

Aideen licked her lips. "Have some more carrots, they've a luscious honey glaze."

19

GOD DEFEND ME FROM MY FRIENDS; FROM MY ENEMIES I CAN DEFEND MYSELF.

Rakecombe speculated if his brain was decaying.

Last night, after dinner, Aideen had personally seen to the pouring of his brandy in the study, plumped his cushions and heaved off his boots. He felt as if a doctor had called and confided that her husband only had days to breathe before cocking his toes – except no one had thought to inform the incipient dead one.

There was no other reason why Aideen should still be treating him with such… He hesitated to say sweetness as that had connotations of charm and he had a horrible feeling it was anything but.

Currently, she was smothering a thick raspberry jam on his breakfast toast. Admittedly, it was excellent jam and divine bread but that was beside the point. He narrowed his eyes and scowled.

His wife was up to something.

A pale-pink day dress adorned her this morning and although it was utterly fetching, he didn't think Aideen was a particularly pink person. Rose ribbons twisted within her hair and she chatted gaily about nothing in particular, ringlets bobbing.

Normally, he avoided breakfast – for the food and his wife – but after last night, he'd been intrigued as to whether the chef could repeat his success and if Aideen would continue to be so…sweet.

Yes, to both.

It wasn't that he didn't like this side of Aideen, it was… restful, but so far he'd been forced to bite his lip thrice to prevent himself from provoking, if only to see that rousing flash of temper.

Another downright incommodious sensation was that he felt wholly unsure of himself.

Always, he'd known the path he trod, the route he would take, but he was aware the path he'd thought to stomp down when he'd made Aideen his bride might have been…uncharted.

He couldn't stay away. That was the truth. He never had.

Aideen twisted his insides, pureed his brains to syllabub and turned his controlled lust into a rabid beast. And if staying away from her had caused the debacle the other night, he'd have to consider a different course of action.

The problem was he couldn't think of one. And that in itself was inexplicable.

"Would you like more chocolate, dearest Alex?" she simpered, and he ground his jaw.

If it was a ploy, all this niceness, he wondered who would break first? Aideen or himself? Neither of them had the temperaments for it.

Well, what was sauce for the goose was sauce for the gander.

"Thank you, my little leprechaun," he purred with a malevolent grin. "I do believe I will. And with one more spoonful of sugar. I really cannot get enough, my cherished cherry."

She smiled, but he detected a curl to her lip as she dumped three spoonfuls in his cup. "Oh, darling Alex," she chirped, sliding it over, "you must also have a biscuit then. They are Irish and so sweet on the tongue."

He nibbled the end. It was rather good. "Thank you, my innocent imp. I do so like an Irish tongue in my mouth. I do beg your pardon, I mean biscuit."

Smiling again, Aideen sipped tea, but he noticed she'd purposely veiled her eyes with those dark lashes. He wondered what curses were rattling through that hasty noddle of hers – no doubt they involved sharp teeth, dogs and his tallywags.

"What are your plans for today, beloved spouse?" she enquired with a Cheshire cheese grin.

"Busy, my sweet sprite. At the House of Lords all morning and then with my steward for the afternoon. I also have to meet Winterbourne this evening, so I'm afraid I shall miss your melodiousness at dinner. And you, my flitting fairy?"

Was there a flash of disappointment in those eyes?

"I am shopping for new night-rails." She beamed, twirling an ebony ringlet around her finger. "I seem to have…torn two of them. Rent beyond repair. Unusable. Have you any colour preference, my cherished husband and master?"

Hell. The winning shot.

His lust burned, and he grinned grudgingly in acknowledgement of a superior…master. "Considering I am being buried beneath your charm and benevolence, my effervescent elf, perhaps a reassuring black might be apt."

Bottomless eyes flashed at last. "Just so, my beloved Alex darling."

. . .

AIDEEN COLLAPSED BACK in the breakfast chair, quite at sixes and sevens as Alex *darling* left the room.

Who would have thought being nice was so tiring?

THE DAY HAD BEEN DEVILISHLY dull and Rakecombe wished he was now home, trading sweet nothings with his wife.

He still had no idea how to reconcile his Crown work with his marital status and keeping his duchess from harm, but something had to give – he was going mad.

"You're very quiet tonight, Alex," said Winterbourne, frowning. "Oh, I should ask, are we on given name terms? I would say so, if we are headed to Charles Street, and... Where was I before I interrupted myself? Oh yes, well, quieter than usual, which isn't saying much."

It appeared *Jack* had been taking wittering lessons from Aideen – or was it the reverse? There must be some rule fifteen about driving your companion to distraction with meaningless prattle.

They strode towards Bluey's home, eschewing the carriage as instructed by the chap's wife. Jack was even clothed in a dark ensemble for once, although he sported hessians – hardly a covert choice as the swinging gold tassels would be visible all the way from the Tower.

"Your boots are unsoiled. Gives you away," Rakecombe grumbled, whacking his cane on his own grubby but eminently comfortable top boots.

"Brummel told me to clean them in the froth of champagne for shine, but I swear my Miggens drinks the bubbly stuff and spits on them instead. I'll tell him to rub in some horse shi–"

"Do you ever feel as though Mother Nature is tossing you

around?" he interrupted. Not that he wanted the rogue's advice, but anything was better than inconsequential babble.

"Hardly," Jack said with a grin, "but if you mean in terms of love, no. Ladies enjoy my company. I enjoy theirs. End of story. They never feel anything deeper and vice versa."

Rakecombe wondered if that was because the marquess only showed the world his annoying *bonhomie* and rascal smile, rather than the warrior he'd seen that night in St Giles or the gentleman who'd pledged a fortune to a charity hospital. He considered saying so, but his own life was in too much of a mess to be spouting forth.

Once, he recalled stating he'd be ten feet under before taking Winterbourne's advice. Well, metaphorically, he now was.

A scotch mist was falling and he wrapped his coat close, wishing he'd requested the carriage drop them nearer. It was not the weather for Shanks's pony as the drizzle soaked into your very bones and there was only one way he could ever imagine warming up.

"If you want my advice, I've a pertinent rule," Jack began, and all at once, Rakecombe regretted opening his mouth, as he now remembered the chap's rules came in two varieties: useless and downright useless.

"Number twenty-four, in case you are noting them down for future use," Jack continued, spreading his arms as though issuing an eleventh commandment. "If your leg is stuck in the jaws of a trap, you have two options: writhe around and cry out or lay still and conserve energy, but either way, you'll lose the leg."

Rakecombe halted his stride so hastily, he almost slipped on the damp cobbles, the cane saving his arse and pride. "That's ludicrous and it's not even a rule."

Pursing his lips, Winterbourne shook his head wearily.

"The rule is don't get trapped in the first place, but once you are...you're buggered. Accept it."

Grumbling, Rakecombe wheeled left and made his way down the back of Charles Street.

His leg wasn't stuck. No, his whole blasted body, head and soul were stuck.

And Aideen's jaws were formed of iron.

BLUEY'S SKIN had taken on a flush and his eyes glittered with fever, but he was vaguely compos mentis.

"I got word," he rasped, "that a couple of foreign fellas 'ave been seen over the river at some Southwark warehouse, so I done a bit of inn-hopping there before I came to yer. It were in the Nag's Head I overheard some fellas nattering French." He shifted and winced. "I could only understand a bit of their parlezvous lingo, and me nous-box feels like it's stuffed with wool, but I 'eard the name Stafford mentioned and" – he swiped a sweaty hand over his brow – "they got somethin' important at that warehouse."

"Documents? Or something more sinister? Gunpowder?" Rakecombe frowned: the plot thickened.

"Dunno. Sorry, guv. It were noisy and..."

"No, I'm indebted again, Bluey. You did well."

"Not that well, I got bleedin' stabbed. Must have heard about my nosing around and followed me. Ta for saving m'bacon, by the way." A female giggled from the adjoining room. "Guv?" said Bluey, frowning. "Can that Jack the lad be trusted?"

"With your life, yes," answered Rakecombe.

"But not with me wife, eh?" He chuckled but instantly regretted it, holding his stomach in pain. Indeed,

Winterbourne had disappeared to help the pretty blonde prepare Bluey's laudanum.

"When did you marry? I didn't even know."

"We keep it hush. For the best in our line o' work, eh? Been hitched seven years now."

Over time, he'd chatted with Bluey about their lives, but never had he thought to ask about female companionship. "And have you never…worried about her?"

"She's got a better aim than me with the pops, but I did nearly end our courting at one point." He twisted onto his side, and those blue eyes of his nickname dulled. "Yer know I was born within screaming distance of St Giles' Church, but I had no intention of dying there. Hard to get out the gutter, it sucks you down." He grimaced. "But I've always been good at…hearing things. She were a touch above me, a teacher, and I told her, I told her I could get her hurt but yer know what she said?"

Rakecombe shook his head. At last some decent advice, even if it was from a dubious character with even more dubious morals. Although whether his were lower than Winterbourne's was disputable.

"She told me her mother died when she were thirteen. Some coxcomb trampled her with his flash rattler and prads. Then her sister died when she were fifteen – the lung sickness. And her father drank himself to death before her sixteenth birthday." He closed his eyes as though the candle lamp was too bright for them. "She said there was just as much chance of Mr Grim carrying you away whilst you lay content and unaware in a soft feather bed than of a blade to the heart. And I couldn't really argue with that."

He nodded. Those words concurred with Jack's advice at the soirée the other night and he silently cursed, loathing it when other people were right.

"Yer have to be careful," continued Bluey, "and we are, very. I've another gaff in the Rookery and I don't introduce her to no one in my work. In fact, yer the first. But my life wouldn't be worth living without Harriet. And I trust her to take care of herself."

That shook Rakecombe to his core.

Did he trust Aideen? His worry was that she would do something perilous like Gwen, who'd been similarly headstrong and wilful.

"I treasure your confidence in me, Bluey. But what of the future?" he asked. "I know you have that farm in Kent but I thought it only for income."

"It's our retirement place. Peace and clean air. I was gonna work here for a couple more years but maybe we'll start early, especially if I'm getting slow and need to lie snug for a while. Never saw 'em coming," he muttered feverishly.

"None of us have eyes in the back of our heads, Bluey." Aware his informant needed rest, he stood and lowered a hand to his shoulder. "I shall leave you to your adept wife, but if you need anything, let me know. Anything at all."

"Will do, Guv. And how's that luscious-arsed wife of yours?"

"She's..." He thought of Aideen's flashing eyes, her soft body, her taunts and syrup words. "...perfect."

WALKING the eerie streets with Winterbourne was becoming a habit but he had to say it was quite pleasant to have a companion for once.

Usually, he tramped home, letting the fog curl around him, and it felt as though he was utterly alone in the world.

A prickling at his nape slowed his stride, a sense of being watched, but as he glanced around, only a stray cat slunk from the shadows, eyes glinting with disdain in a lantern's glow.

Early on the morrow, they would investigate this Southwark warehouse, but there was nothing to be done tonight. Only a fool – or Bluey – went to those areas of town after dark asking questions.

"Nice couple," mused Jack.

Then again, being alone did have its advantages. He merely grunted.

"Very…close."

Rakecombe halted in the murky street, stabbing his cane on the cobbles. "Spit it out. I can hear something jangling around in that empty brainbox of yours which you can't wait to share with me."

"Very well. Since you asked so nicely." Jack rocked on the heels of his hessians, the blasted tassels swinging like a doxy's arse. "I realise you are trying to keep Aideen at a distance because of the danger, but those two make it work. You just have to try."

"There are reasons–"

"I may be the most genial rogue in town – Lady Sutherland's description, not mine – but I am not senseless. I know something dreadful happened to your sister, something you obviously blame yourself for as Kelmarsh mentioned it. But you cannot live life on past regrets."

Rakecombe hated tête-à-têtes. His mother had always wanted him to talk about it too.

"I held Gwen in my arms as she died." He couldn't hide the hoarseness in his voice, even after twelve years. "I can't forget it. You don't understand. What if–"

"What if it doesn't?" Jack interrupted. "What if you lead a full life with all its normal trials and tribulations?" He glared. "You want to be melancholic? Then what if you get mauled by a bear next Tuesday afternoon whilst promenading Grosvenor Square? What an utter waste of all the time you've spent married. You could've been happy but instead you were a miserable old curmudgeon."

Rakecombe stomped on in silence for a while, the streets gradually filling with more frequent pools of yellow glow from the Mayfair gas lights.

But there was one niggling detail he could not and would not let go of.

"There are no bears in England."

"That is where you are mistaken, my dear Rake. Happened at a fair I attended last month. The bear escaped and ate three people. I managed to save the bearded lady, but the fortune teller never saw it coming. Last time I ever venture forth to Hampshire," he grumbled with a wink.

20

THERE'S TRUTH IN FICTION.

Socially awkward, few friends, bad-tempered and haughty.

Yes, thought Aideen as she sat in bed reading, there were more than a few striking similarities between her husband and Mr D, but unlike Miss Elizabeth, she'd had to marry the man before violent love had been proclaimed.

She plonked her well-thumbed volume on the bedside table and instead picked up the letter she had received earlier today. It was from an ecstatic Cordelia. An ecstatic Cordelia, who at the time of writing had been passing the night at an inn near Northampton *with* Lord Oakdean.

My dearest friend,

I apologise profusely for not bidding you farewell, but this past day has been somewhat of a rush as James and I have decided to marry at Gretna Green!

I have always wanted to visit Scotland, but Aunty warned me it was full of barbarians. James assures me, however, this is not the case.

We are at an inn. ALONE.

Why did you not alert me, dear friend, that nightcaps would be the least of my concerns? It was quite a shock, I can tell you, but oh what a rapturous one!

James and I still have much to learn about each other, but our deepest emotion is the same – Love.

I do so hope you can find this with the duke, as I have beheld your anguish when you think no one is looking. I know he feels equally for you as his gaze possesses that same anguish when it catches in your direction – which is A LOT.

I had better end my letter there, dearest friend. James has got that look in his eye again.

All my love,

Cordy.

Obviously, Mrs Greenwood had succeeded in subduing the news that her pristine daughter had eloped to Gretna Green, as nothing had reached the papers or been gossiped about at tea.

She was happy for Cordelia, for the excitement and love her friend had found, but she also couldn't help feeling bitterly, wickedly jealous.

It was awful to bear such an emotion but so it was. She could pretend otherwise but there was no point lying to oneself – or maybe there was. Maybe if one repeated something enough it would come true.

Aideen took a deep breath. "I am not jealous as my husband will enter through that door at any moment and declare undying love."

The adjoining door opened. "Aideen, are you awake?"

Well, one out of three wasn't bad.

"Yes."

Alex strode in – as if he ever walked in any other way – and then stood by the fire, even though it was unlit. He wore that black banyan again and she couldn't help the tremble as she remembered pushing it from his shoulders, kissing that odd tattoo. The curl of hair had returned, draping its way across his forehead in defiance of its strict regime.

Why was he here?

A glass of brandy sat cradled in his palm, but he placed it on the mantel and swiped a hand over his face. If she didn't know better, she would say he was nervous.

"What are you reading?" he asked.

"Oh, nothing important, darling husband." She twiddled with her plait, unsure about continuing with the sweet act as her fists ached from all the clenching…as did her jaw.

A smile surfaced. "You do tell fibs, don't you, my mavourneen?"

Now there was an agreeable endearment, Irish and loving. "Only trivial ones."

After crossing to the bed, he sat on the very edge and expressed…nerves again. It was infectious. Had he come to give her bad news? Was he leaving for the Continent on a mission?

RAKECOMBE PUSHED HIS HAIR BACK, although that ridiculous curl he'd never been able to get rid of slipped down. Thorn had once suggested egg white as a remedy – never again.

Walking home with Winterbourne – when he'd been able to get a thought in edgeways – he'd decided to talk to Aideen this very night. He couldn't bear it any longer.

Attempting to stay away from her resulted in failure and frustration, so he'd have to do the complete opposite. But in order to keep her safe, and far from the danger he brought to those close, he needed Aideen to understand a few matters, comply with a few…instructions.

So, whilst eating supper, he'd written a list with twenty-three… He hesitated to say rules, more like codes of procedure which must be followed.

Compliance with instructions, he knew, wasn't an Aideen trait but surely if she understood the reasoning behind his list, all would be well.

But where to start? She looked so young and innocent with her hair plaited into submission, hands folded saintly, although the gossamer night-rail belied her true colours. Black, of course – the wicked wench.

"I told a falsehood," he confessed.

She didn't reply, scarcely raised a brow, and he realised his wife wasn't going to make this easy for him. But then again, it was exactly that prickliness he adored.

He coughed. "I stated that I married you for an heir. Gave the impression I was forced because of that kiss at the Beckfords'. But you were right, I could have bundled you off somewhere, and if I wanted an heir so desperately, I would have married some horse-faced debutante with excellent bloodlines."

Silence met his confession. Was she really not going to help at all?

Obviously not.

"However, I was extremely worried about my vocation affecting your safety, so decided we should live…separate lives."

He waited.

Silence. She pursed her lips and…

But no, they rested again. Mute.

Damnation, this was more painful than being tattooed.

Clearing his throat, he continued, "I have realised since our wedding that this is not feasible. Our attraction is too great, and we are both…discontented, are we not?"

Surely, she would have to answer a question?

She merely nodded.

Bugger.

"So, I hope to…begin our marriage again. Start anew. Spend evenings together. Read. Dine. The theatre and so forth." He fiddled with his signet ring and then hastily thought better of it – fidgeting and fiddling were a sign of worry, and he wasn't…at all. In any way.

A horrible thought occurred.

What if she didn't wish to start anew? He didn't mean to sound arrogant but he naturally assumed she would be amenable. But her silence was speaking a thousand words and none of them were "that sounds lovely, Alexander, get into bed".

"Erm, to facilitate your safety, however, I have come up with a list of–"

"What do you feel for me, Alex?" she interrupted at last.

"Feel?" He frowned. What did that have to do with anything? "Er…"

"Is this *attraction* you speak of purely lust which will diminish with time?"

God, no. He adored her smiles and kindness, her vibrant eyes, and he liked simply watching her restless energy. He also adored it when she got annoyed and waved her arms around like a mad windmill. But telling Aideen that was a bit like stuffing your hand in an escaped bear's mouth and expecting a lick.

"Not at all. I very much enjoy your company." There, that sounded good. He also relished and craved it, but steady on.

"Hmm," she replied.

He tried again. "I have a list, Aideen, which I hope–"

"Why did you pretend to be a Welsh seducer? And please be aware only one answer is correct." She flipped the plait over her shoulder and crossed her arms.

Blast. Why *had* he done that?

"I was jealous?"

She unfolded her arms and smiled. Phew.

"Absurd but correct."

Good. Now… "Aideen, I have a list–"

"What happened to Gwen?"

Although she had been rather uncommunicative so far, Rakecombe had felt he was at last getting somewhere until that question. Just the name on her lips caused his throat to dry and blood to chill.

"Gwen?" he stalled.

"Gwen," she repeated.

"She was my sister. She died." *Don't ask,* his heart rapped out. *Please don't ask.*

"How did she die?"

"I do not wish to discuss the matter," he replied, using the tone that petrified worldly matrons and made young cubs wet themselves.

"But I do," Aideen said, "because I have a feeling she influences everything you do, everything you say."

Glaring at the rust coverlet, he considered leaving, but a supple hand swept his face, pushed that bloody curl back and then slipped down his neck.

He'd never told anyone – not properly. His mother had been given the barest of details to spare her the pain, and his leader at that time had received a report devoid of emotion. Kelmarsh knew the most but the words had been garbled out with anger and pain.

"I can't..." But he couldn't leave either because fingers delicately caressed his nape and he craved more.

"Join me in bed, Alexander," she whispered, and he knew. He knew he'd reveal all if she continued to whisper in his ear, that beautiful Irish lilt soothing his soul.

Aideen brought him vexation and worry and barbed words, but she also brought peace and contentment and gentleness. Such a dichotomy. He had to protect it, treasure it.

Throwing his banyan to the floor, he clambered into bed as she shifted over to make room, but he didn't want that, and pulling her back to the centre, he laid his head on her breast – so soft but with a heart thundering his presence like cannon fire.

A sigh reverberated through her and then those fingers returned, brushing his hair, nails lightly scratching.

"Mother said Gwen was daring from the moment she was born. Always getting into scrapes, crawling where she shouldn't and generally twisting everyone around her plump little fingers. She was utterly spoiled by us all."

"What was the difference in age?" she asked, now stroking his shoulder blades.

"Four years but we were close. We went rambling in the woods, fishing. I treated her as a brother, which maybe was a mistake."

"No regrets, Alex. If she enjoyed it, then it was her nature. It all sounds idyllic and I wish I'd had siblings."

"Your father has never remarried?" He played with the black velvet ribbon of her bodice.

"No. I thought he loved my mother too much to remarry, but now I believe it to have been a jealous love. He buried any feelings with her, including those for me, his own daughter. Da would make another wife miserable as sin."

From the little Mr Beckford had told him, Aideen's father was a loud-mouthed bully. A daughter might have wilted under such treatment, but his Aideen had grown strong and fearless.

"So, then what happened?" she whispered.

"Whilst in the final year of Oxford, an elder peer approached me. After the French revolt, they required men from the aristocracy to assist. Intelligence work is not normally undertaken by dukes, you realise, but there were whisperings of revolution and treason here within the *haut ton*, especially with the King's supposed lunacy, so they asked certain people to…"

"Spy?"

"Yes, in a word. I… I wanted to warn those closest to me, to let them know I was undertaking potentially dangerous work. Father was pleased as he'd always worried I would fall foul of the Rakecombe gambling trait and he thought it would keep me from trouble. Mother was anxious, as all mothers are, and Gwen…" He swallowed. He should have known. But he'd been so deuced young and naive.

"Hmm?" Fingers stroked his forehead, encouraging and sensitive.

"Gwen was excited. She considered it a thrilling adventure. Of secret codes and misty twilight. She'd badger me night and day about missions, and I'd try to instil a note of caution but… She always liked to be the boldest and the fiercest and it became worse after Father died. She was the one to ride the largest horse from the stables, the one to rescue the weak pup from the tormenting lads, and I loved that bravery, that verve for life."

"I think I would have liked her," Aideen said quietly.

"There was a mission that winter, involving a group of revolutionists. Information came about a meeting in a Seven

Dials tavern, and I inveigled myself an invite. Fairly standard job. Keep my mouth shut, eyes open and ears flapping."

He closed his lids, remembered his jaunty pride. "She pestered me that morning. Beaming and prodding for details, so I thought what the hell and told her about the mission, about the meeting. Where was the harm? She would never encounter these men or repeat my words. In retrospect, maybe I enjoyed playing the hero, swaggering in youthful pride."

Aideen's hand brushed his cheek. "To want to share is natural, especially with someone so close as a sister. There is a difference between vanity and candour, my Alex."

Burying closer, he nodded. "Perhaps. But...another spy came to the house. I was not at home and so he left a note – stupid bastard – as he'd found out more about the group concerned. I didn't return that day and so my sister read it and..."

He could imagine her excitement, Gwen's fervent anticipation at aiding her elder brother. There would have been no hesitation on her part. "I believe she thought me in danger. Thought I needed the information, so she sneaked out to waylay me on the way to the tavern and hand me the note."

"Did she take a weapon?"

"A...a walking stick. One of my old ones. Ordinary."

Fingers drifted down his back, caressing his skin, then holding tight, and he realised that, although hideously painful to talk of Gwen, he needed Aideen to know, to share his burden, to listen.

"I was almost at the tavern when I heard my name half-spoken, half-whispered. I looked back and...and there was my baby sister standing in the middle of that vile Tower Street, in an expensive velvet cloak and fur-trimmed bonnet.

I have never felt so bloody angry and was about to vent my fury when a man grabbed her from behind."

The image overwhelmed him, and he had a sudden compulsion to flee, to escape this bed and the calming touch he didn't deserve. An embrace crushed him to soft skin, and fingers laced through his hair, but still he envisaged sweet Gwen's face as the whoreson held her, skin pallid, her excited eyes shifting to horror, walking stick clattering to the filthy cobbles.

Why did it still damn well hurt so much? He'd seen many a man and comrade die since then.

"He…he was crazed. I could see it in his slack face. Gin or opium, I know not. He held a blade to her throat. I could see it pressing against her skin, indenting under the bright moon. All I had was a short sword under my cloak, no pistol, and I was inexperienced, and this was supposed to have been a simple mission. I didn't…"

Arms squeezed, and he buried his face in Aideen's chest, aware the material of her night-rail was already wetted. "He screamed for money, and I scrabbled with my signet ring and fob watch, pushing them into his greedy fist. I would have given him my shirt but a shout from down the street distracted him and… I still do not know if he meant to do it, but his hand tightened… I saw blood and then he drew his arm away, the knife slitting her throat."

Abruptly, he rolled onto his back, dragging Aideen tight to his chest, unyielding.

"She fell like a doll. A puppet let loose of its strings, her face falling in the dirt. The whoreson ran, but I paid no heed." His gaze flitted to the bed canopy, red, awash with blood. "The sound, Aideen, Christ. It haunts me. She struggled for breath, and I could do…nothing. A prostitute came to my aid, tearing her skirts for linen, even though that was all she had to her name, and we tried. God, we tried…"

He veiled his eyes in Aideen's hair, aware tears fell but unable to release her to wipe them away.

"One last awful breath and she left me…alone."

Wetness trickled over his chest as he felt Aideen's own tears fall against his bare skin. They clasped each other close, unmoving, the sheer futility of a life lost in such a way encasing them in silence.

At length, Aideen pulled from his clasp, kissed his lips, his cheeks, hands pushing back his hair and brushing her mouth over his forehead. And although the memories would always remain, he felt some of his hurt released by her compassionate touch. "Alex, my poor Alex. To see your sister die in such a way, I have not the words. I am so very sorry."

Staring into her wet sable eyes, he continued, "I carried her home with Mary Lane, the prostitute who'd aided me. It felt like forever and yet no time at all, carrying her through the frozen streets. I felt numb. And since then, I've always felt so numb. So cold."

"And the madman that killed her?" she asked, hovering over him and pressing lips to his hair, violets teasing his mind from the raw horror.

"I asked Kelmarsh to find him for me. I was in no state and my hands were full with Mother's grief and the funeral. A day later, Kelmarsh said he'd found the bastard dead in his hovel, brought me back my signet ring. I often wonder if Kelmarsh…" He shook his head. "It matters not. I felt no vengeance or satisfaction. I felt…nothing."

She placed her face next to his, so close he could feel her warm breath. "My dear Alex, you have no need to blame yourself for her death."

"Everyone denies my culpability but I cannot." He

stroked her cheek with the back of his hand – such fragile skin. "Kelmarsh had chosen to keep silent with those close to him, nearly lost Sophie over it, as you know, but I'd blabbed. If I had never told Gwen about my vocation or about that mission, she never would have come after me."

"Or she might have gone searching anyway," Aideen whispered. "Or followed you one night in suspicion. It is a shocking waste and loss of a brave young girl's life, Alex, but the blame lies with the man who carried out the needless deed. It is he that is the culprit. You were and are a loving brother."

He began untwisting the tight plait, watched her hair unfurl. "I have heard it all, Aideen. From Mother, from Kelmarsh, and my mind heeds their words, but my heart – that believes something else entirely." He finally freed the knotted mass. "I could not bear it if you came to harm due to my own selfish need to have you a part of my life." He pulled her close, kissing her, a delicate brush of lips. "I have already hurt you." And he stroked the fading dark-red mark on her neck.

"Only my feelings, and if you'd kept your bog mouth shut, all would have been well. But I knew, Alex. I knew you were pushing me away for a reason."

"Is that why you were smothering me with sweetness?"

"Mayhap. Did you like it?"

He fingered the ribbons on her bodice. Exhaustion blanketed him, emotions a deluge, and yet he needed Aideen to banish the shadows and ghosts that haunted him. To clear the blood from his vision. He needed her so very much and in every way.

"I did, but perhaps, after the other night, I should show you gentleness. How desperately slow I can love."

"I enjoyed the corridor," she whispered, arching to his touch.

He thought about the list he'd meant to talk to her about, but that could wait until tomorrow. For now, he needed the peace that only Aideen could provide.

And he began to show his wife how very sweet he himself could be.

21

RULES ARE MADE TO BE BROKEN.

In a thoroughly agreeable mood, Aideen wandered down the principal staircase to the sound of voices from the breakfast room – Alex and his mother if she wasn't mistaken.

Yawning, she stretched in a most un-duchess-like manner and groaned lightly. Certain areas of her body ached this morning, but she wouldn't change it for all the whisky in Ireland.

Her husband had been true to his word last night and loved her gentle until she'd been driven mad with pleasure.

Understanding his past explained so much. He shied from intimacy like a beaten hound, snarling from the corner after a harrowing experience. But quite honestly, she didn't want him to change – she adored his cold glances and brusque demeanour, his teasing taunts and malevolent smiles.

There might be something awry within her character for liking such conduct, but then there weren't many gentlemen who would enjoy her own pert retorts or lack of reserve either.

How odd, but they matched – despite station in life and their squabbles, they matched.

And she loved him. Completely and deeply.

Meghan's raised voice could now be heard from the hallway, and Aideen paused to listen. They were arguing, and it didn't sound good.

"I've never seen anything quite so ridiculous, Alexander!" the dowager duchess stated, with the tone of a governess to their ill-behaved charge. "She is no senseless young miss!"

Staying her entrance, Aideen wondered who they were talking about.

"Of course not," Alex replied smoothly, "and hence I am sure she will not be offended by some…guidance. Aideen understands my worry."

Oh.

"*Number one – Do not speak to strangers*!" the ever-elegant dowager duchess screeched at full pelt. "Breadcrumbs and fishhooks, Alex, you'd lock her in a box if you could."

Oh dear.

"*Strangers* could be undercover spies or assassins."

"And strangers could also be nothing like." There followed a raft of Celtic babbling.

"Mother, I do understand Welsh and that is not anatomically possible."

"That is rather the point, *twpsyn*."

Aideen couldn't bear mother and son to be so at odds, especially over her, thus she pushed open the door.

Her husband was sitting at the breakfast table, a hunk of bacon stuffed between thick bread paused at his mouth whilst the dowager duchess paced the blue Aubusson rug.

"Good morning, Meghan, Alex."

They both nodded, Meghan with features tight, but the duke…

Although fully starched and wearing an even deeper black, if that was possible, he appeared slightly more... relaxed was going too far, but certainly more at ease.

Meghan grabbed her reticule from the sideboard and dashed over. "I must go or I shall cosh that thick jolter-head with my coffee cup." She bussed Aideen's cheek. "I'll never know how I raised such a dogged numbskull, and if you can't bear it, dear, then come and stay at my house and we can peruse maps of Egypt. Once Napoleon has been seen to again, I've a particular fancy to go hunting the lost emerald mine of Cleopatra."

Nodding as Meghan breezed through the door, Aideen shifted from foot to foot, now a little unsure. She may feel at peace with the world this morning, but Alex had a bad habit of blowing hot and cold for inexplicable reasons known only to himself and God... And even God was probably somewhat perplexed at times.

"Egypt?" He rose from the table, eyebrow raised, lips twitching at the edges, and her insides burbled their delight. She chastened them severely.

"Your mother wishes to visit Egypt and has said that if you annoy me, I can join her."

The duke came to stand close, looming over her with masculine intent. Placing his hands on her shoulders and bending down, he gave her the most searing, deep kiss that surely anyone had ever experienced before nine in the morning.

"Do I annoy you?" he whispered against her lips.

"Yes, but I rather like it."

He smiled and backed away to return to his bacon. "I am grateful to you for the vast improvement in cuisine. It's superb. Did you dismiss the last fellow?"

Wandering over to that superb selection, Aideen debated

telling him the whole story, but she could imagine her haughty duke not being best pleased with charlatan staff. "We have an Irish chef now. Very talented."

"Well, my duchess, I am indebted."

She loaded her plate with a sample of everything and took Meghan's vacated seat. It felt odd taking breakfast with her husband when they were in accord. A mite…unnerving.

"What were you and Meghan discussing and why are you a numbskull?" Perhaps a light bicker would settle those nerves.

"Ah. Hmm. Yes."

Having never heard Alex hum and haw, Aideen glanced up from a perfect fluffy egg, solid in all the right places. "Is it so bad?"

"No. Well, I didn't think so, but Mother…" He perused the ornate plasterwork on the ceiling before straightening his serviette. "As you know, I worry greatly about your safety."

Slathering butter onto the thick yeasty bread, Aideen nodded. Nothing wrong with that. She equally worried about his, despite knowing he was fully able to protect himself with sword, fist or boot.

"So, I have compiled a list I would like you to…observe. In order to keep safe."

That didn't sound too bad, but…

"Can I see it?"

A sheet of paper with an inordinate amount of script was nudged across the polished table. It was numbered from one to…twenty-three.

Oh, Saint Tuda's relics, what was it about men and their lists?

She scanned the paper. Some were eminently sensible:

12 – Take two footmen on all outings.
Practical, as they could carry hat boxes.

21 – Always take the enclosed ducal carriage.
Useful for inclement weather.

16 – Wear that garter knife AT ALL TIMES.
Tolerable, but was that solely for her benefit?

Other rules were not:

5 – Do not go out after dark unless accompanied by myself or Lord Winterbourne.
Dusk arrived at the hour of three on a winter's afternoon. She'd never leave the house.

11 – Take one footman INTO the modiste.
Madame Chevrolet would be rightly outraged.

8 – Learn how to swim.
What?

"I…" she began and then stopped. Her temper wanted to assert its irritation. Tell her husband he was being absurd, but her reason cautioned because at the base of it all sat Alex's anxious fears.

He worried for her. He didn't want to lose her. He…cared for her.

But equally what he didn't do was trust her.

Gwen had been eighteen and, by his own admission, a headstrong girl. Aideen was no schoolroom fledgling and although bold, she understood caution.

Despite Alex's regrets over confiding in Gwen, Aideen *did*

believe forewarned was forearmed, and after being kidnapped last year, she never travelled anywhere without certain…accessories.

She also knew how to shoot a pistol and how to whack a man in at least five extremely painful places – perhaps she should make a list.

"Erm. I can swim. I learned in the River Suir."

His shoulders visibly relaxed. "Ah, you can cross that off then."

"So, the list is…adaptable?"

The shoulders stiffened, his narrowed eyes as dark as ivy this morning. She could tell he wanted to say no, but it seemed they were both seeking to foster the trait of patience. "It depends," he finally bit out.

"So, if I cross out those which I think are" – absurd, outrageous, suffocating – "not applicable, and then give it back for your perusal, maybe we could…compromise?"

The unpleasant word stuck in her throat and she had to slosh it down with tea.

"There are not many I would…compromise on," he said tightly, also gulping chocolate, she observed.

"I see there is no rule about learning to defend myself."

"Unnecessary if you are not placed in a potentially hazardous situation. Which adhering to this list precludes."

"But, Alex, what this list doesn't take into account is that I *can* shoot. I can also wield a knife and over winter, Uncle Seamus taught me how to defend myself if need be."

He stiffened further. "My wife shouldn't need to–"

"Too late. You have a wife that can. Your mother was right, this list is for a schoolgirl. I wouldn't even give it to Cordelia." She mentally apologised to her friend. "Some are sensible, but… *Number fifteen – Don't stand by windows?*"

"Maybe that is–"

"Alex, I will take every precaution, but I would drown under such rules. Can we at least talk about–"

Abruptly, he rose, and she didn't like the way his eyes deadened, the green ivy frosting with the encroaching cold.

"Perhaps we will have to revert to our previous marital arrangement then. Separate."

The blackmailing dullard.

She also stood, leaning forward, hands on the table. "And to be sure, that was *so* successful." Desperately she tried to recall Mrs Beckford's advice on patience but never was it mentioned how one acted if one's husband was a controlling, obstinate mule. "Can I amend the list and we'll discuss it tonight?"

"No," he thundered. "The list is–"

That was it. Patience be damned. She'd tried, she really had, but enough was enough. "Listen to me, husband," she said, hands now on hips. "If you wanted a milksop wife then you should have married one, but I believe you like my fiery nature. Am I right?"

No answer. He just glared that glare he typically cast upon pallid debutantes, causing them to quake and quiver.

"Am I right?" she repeated, only quivering with sheer temper. "Or heaven help me I will curse you to hell and mean it."

Finally, a nod.

Stalking over to him, she grabbed hold of his immaculate cravat and yanked him close, fisting the material. "Then don't smother it, Alexander. For it will go out."

She released her grip and stomped from the room with the dratted list clutched in her fingers.

RAKECOMBE SCOWLED into the large mirror above the mantel.

Creases. Goddamn creases.

Did she not understand how long it took Thorn to fold the bloody neckcloth, despite his preference for this simplest form? Not only that but there was now a small splodge of bacon grease on it from his wife's grubby fingers.

He raised his eyes to his own in the mirror and hated the angry hard look in them compared to when he'd woken.

As Aideen had quoted some of his guidance, it had sounded a dash extreme, but surely one had to begin strict in order to then loosen. He didn't want to quench Aideen's fire, but she must see his point of view.

Yes, avoiding windows might seem marginally outlandish, but when he'd written the list, he'd thought of all the ways that fellow spies had met their untimely end over the years.

Harris had been shot whilst standing at a brothel casement window.

Middleton had been drowned in his bath tub.

Gilmore had been stabbed at the tailors with a pair of cutting scissors.

So, it wasn't as if he'd invented them.

22

DECISIONS, DECISIONS?

The crumpled List of Gloom, as Aideen now called it, was smothered with scribbles, crosses and the very occasional tick.

She felt for Alex, she really did, understanding his rationale and concern, but he may as well lock her out of harm's way in the bedchamber forever. And even then, she may injure herself, thumping her head on the dressing table at her husband's need for control.

So should she do away with the list now? Burn it? Take a stance at being dictated to?

But that seemed so cruel when Alex had suffered such loss. Despite his frigid exterior, he was a man who cared profoundly, for her and others.

Still waters did indeed run deep, and she had a suspicion he was deeper than the River Suir at full flood in February.

Should she try and compromise? Maybe with time he would mellow as he recognised her capabilities?

Worrying her lip, she stared at the lively square from the drawing room window – in flagrant breach of rule number fifteen.

Did Alex see every man, woman and child as a potential threat? The lad crying out the news? The two girls from the east side of the square bustling along? Their footman scowling as he juggled four packages?

Of course her kidnap by that Frenchman last year hadn't helped the situation. Alex doubtless viewed her as weak and defenceless, but she was wiser now. More vigilant.

Aideen sipped her tea and grimaced; it was cold.

Perhaps it might be worth visiting Meghan for marital advice with – she consulted the list – two footmen, the ducal carriage and appropriate footwear.

The appropriate footwear rule had a large tick. Intriguing. Would it involve boots with hidden blades?

"Your Grace?"

Turning, she found Rawlins staring down his haughty nose. He was a fixture of the house she quite liked, and she suspected, deep down, that he might like her too, but you'd have to dig deep…very deep.

"Yes, Rawlins?"

"A…lady has called. She seeks His Grace, but in lieu, she has requested your audience."

What a lovely way to put it. Was there a butler school where they learned such terms? Her father's man had always been a rather jovial fellow with no polish except on his shoes.

"Show her in, Rawlins."

Belatedly, she recollected rule number one concerning strangers. But surely the list hadn't been fully approved, agreed upon or signed in blood yet. It was at…consultation stage.

And besides, she had her green beribboned reticule strategically placed on the table.

A pretty, blond woman crossed the drawing room.

Dressed simply but with quality cloth, she had no maid, which explained Rawlins' hesitation.

Aideen noted a stubborn chin, much like her own, but the lady had a pleasant complexion and intelligent brown eyes, although a weariness could be detected in the shadows beneath.

"Your Grace." The lady curtseyed, and Aideen motioned her sit, dismissing a wary Rawlins.

"Tea?" She omitted to mention it was cold.

"No, thank you." The lady's speech, although not of the upper classes, was nicely formed. "My name is Mrs...Blue. I had hoped to catch His Grace before he left as I have some...information."

Aideen realised the woman was trying to admit as little as possible whilst still probing. "How essential is this information? Can it wait until tonight?"

"No, er..."

"I am aware of my husband's...service."

"In that case, I– I will be blunt. Although I do not usually involve myself, perhaps you can pass a message to relevant people."

Aideen nodded. She had no idea where Lord Rainham spent his days, but it must be somewhere at Whitehall.

"My husband," Mrs Blue began, fiddling with the stitching on her tan gloves, "overheard a conversation in French. He was badly hurt but recounted what he could to His Grace last night. However, this morning, he has remembered more and repeated some of the French words to me. I understood a little and... As I said, I would not normally involve myself but..."

Evidently, the lady was worried for herself and her husband's safety. And who wouldn't be? Napoleon's escape had put everyone on tenterhooks.

"I will not reveal your presence to anyone, and as far as the servants are concerned, you are here from a charity requesting donations."

"Thank you. Your husband, I believe, is searching a warehouse today in Southwark. He supposes vital information or even weaponry is being stored there, but...he needs warning. I'm sure His Grace will be careful, but the situation is more delicate than he realises."

Confusion creased Aideen's brow, but Mrs Blue swiftly continued, "It's a child, you see, and your husband does not realise this. It is not gunpowder or weapons or documents; the men are holding a little girl. From what I can gather in blackmail."

Aideen's eyes closed. "May God help the poor girl." She stood and paced, fists clenched. "And you think they may harm her if they've the slightest inkling someone is nosing around?"

The blonde's shoulders eased. "Exactly so. As I said, I am sure His Grace will take care, but my husband said no one is expecting a kidnap – especially of a child."

Pacing more, Aideen's mind cogitated, reasoned and considered but it still only came up with one idea. One which Rakecombe would detest, that would combust his list to ash and potentially destroy her marriage.

But this lady sitting before her had also unwillingly embroiled herself for the same reason: an innocent life was at stake. And weren't they always the ones who ended up hurt? Like Gwen. Innocents caught in the brutality and machinations of mankind.

Aideen was all too aware these circumstances also resembled those of Gwen, but Aideen was neither heedless nor an artless young girl and she had more than an old walking stick. "My husband must be alerted. Do you know exactly where this warehouse is?"

"YOU THERE!"

The burly young man leaning against railings opposite the Rakecombe residence peered over his shoulder, but Aideen pointed again. "Yes, you. Come inside now."

With a shrug, he sauntered across the street, narrowly avoiding a high-perch phaeton clipping quite a pace for a residential square.

Aideen turned back inside to Thorn, who stood ready with missives in hand for Whitehall, in case they could reach Southwark quicker. She knew Alex trusted his valet completely and Thorn had admitted his knowledge of where Lord Rainham could be found.

As per the rules, two of the brawniest footmen had been selected, and the carriage had also been loaded with the pistols normally reserved for evening rides. Not strictly a rule but a wise precaution, Aideen felt.

She hoped no weaponry would be needed, that her husband would be situated in some ale-house opposite, merely surveying, but luck wasn't always so obliging.

The guard entered, his huge frame filling the doorway. "What yer want?" he asked nonchalantly.

"I know you work for my husband."

He remained silent but shifted uneasily from foot to foot, eyes flitting anywhere but her.

"I am departing for a warehouse in Southwark where there is potential danger. I thought I'd tell you and then you can join me in the carriage rather than hailing some grimy hackney to follow. I presume you have weapons?"

The guard appeared somewhat dumbfounded, mouth

open like a gasping fish. "He'll throttle me. You tell me the problem, and I'll go to Southwark. Ain't no place for a lady."

Aware she didn't know this *stranger* from Adam and thus dare not entrust him with such information, she shook her head. "If you go, then I will be alone here, and then my husband will throttle you anyway. Which site of execution would you prefer?"

Alexander had obviously chosen brawn over brain when he'd selected this guard as the fellow took an inordinate amount of time thinking it over, but finally he jerked his head to the carriage.

"But don't die," he muttered. "I'll lose my job."

"I'll try not to. Now wait here one moment."

She dashed up the stairs, along the corridor to her bedchamber and headed to the smaller wardrobe at the back of her dressing room. An array of cloaks met her view, but she ignored them and instead kneeled to unlock the oblong box at the very bottom.

Now, the red or the blue?

23

A MIGHTY HOGO.

"Me deft ole conk detects some'in fishy, Alex, me ole duck."

The riverside location of the warehouse suspected of being a centre for nefarious dealings did indeed whiff, but his companion's attempt at the local flash lingo was truly appalling. If Winterbourne favoured him with the appellation "duck" one more time, he'd stuff that grubby neckcloth down the man's gullet until he quacked.

Bluey had mentioned the area was employed in fish storing and gutting, and assuredly, the rank smell was enough to daunt even the most hardened of spies. Thankfully, after stomaching the previous chef's creations, Rakecombe felt himself wholly hardened.

Currently, the two of them were ensconced across the street, leaning against a loaded cart, the fruit seller amenable to their leanings once she'd been handed – as his companion called it – "hush blunt".

For two hours they'd loitered without anyone coming or going, until finally three men had entered the building. They had yet to leave and hadn't been wearing the garb of fishermen. In point of fact, one had a suspiciously familiar pug nose.

Rakecombe scratched his neck, feeling…watched again.

Glancing around, he spied no one, but the hairs at his nape stood to attention. Friend or foe? "Let's wander around the back and see what we can find."

"Plummy idea, me ole–"

Accompanied by a curl of the lip, he cast his coldest glare, and Winterbourne silenced his trap. Thank the devil that glare still worked; he'd been worried as his ruthless scowls didn't seem to affect Aideen in the slightest.

Strangely, she…liked them.

As they idly strolled the side of the large brick-built warehouse, circumventing numerous stray cats, he pondered on that realisation.

Most women wanted to change a man such as himself. They'd berate him for his taciturn manner, but Aideen appeared to like him, more or less, as he was. Yes, he softened in her presence, but he didn't have to think on his words or attempt to cajole her with false flattery.

Was it worth losing that because she wouldn't adhere to his guidance? Perchance he could negotiate a little.

Stacks of empty barrels squatted around the back, but hidden amongst them was a small door in the warehouse wall. They sauntered over, and he was about to rummage in his pockets for his lock-picker when Winterbourne wafted a suitable device under his nose.

Better crafted than his own, it was silver and superb in every detail. It even looked to have a sprung knife within. "Where did you get that?" he asked grumpily.

"Yer bit o' lawful blanket," Winterbourne replied with a wink. "Thought we might be out on the dub."

He had to think on that a while as his comrade fiddled

with the lock. "Aideen lent it to you?" Should he be more irritated that she owned such a magnificent picker or that she'd lent it to the marquess?

"'Aven't you jabbered with yer rum rib 'bout her Uncle Seamus – clever cull by all accounts."

No, he hadn't. This is what he'd missed when he'd been too intent on ignoring her, and he called himself all types of fool, although this did explain how his "rum rib" had invaded his locked chambers to pin a note to his bathing device – the little minx.

Despite Winterbourne making a bodge of it, the lock clicked, and they gingerly poked their heads in.

The place stank to high heaven and all he could make out were barrels stacked to the rafters.

A faint light shone in through high up dirty windows casting a murky grey, but as his eyes adjusted, he could see the warehouse was divided into two sections with a separating wall preventing him from seeing beyond.

They skulked in and paused behind the first stack of barrels, taking in the layout of the warehouse. With some trepidation, he rubbed his finger over an oozing stave and brought it to his nose: no gunpowder, only fish.

A sudden creak and Rakecombe spun but saw no one. Dust danced in the faint gloom, mocking his racing heart.

Both he and Winterbourne glanced at each other, frowning, and he signalled they split up. Rakecombe took the left side, quietly approaching an opening in the division, but as he trod softly, a voice rent the air.

"Non, je ne le ferai pas."

And Rakecombe wondered what exactly the man *wouldn't do*.

Fierce rattling echoed around the warehouse followed by

a vague unidentifiable cry of distress from the other side, and he was tempted to storm in.

"Non, je ne peux pas." That same voice repeated its non-compliance.

Rakecombe slipped his pistol free and stepped closer behind a cluster of crates. Winterbourne crouched on the opposite side, but as he nodded, his comrade's gaze promptly shifted to the fishy barrels behind them, eyes rounding in horror.

That feeling, that feeling of being followed and he sharply twisted.

A hand knocked his pistol muzzle to one side and a knife immediately dug into his lower regions. He stopped dead.

His wife stood before him, hair bundled beneath a cap. She wore an open black redingote, from which a slender arm protruded holding one of the wickedest blades he had ever seen. It had a bloody curve to it.

"What the hell are you doing here?" he hissed. "Get back to the house."

She leaned close; the blade dug a fraction deeper. "Listen, you dolt," she whispered, "I'm purely here to warn you that a child might be in there, held for blackmail. I'm bringing you information from Mrs Blue."

"What child? Damn it," he rasped in her ear. He'd take umbrage with "dolt" later.

"She said that Mr Blue didn't catch a name. It's a girl. And you should also know a dark-haired man with a red scarf has been following you. He's behind that barrel stack to the left."

The knife shifted away – a mite too slow for his liking – and she stepped back.

Not that now was the time for noting fashion, but she seemed to be wearing an overwide skirt in plain wool, akin to a riding habit, also in black, and he briefly, very briefly, wondered if she'd followed his instructions and stowed that knife in her garter…and if said garter was black.

Quick as a wink after that disquieting thought came downright anger. Her arrival must have violated every single rule on his list. And they *were* rules. They *had* to be rules, for her sake.

"Aideen, you–"

"At home," she spat.

His retort was forestalled by another rattling and muffled cry, but the terrified whimpering now took on new meaning – a child. It mattered not who she belonged to, French or English. The red-scarfed stranger would also have to wait his turn.

"*Je ne lui ferai pas de mal,*" a voice yelled.

"*Je le ferai alors.*"

"What was that?" whispered Aideen, leaning over his shoulder.

"One man said he won't hurt someone and the other said he'll do it himself. We have to go in. Stay here, Aideen." He waggled his finger at her mutinous eyes. "Do. Not. Move."

Waiting until she bobbed her head, he and Winterbourne then snuck from behind the crates and edged to the opening in the partition wall.

Glancing through, he saw a large storage expanse, empty save for a makeshift sleeping area to one side. A grubby stove and an overturned crate as table were shoved against the brick wall and in the corner sat a small bed.

Three men blocked his view of the occupant, but the bed frame rattled as the person upon it drummed their heels.

Bloody hell.

A shrill child's whimpering raised the hairs on his arm, and he braced to burst in, when a sudden pounding footfall from behind grew louder. The French startled, and before he could act, a huge man with a red scarf brushed past him, storming through the door, pistol aloft, and Rakecombe was left cursing the loss of their element of surprise.

"You bastards, get off my girl," the man roared.

Pandemonium ensued, the three villains spinning, one with a knife, another with a pistol, as he and Winterbourne charged in.

Raising his own pistol, Rakecombe aimed but not before a shot rang out.

With no time to look around, he fired and the villain reeled, falling to the floor in a cloud of dust, arm outstretched with a bloody hole to his guts.

The knifeman he recognised as the pug-nosed bastard who'd slashed Bluey, and throwing his spent pistol to the ground, Rakecombe came forward with his own blade, determined to finish the job this time.

From the corner of his eye, he saw the red-scarfed man in a crazed struggle with the other Frenchman, and the part of his brain that wasn't watching pug nose realised it was the grizzled butler from Stafford's house.

"I kill you this time, English dog," sneered pug nose, "then I finish the girl. I cut 'er fingers, toes, one by one."

Ignoring the taunts designed to rile, Rakecombe circled the whoreson. Maybe he would go for the same trick as before, but pug nose remained wary – not lurching too soon.

Rakecombe swiped, a horizontal arc of sharp blade slicing the air, the merest sliver between it and the man's stomach. The rank smell of sweat and fear even overwhelmed the fish. He repeated the movement, but pug nose slashed out with his own knife, sending Rakecombe's blade airborne.

The Frenchman grinned, and without mercy flew at him, dagger held aloft, curving it down for the killing blow, but

Rakecombe yanked for the cane affixed to his side, thrusting a thumb to the jade eye. A deadly stiletto sprung from the silver head, and he didn't even have to slide it forward, the man's own momentum drawing him onto the shard of blade.

The dagger meant for Rakecombe's own heart clattered to the floor, surprise etched on pug nose's face. He crumpled without a whimper, blood seeping from his lips.

Panting, Rakecombe's eyes focused on the bed, to see the grizzled butler pulling a small girl into his arms, both their eyes streaming. "Papa," the little one screamed.

"Aimée, my precious Aimée."

Rakecombe twisted but another pistol shot tore the air, the crack echoing and sending pigeons scattering once more in the roof. His skin grew cold and ice threaded his veins at the female scream of "No" which had accompanied that cannonade of sound.

He couldn't bear to turn. Couldn't bear to look. His closed eyes saw it all.

Blood. Aideen. Hushed forever.

His world black.

Numb once more.

A cursing Frenchman…cursing an English whore, ripped through his numbness and Rakecombe dared to turn, eyes snapping open.

Amid the smoke and dust, a stocky blond fellow lay on the ground clutching a bloodied knee, screaming in agony and blaspheming until Winterbourne kicked him in the mouth with a stout hessian.

In the opening stood Aideen – scratching her nose and damn well smiling.

Too raw, too angry and too relieved, he did what he always did in these circumstances and ignored her, when all he really wanted to do was crush his wife to his body and feel her breathe.

"I'm indebted, Jack," he merely groused.

"Wasn't me, old chap. In case you hadn't noticed, I got shot and before I could reach for my other pistol, your talented wife saved your hide."

"Wh-what?" he stuttered, and Winterbourne, he now noticed, held a hand to his upper arm, blood seeping through his fingers, jacket torn.

He turned to Aideen, whose expression was smug. She held out her hand in which lay…

"My four-inch lady's pistol with poppy-red enamel and inlaid pearl handle. Light, trim and well-balanced. Deadly, of course, but I only aimed to injure…although if he calls me English again…" She glared at the Frenchman. "He had a gun pointed at your back, and however bothersome you can be, I didn't want you in the seven dirges of hell…quite yet."

"You should see her reticule, Alex," interrupted Winterbourne. "I made the mistake of surprising her in the street the other day and she very nearly removed my noggin."

"Uncle's finest," she said, swinging a beribboned item of female frippery from her wrist. "My favourite Saxon-green reticule contains a four-pound iron weight sewn into the bottom – I never go shopping without it. Now, shall we all go home? As instructed, I brought the ducal carriage. It's waiting with the footmen and that guard you have following me. To be fair, I did follow your rules, Alex… Most of them."

Rakecombe yearned to simultaneously kiss, crush, scold, spank and swive Aideen until she couldn't stand…and he didn't care in which order.

"Thank you all," a deep voice rumbled. "I am in your debt."

Rakecombe swivelled to find the bloody butler, a bundle of quivering, dirty white in his embrace, thin arms encircling his neck.

"Stafford, I presume?" Rakecombe queried, brow raised. "A chameleon indeed."

The man nodded, and Winterbourne came forward, stroking the little girl's hair with a bloodied hand. "And who are you, little one?" She was young, six if that, but even she gave his handsome face a hesitant smile.

"I am Aimée Stafford," she whispered in a French lisping accent, hugging her papa close.

Rakecombe pinched his forehead.

What an utter bloody mess.

The warehouse door flew open, rattling on its hinges, and they turned as one, pistols and daggers raised, to encounter Rainham striding in followed by five men with necks as thick as tree trunks.

"Rakecombe, Winterbourne," he acknowledged with a nod. "Duchess." He bowed, seemingly with no surprise. "And…Stafford," he said with a sigh. Their leader took in the situation, eyes lingering on the child. "Is everyone unharmed?" At Rakecombe's nod, he got to the heart of the matter. "And where are those cursed documents?"

Stafford hung his head. "They're in my coat," he replied softly. "I… I held off as long as I could, sir…"

Their leader approached and placed a hand to Stafford's shoulder. "I know you did, Gabriel, but I'm afraid we need a long talk back at Whitehall."

With remorse obvious, Stafford nodded as the tiny Aimée patted his cheek.

"Rakecombe, take your remarkable duchess home, and Winterbourne, get that scratch seen to."

"At last, someone acknowledges my pain," Winterbourne

grumbled. "But do not disturb yourselves as I'm sure I can find a willing widow to patch me up and soothe my fevered brow…if they're willing enough to ignore the fishy stench."

But Rakecombe wasn't really listening as they stepped into the light, leaving Rainham to sort out the mess inside.

Instead he studied his wife, stood biting her lip and rubbing a smudge on her nose but only spreading it further. The black clothing suited her, and he noticed that the unusual skirt gave her more freedom of movement in the legs. She carried an air of downright menace.

He didn't quite know what to say as they walked up a narrow lane to the carriage:

Thank you for saving my life but never do it again?

When I believed you dead, my heart ceased beating and I didn't wish it to restart?

I adore you, but the thought of you in danger tears me asunder.

Slowly, he opened his mouth, but all those thoughts refused to voice themselves, so he clambered into the carriage.

Aideen sat opposite, skirts brushing his legs, and he longed to touch her delicate cheek, peel off those black clothes, hold her skin to skin.

Her warmth, her passion. Her vitality.

Yet as his eyes skittered in her direction and the carriage moved off, he heard that scream of "No" in the warehouse, he heard Gwen's terrified cry, and fear squeezed his lungs until he could scarcely breathe.

But for a quirk of fate, a slip of someone's hand, he might have been holding Aideen's cold motionless body in his arms at this moment…or she his.

He shifted his gaze away.

24

IF YOU FEEL SOMETHING'S WRONG, THAT'S BECAUSE IT IS.

The newspaper twitched.

And then rustled. But didn't lower.

So Aideen fell silent.

She glared at the portrait of her scowling duke, the only likeness she was liable to view over breakfast as the real one hid behind *The Times*.

After the carriage ride from Southwark yesterday, he'd escorted her into the house without once catching her eye and then gone out for the remainder of the day.

That was until a half before midnight.

Not feeling like reading, she had simply lain in the darkness, not regretting her actions, as ultimately she had saved her husband's life, but saddened they couldn't seem to find a middle ground, a…compromise.

Then the door had whispered open. A light tread. The covers had been drawn back. A cold body had joined her.

She'd opened her mouth to speak but words had been taken by a gentle kiss and he'd clasped her close, sighed and then slept, warm breath disturbing the skin of her neck. For the whole night through she'd been lost to his tight embrace, holding her as if it was the last time he would ever do so.

But even though she'd awoken a mere smidgeon after dawn, the bed had been bereft of warmth. He'd left.

As a consequence, Aideen now felt befuddled, annoyed and generally quite out of sorts, as it seemed the duke of glowering rigidness had returned.

Maybe that tattoo stood for Dogmatic or Despotic or Downright pig-headed.

She'd dressed hideously early in order to catch her husband at breakfast, and even Rawlins had cracked a surprised expression, but the duke had merely greeted her courteously and then disappeared behind that dratted newspaper.

Indeed, the sole reason to suppose there was anyone there at all was the vanishing of two slices of toast, one sausage, three pieces of bacon and three cups of chocolate.

"I don't suppose," she tried, "that anyone fancies kippers this morning?"

A vague grunt came from behind *The Times*, but it didn't lower, and no stern glances edged over the top.

Tea, Cordelia had forever declared, was the cure for all woes, but Aideen craved something stronger – like Uncle Seamus's home-distilled whisky. It didn't cure woes, but you did forget about them for a week.

Aideen opened her mouth to tell Alex about it, but he must have heard her intake of breath as the newspaper shook and rose higher.

Instead of the usual fury churning within, however, weariness now pained her heart and utter exhaustion beset her limbs.

She closed her lips.

Another slice of toast disappeared behind a front page

article about an escaped bear mauling the crowds at Winchester fair, and she nibbled her own breakfast. The chef now baked her favourite Waterford buns every morning and she bit into the soft white dough, relishing the taste of Ireland.

She missed home.

When she'd thought Alex felt something for her, living in this marble mausoleum had been worthwhile, and of course, she had made fine friends here – Meghan, Cordelia, the Beckfords, Jack and Lily.

But she missed the open green fields and Uncle Seamus's slathering hounds, booming laugh and enthusiastic hugs. Even her da's sarcastic rebukes kept her on her toes. She missed the wild River Suir and the slate drizzle that dripped into your soul like love.

She considered staying with Meghan or the Beckfords for a while, who she knew would welcome her with open arms, but the duke would no doubt call and command her home.

A change of scenery was what she required. To breathe deeply without choking on grimy city fog. To regather her strength and thoughts. To feel the wet grass of Ireland beneath her feet and the blustery wind in her hair.

She would visit Waterford. Just for a short time.

"Alex, I think I may–"

"Not now." The newspaper lowered and, after an unwarranted amount of folding, was placed carefully on the table. Then her husband stood. "I have an early meeting with Rainham. I apologise, but you understand?" he said, not appearing in the least apologetic.

And she did. She really did. Because all of a sudden, comprehension besieged her. Caressing his stern handsome face with her gaze, she finally understood.

Last night, Aideen had received another letter from

Cordelia marked *Somewhere in Nottingham*. She'd written of Oakdean's teasing nature and caring ways; she'd written of love and laughter and everything which Aideen's marriage lacked. She'd signed off with:

> *Trust your heart,*
> *Love, Cordy.*

But Aideen trusted her heart no longer. It thumped for a man that didn't need her.

Always, she had thought themselves well matched. Their tempers may flare and clash, but a more delicate woman would have shrivelled beneath Alex's fierceness. Equally he didn't back down from her pert words and brashness.

But none of that mattered. Because ultimately, the duke did not need her.

He had his vocation, his two friends – if you counted Jack – and his title. But he didn't need *her*, didn't need a wife. He'd tried to explain this once before, at the Bucklands' soirée, but she'd thought him dissembling.

Previous to their marriage, his life may have been lonely, but he'd been comfortable and content with only himself to worry about. He may "enjoy" her company and be "attracted" to her body, but it only added complication and strain to his life.

She disobeyed his rules and caused him to fear and ultimately...

He didn't need her.

He didn't love her.

"Yes, Alexander," she said softly. "I do understand you."

As THE CARRIAGE clattered to Whitehall, so Aideen's last words clattered in Rakecombe's skull.

For God's sake, he knew hidden meaning when he heard it, but for the life of him, he couldn't decipher what she meant.

This morning he'd acted a beetle-headed arse, he knew that.

He gritted his teeth and exhaled heavily as London flew by the carriage window, his thoughts as dull as the weather – no rain, just the dreary grey that England seemed to specialise in.

Yesterday, after the Southwark jaunt and the patching up of Winterbourne, he'd headed to Bluey's house to impart his thanks but ended up staying for supper, aware he might have been... He hesitated to say hiding.

Whenever he beheld his wife, a savage desperation arose to ask Madame Chevrolet, the extortionately expensive modiste, to permanently double-stitch Aideen to his side, finishing with a quadruple knot.

But all that kept tumbling over him every moment of the night and day when not with her was the fear and numbness he'd felt on hearing that scream and thinking her dead. Then, swift on its heels came the fact she'd saved his life, with a bloody lady's muff pistol...in poppy-red enamel.

Last night, he hadn't meant to visit her bedchamber, but he'd needed to touch her, to see she was safe. He laughed, a mocking tribute.

But then he'd been unable to get close enough, unable to hold her enough, unable to cherish her enough.

Dawn had broken, and she'd looked exhausted, so he'd left the warm bed, but over breakfast his thoughts had still been a hotchpotch jumble of turmoil, and he'd barely managed a grunt in response to her words, hardly tasted the food he'd shovelled into his mouth and hadn't read a word of the newspaper.

She'd disobeyed every rule on his list...except for the carriage and footmen.

She'd put her life in danger.

She'd potentially saved a child's life.

She *had* saved his bloody life.

She could shoot better than he could.

The very characteristics he loved about her, he had sought to suppress with that futile list – her caring, her boldness, her strength. But to have Aideen and all those attributes close also meant living with the possibility of losing her. Or likewise, the possibility of his duchess losing him...and he knew what loss felt like.

All of which had kept him silent over breakfast.

Part shame. Part Gwen. Part confusion.

What an arse he was.

And what *had* his wife meant by those last softly spoken words?

"You are an arse, Rakeshame," said Winterbourne, a needless red silk sling fragranced with jasmine garnishing his person.

Rakecombe ignored him as they sat in Rainham's office awaiting their leader's return. He'd left for a brief meeting with his superiors but obviously got stuck.

Another white lily bloomed upon the table and he scowled. Had he ever bought Aideen flowers?

"I wager," Winterbourne drawled, "that you haven't even said thank you to your lady wife for saving your posterior."

No, he hadn't. "I...saw her last night."

"Tupping is not the same," the insolent rogue replied.

"I did *not* tup."

"Well, that's where you are going wrong. I can–"

"Gentlemen," Rainham acknowledged as he strode through the door to Rakecombe's eternal relief.

Their leader sat, spreading his palms over the desk. "Where were we?"

"Stafford and Aimée. How are they?" asked Winterbourne, being blunt for once. "Surely he will not be accused of treason as no one should have to choose between a daughter and their country? The poor chap was driven to it and he hadn't *actually* handed anything over."

Not so blunt then.

Rainham steepled his fingers, never a good sign. "I have managed to convince the grumbletonions on high to leave him be…for now, although he is, of course, suspended and to be watched."

Smoothing a thumb over the dog's head finial of his cane, Rakecombe mulled.

Love, seemingly, had no respect for borders, as Stafford had fallen for his wife when working in Paris. Worried about retribution from either side, they'd married in utter secrecy but a mere ten months later, she'd died giving birth in a remote village in France, where Aimée had remained with her maternal grandmother, Stafford visiting whenever he was able.

But someone had found out and she'd been snatched, the information demanded for her return.

"And the butler act?" Winterbourne pressed. "I bought the deuced fellow two pints of porter."

Their leader smiled. "I *do* choose codenames with forethought, and in that disguise, he could remain unseen in London and still search for his daughter. Reminds me of someone with that dyed black hair, but no matter. Apparently, he has been following a certain…bloodhound."

"I…" Rakecombe trailed off.

"Hmm. He knew of your reputation and hoped you would pick up a scent, leading him to Aimée."

That explained the feeling of being watched, and the only consolation for not recognising the faux butler was that Stafford was – or used to be – one of Rainham's finest.

Clearly, Stafford should have told them of the blackmail, but who could blame him? Mason had done that and it had ended in tragedy.

"It is obvious," Rainham said, interrupting those grim thoughts, "someone is coordinating these kidnappings. Rakecombe, you shot *La Chauve-Souris* last year, but his body was never found. Could he still be alive, I wonder? Finding out is the priority."

He nodded. "I'll begin at once."

"No, no." Rainham waved a hand. "I think you should take some days off first."

"I beg your pardon?" The suggestion riled him. "Napoleon is on the bloody loose and you want me to take a holiday? Where? Paris?" he snarled.

"Amusing, my friend, but you never even took your wife on honeymoon. Bit lax and you worked your wedding afternoon. Winterbourne can make a start."

Rakecombe had never felt so disgruntled.

"I agree," Winterbourne said, winking, "it might give your duchess a chance to penetrate that thick hide of yours and find the inner softness."

"If only that bullet had grazed your mouth and given us all a rest," he grumped.

"Quite so," murmured the marquess, "a weak arm is very

debilitating for a celebrated rogue. There are certain tasks I can only accomplish with my rig–"

"If a woman says she understands you, what does it mean?" Rakecombe barked abruptly. He'd rather kiss a snake than ask these two for advice, but it was driving him insane.

"Hell and damnation, your wife said that?" Winterbourne frowned. "Why didn't you say? It means get home quick and don't spare the horses." He looked Rakecombe straight in the eye. "Rule eight. It means trouble."

THE DUKE OF RAKECOMBE slumped in his study, a bitter coldness seeping through his body as he re-read Aideen's stark note once more.

Already the house felt her absence. No books were strewn over the drawing room table and the scent of wax polish had doused the violets. Deep silence had fallen.

She'd left him to visit Ireland.

Except the note didn't say visit. It said *stay*.

A peculiar sensation had caught in him when he'd first read her words, his heart skipping an odd pattern, his head woolly. Disbelief and anger. He'd stalked to her room, but the lady's maid had been packing trunks to follow on, and he'd been informed that Her Grace had left three hours ago in the enclosed coach with two footmen, the guard and a maid.

Then the anger had swiftly departed, and not since Gwen's death had he felt such...desolation.

Deadness stealing into his limbs and snatching his breath.

She'd left him.

And the note merely said she would return *after a while*.

What did that mean? A week? A month? A goddamn year?

Why had he been such a clumpish lout this morning?

Why hadn't he thanked her for saving his miserable hide?

Why hadn't he got down on his wretched knees and told her he loved her, because the fear of losing her to Ireland forever was now more pertinent and real than losing her to tragedy.

Death, as Bluey had suggested, could snatch a beloved at any time – unseen and unpreventable – but it was *he* who had driven Aideen to Ireland.

Him and his cursed fears.

Rawlins knocked and entered with a decanter.

"Leave it on the desk," he snarled. "And I don't want to see anyone for the rest of the day."

He tugged off his cravat and flung it across the study, but it caught on the statue of Orpheus. How bloody apt. Ireland may as well be the underworld.

After glugging a stiff measure in one, he stood and paced, squinting at the note.

Of course, he knew what Winterbourne would say. Go after her. Get off that stuffy arse and pursue her.

But her last line precluded that. *Do not follow me. I do not need you.*

An ache, so painful he had to hold his chest, twisted inside him whenever he spied those brutal words.

Finally, he'd done what he had always meant to – frightened Aideen away with his cruel remarks and scowls, caused her to flee his chill disposition.

He hurled the empty brandy glass into the bare fireplace, the glass splintering and shattering like his heart.

25

DYFAL DONC A DYR Y GARREG.

PERSISTENT BLOWS SHATTER THE STONE.
(WELSH PROVERB)

Coquettish giggles shrieked through the Duke of Rakecombe's skull and he whimpered at the sharp stab of pain.

Where the deuce was he?

His eyes refused to open, his face was stuck, and his mouth felt like a pit of ash.

Hell, he'd not indulged in a drunken spree like this since…Gwen.

At a boomed male chuckle, Rakecombe attempted to lift his head. A tearing noise made him realise his cheek was flat to his study desk and that he'd drooled on his blotting paper, gluing it to his skin.

"Oh, you naughty scoundrel… And a dog called Roger? Then the highwayman?" a female squealed from somewhere across the hall, causing every nerve to tear and thump alarmingly. "You couldn't make it up…"

More sniggers.

A pistol sat on the desk and Rakecombe frowned, eyes slitted.

Ah yes. Winterbourne had yesterday – or had it been the day before? – attempted to extract him from his study, and so he'd warned the fellow off with his trusty Ketland brass-barrelled *unenamelled* flintlock. No one had believed his threat until he'd cocked it and blasted the bust of Orpheus to smithereens.

Damn, how utterly unconstrained, and what must the neighbours have thought?

Not that he cared. They could bugger off. He was a duke.

Vaguely, he recollected gathering two more decanters of brandy, some bread, requisitioning the only spare key from Rawlins and then locking himself away to read endless volumes of the most depressing Blake poetry he could find.

His head swam and his stomach felt set to cast up its meagre contents at the thought of not hearing that Irish lilt or smelling violets or reacting to curses, for however long Aideen wished to stay in Ireland.

Another male burble interrupted his anguish. "You *must* call me Jack," the rogue purred to much vapid tittering.

Was Winterbourne really seducing some lackwit maid in his drawing room?

"Oh…Jack, well, if you insist, and you *must* call me Meghan."

Rakecombe's head jerked up, hand held to said appendage to avert it from tumbling off.

Mother?

"Such an enchanting name," Winterbourne's deepest drawl replied. "And I would be honoured to whisk you to the pyramids, Meghan. We could explore all those…forbidden delights together."

Rakecombe scowled. He knew what they were doing even

in his current state. Well, it wouldn't work. He would never open that door.

"I'm a little old for you, Jack." His mother *giggled* again.

"Au contraire, my delightful flower. You are a rose of late summer, the most fragrant and lush of them all."

Rakecombe ground his jaw. He visualised those flashing ivories and molesting fingers.

"Oh! You handsome flatterer, but Lord Fotherington has finally offered to take me, and he is more of my age."

Hah, take that, Witterbore. A Rakecombe woman doesn't fall so easily for glib tongues.

"But," the rogue rasped, "Lord Fotherington would not have the...stamina to squire you around all those sights. Whereas I can persevere the entire day should it be necessary, *fy nghariad bach."*

Toadying, dissolute buck fitch. Welsh endearments would not sway Mother, the pronunciation was appalling, like a honking goose.

"My oh my, such exquisite Welsh," she squealed girlishly. "So flawless, the very rumble makes me all–"

"Get your rancid mittens off my mother," Rakecombe yelled from his desk, using both hands to hold his head still.

Giggling of the male and female variety answered.

Why couldn't they leave him alone? His beautiful wife had left him, and he wanted to wallow in his own pit of shame, self-hatred and, he realised, stench.

Murmurs now seeped through his door and scowling, he struggled to stand. He looked to be clothed in only breeches and shirt, and his feet were bloody freezing but there was no sign of stockings nor jacket.

With a shrug, he stumbled into the sharp corner of the desk, relishing the pain, and with shuffling steps, crossed to the study door.

Whispers. Another giggle. What were they doing? A voice louder.

"If only Aideen had married you, Jack." His mother sighed low. "Perhaps *you* ought to follow her to Ireland. She enjoys your company after all, and I've heard–"

Rakecombe flung open the door. "And keep your licentious paws off my wife," he bellowed.

Expecting them to cower from his words or cast admonishments, he frowned as they instead stared aghast from the drawing room opposite.

He peered down at himself.

Bare feet, well he knew that. Creased breeches with a suspect stain, but he had a feeling – or hoped – it was spilled brandy, and a shirt that looked and felt somewhat putrid. There might even be…stubble upon his visage.

How very un-ducal.

"You have bits of paper and sand stuck to your cheek," observed Winterbourne, expression appalled.

Rakecombe slammed the door on their stunned faces and stumbled to fall on the chaise, head in hands.

A timid turning of the handle and his heart plummeted. If Winterbourne prattled rules, he'd… Death wouldn't be punishment enough – it would have to involve coquelicot waistcoats and slashing blades.

An orange blossom scent pervaded the room and then the chaise lightly depressed at his side. He waited for the condemnation, but instead a soft hand stroked his hair and he wanted nothing more than to turn to Mother like a schoolboy on his first day at Eton and bawl his eyes out.

He didn't, obviously.

"I was going to berate you, Alex dear, but seeing the state of you – a state I have never seen before, I hasten to add – it seems you are loathing yourself quite adequately."

"I chased her away, Mother." He rubbed his face with rough hands. "With my rules and control and surliness. She detests me and I deserve it."

"Aideen does not detest you. She..."

"Despises me?" he suggested, raising his head.

"No, dear," she answered, picking paper from his cheek. "She loves you, I believe, but even the most fervid love needs sustenance and you have given her nothing."

"I know, but Gwen–"

She held his cheeks in her small palms, eyes so direct they stung. "Alexander. I loved Gwen deeply – we all did – but she was a resolute girl who never should have followed you that night. I know you blame yourself, but..." Tears came to his mother's eyes and his own closed to them. "I could just as easily say it was my fault – for indulging her, sheltering her too much from the dangerous world, and your father equally never denied her anything, be it the enormous harp she insisted upon at seven years of age or that dashed great horse she had at thirteen."

"'Tis natural, Mother."

"Maybe, but my point is we can blame ourselves or each other or the man who did the deed or God – it makes no difference. It happened, and all we can do is accept and live the life that Gwen would have wanted. And being Gwen, she would have wanted laughter, love and joy for us all. Passion for life and the living."

"But I couldn't bear it if anything happened to Aideen."

"Silly man." She smiled and shook him...rather hard, tears retreating. "We cannot live in such fear. I married your father knowing his lungs were weak, knowing they could kill him at any moment and yet we had twenty-three glorious years together. I would not swap them for anything – the memories, the joy *and* the sadness. We were together. And if you are in love, well, nothing else matters. Do you love Aideen?"

He wanted his wife to be the first to hear those words from him, but she was clattering along the road somewhere towards the port of Milford Haven. "Yes," he said simply.

"Then all will be well. Aideen is audacious, yes, but she is not senseless, and I believe she would make an excellent wife for you – strong and caring, capable and ardent."

Rakecombe nodded. When bouts of soberness had intervened, he'd thought on all these matters and come to the same conclusion. He could trust Aideen implicitly. With his life. And her own. But then he'd drowned it all in brandy.

"I realise that now."

"Then why haven't you followed her, you great numbskull?"

Rising and feeling his stomach roil, he bumbled to the desk and grasped her note. "Read this."

His mother scanned the brief words before raising incredulous eyes. "This says *do not follow*."

"I have obeyed. It is the least I could do for her..."

"You bird-witted, jug-bitten, bacon-brained pigwidgeon! This says heave your stately posterior onto your fastest horse and go after her. Oh, good grief! I always thought you took after me, but now I begin to doubt it." She huffed. "I had to suggest Gretna to your father in the end. Honestly. Men!"

"But it says..."

"If you tell Aideen not to do something, dear, what does she do?"

"The exact opposite, but–"

"Lord Winterbourne is with Thorn, sorting out food, a bag of clothing and your favourite gelding, and if the weather is good, you may make the coast before Aideen leaves our shores. After all, she is in that rickety carriage of yours rather than our spanking trim gig. Go, go," she said, bussing his cheek and shooing him from the door.

With head still thundering, he plodded up the stairs whilst still trying to decode the hidden meaning in a note that said *do not follow*.

Thorn greeted him at the bedchamber door with another dismayed expression – was he that bad?

Winterbourne stood perusing his wardrobe contents – God forbid.

"I'm not wearing parrot green, coquelicot or lilac," he groused.

"I agree," stated Winterbourne, "love doesn't bring about miracles, and Aideen likes you in black for inexplicable reasons, but where's that off-black waistcoat with the charcoal thread?"

"At the back, I suspect."

"Hmm. Now I don't usually advocate running after women or grovelling – it breaks two of my foremost rules – but in your case, I make an exception. Abject grovelling might be advisable."

Accepting a foul-looking brew from Thorn, he looked up puzzled. "Why would one write *Do not follow. I do not need you* if one desired the opposite."

"Hah, rule eighteen. The lady doth protest too much, methinks."

"That's ridiculous," he argued, his stomach gurgling the arrival of Thorn's restorative.

"Yes, but plainly love can be ridiculous. How have you not realised this? I mean, look at you? The staid, priggish, impeccable duke turned slovenly shagbag in a matter of days." He sighed, shaking his head.

Rakecombe peeled his shirt off and Thorn apprehended

it, fingers at the very edge as though it crawled with fleas, and he'd a feeling it was set for the fire.

What a fool he'd been. He should have set out the moment he'd read that note – her words be damned.

But he'd been spineless. Afraid of losing her regard for good, afraid to see her eyes glitter with hatred, or even worse, no feeling at all. But no more.

There was one other matter to address first. A matter of some consequence.

"Winterbourne, if you repeat to anyone what I am about to say, I shall render you ineffectual for any widow's pleasure ever again."

"Hmm?" The marquess glanced up from the off-black waistcoat he'd found, eyebrow raised.

Rakecombe swallowed. "Thank you, my friend." He raised a hand to Jack's shoulder. "For remaining at my side. For your aid, advice and…rules."

A pause.

"All my pleasure, Alex." Winterbourne gave a roguish wink, eyes lit with joy. "Now you do indeed smell like an old dog, so off to that contraption of yours."

He let himself be herded to his bathing device, not caring the water was cold as sleet.

Now he would revert to type.

He would be ruthless in declaring undying love for his wife. Pitiless in claiming her. Merciless with his touch. All control focused on winning her back. Aideen wouldn't stand a chance in the well of ashes seven miles below hell.

26

'HE WHO KISSES JOY AS IT FLIES BY WILL LIVE IN ETERNITY'S SUNRISE.'

(WILLIAM BLAKE)

For two days, sideways slashes of rain had pounded the Welsh harbour town of Milford Haven and even when it had taken leave for a moment, a heavy fog had descended in its absence. All-pervading and dense.

But that wasn't why Aideen wished she was in London.

During the endless hours in the carriage, which she now realised needed to be re-sprung as a matter of urgency, she had passed an inordinate amount of time reflecting on her short, married life. There had been little else to do, as attempting to read in the swaying box had become unbearable, nausea looming every time the words bounced around the page like scuttling ants.

No, she wished herself back in London because she felt a coward.

Never had she been one to run away from problems. In fact, quite the reverse – she normally confronted them head-on, relishing the contest.

But she had run from Alexander.

She consoled herself that it was only for a short while, to gather her strength and visit home, but the devil on her left shoulder scolded that she should have ripped that newspaper from Alexander's nose and swatted him over the head with it.

Scowling at the dawn sunshine, which now beamed through the Nelson Inn's meagre window, she gathered her valise.

The packet boat's departure had been delayed due to the weather, but this morning, at this unspeakably early hour, the Welsh stone glittered under a low sun and the trees had begun hauling themselves to upright after the storm's battering.

She had thought...maybe... Perhaps... Alexander would...

But he hadn't. And why should he? She'd told him not to follow after all, and he had his ordered life, his vocation and he needed very little else.

Perturbed at her contradictory thoughts, she meandered from the inn, the poor maid and guard who had accompanied her to Wales dragging their feet behind.

Puddles of water sluiced the lane to the harbour, forcing one to hop for dry ground, but people bustled briskly after the rain, and she spied several of her fellow inn guests waiting by the modest packet boat.

Her title had procured one of the few cabins aboard – or the captain's, she suspected – and she couldn't quite believe that barely a few months earlier she had made this trip to England a mere Miss Quinlan, taking the stagecoach to Fetter Lane and the White Horse Inn.

Such mundane thoughts, she groused, as the passengers manoeuvred to board, and she glanced back at the harbour wall, a light salt breeze fanning her cheeks. A few onlookers waved from the stone quay and she scanned the heads for no good reason.

Straightening her shoulders, she vowed to enjoy the voyage on a rippling sea, to take pleasure from sighting Waterford's coast and being greeted warmly by her uncle and his hounds.

The Irish captain, with flashing smile and weather-beaten skin, personally helped her aboard – little wonder with the amount she'd paid for the cabin. Her maid scrambled below but Aideen remained on deck, a rosy Irish woman making room for her at the bow rail.

"Are ya off home then, darlin'?" She nudged Aideen's elbow.

"I... Yes, madam."

"The name's Mrs O'Driscoll. And did ya like England? The bread's appalling but the shops are mighty fine."

Aideen smiled. "You have the way of it," she replied, watching as they hauled up the boarding plank.

"And the fellas? What did ya think?" the woman asked, blue eyes bright.

"I think..." One of the sailors gave the word to weigh anchor and panic rose within her. "I think I'd like to get off." But it was too late and too crowded. Passengers pressed from behind, waving to well-wishers, and a few pigs had joined the laden boat, which two boys chased while a lady shrieked.

"Ya canna, darlin'." And the woman patted Aideen's gloved hand, cold despite the leather. "Did ya leave a handsome English lad behind, then? I've noticed they're hopeless with feelings, although our lads could do with saying less and meaning it more, I'd sa–"

A commotion at the harbourside caused the woman to pause, frowning, and assuredly a hulking white horse was causing the well-wishers on the quay to scatter like seeds.

Aideen's heart skittered for a moment, her fists clenching on the rail as she leaned over.

Could it be…

With frantic shouts, a man leaped from the enormous animal and began jabbering at the harbour gang… A small man with chestnut hair, and Aideen drew back, feeling stupid at her worthless thoughts.

One of the gang threw a line out to the boat whilst the captain grumbled his annoyance. A lad caught the heavy rope and hastily lashed it around the rail as passengers and crew alike babbled with either interest or frustration.

The captain cleared the way and strode to the rail, hands on hips. "Who in the hell has stopped my boat from leaving?" he bellowed for both hell and the heavens to hear, causing mothers to close hands about their children's ears.

Another commotion and the poor well-wishers were once again forced to flee as an immense sweating black horse galloped onto the harbour quay.

A gentleman sat atop, dark hair gleaming in the low sunlight, features taciturn and stubbled, raven-black cloak shrouding him.

Mrs O'Driscoll crossed herself. "Mother Mary, protect us. The devil himself has come to toss us all into the abyss, I never should have flirted with that soldier."

But Aideen couldn't answer or agree or even nod at the apt summation.

The devil on horseback glared at the captain, the spirited animal spraying the crowd with lather. "The Duke of Rakecombe has. And you won't have a boat unless you drop anchor this instant. You have something which belongs to me," he snarled.

Wisely, the captain muttered his acquiescence.

"What do ya suppose it is?" the woman asked, nudging. "A crate of whisky or… Ya've gone awfully pale, darlin'."

Excitement, fear, anxiety and a hundred other emotions fluttered within Aideen. He was here. Why was he here? Saints in their cowls, he looked handsome and dishevelled and…angry.

He swung a leg from the horse, ably dismounting to the quay, and Mrs O'Driscoll goggled as he flung his cloak back over his shoulders to reveal…more black, except for a dusty white mangled cravat. An ebony cane was dis-attached from his horse's saddle and clenching it firmly, he strode towards the packet boat.

"Duchess!" he bellowed from the quay, even though only twelve feet separated man from vessel. She tucked herself against the substantial lady. Not that Aideen was faint-of-heart but…

"Have you the Duchess of Rakecombe aboard that boat?" he yelled again, ramming his cane to the stone.

"Aye," the captain agreed. "Black-haired young lady in red. A fair fetching little pi–"

A dead-eyed stare halted his words.

"Oh," Mrs O'Driscoll gasped, staring down. "That sounds like you, darlin'. Coo-ee, Mr Ya Grace Duke? She's here."

Being tossed into the limpid abyss presented more appeal than her husband's wrath, but a Quinlan *never* hid, so she straightened her shoulders and tipped her head up.

She would not step off this boat, however, unless some very pertinent questions were answered to her satisfaction.

"Your Grace," she said. "How may I help you?"

The passengers, crew and well-wishers fell silent, breaths held, and for a moment, he simply stared.

"You will remove yourself from that vessel and return home with me," he stated.

Mrs O'Driscoll clucked her tongue and Aideen could only agree.

Overbearing buckeen.

"Why?" she asked, and her fellow Irishwoman nodded, pursing her lips.

A fluffy cloud shifted, allowing a beam of morning sunlight to tinge his black hair with red, the wind blowing it awry, and even Mrs O'Driscoll sighed at the handsome sight, but his face tightened, and he placed fists on his hips, looking for all the world like the autocratic haughty duke he in fact was.

"You are my wife and belong at my side. 'Tis your duty."

"Ooh," murmured the passengers. Not the answer a boat full of romantic Irish folk were looking for.

She tapped her finger on the rail. "Not acceptable. Give me one good reason why I should step off this boat?"

"And get on with it," a voice belted out bravely from the back, "I wanna get home to my own colleen."

"I…miss you," he growled low, but the light sea breeze wafted his words for all to hear.

Mrs O'Driscoll nudged her. "Not good enough, I'd say. I miss cake and my best friend Dierdre but 'tisn't the same."

"And?" Aideen prompted.

He scowled. "Do you really wish me to speak my heart in front of the residents of Milford Haven, a boat full of scurvy sailors and a disparate group of nosy passengers?"

Everyone nodded, pressing closer. "And who's he callin' nosy?" someone muttered.

Well, when the duke put it like that… "Yes, I do."

His shoulders slumped, and she suddenly worried that maybe she'd pushed him too far. He was a proud duke after all.

Yet Alexander could jibber about wifely duty all he

wanted as a man didn't follow that rutted road on horseback for days on end, endure a soaking and end up saddle-sore unless he felt...something.

She would be brave and reveal her heart first.

"I love you."

But her words had been overlaid by his deeper tone. The same admission, the same pledge, the same truth.

His head lifted and shoulders eased, gaze directed solely at her from the quayside. "I apologise, Aideen. I apologise for being an utter arse. For not telling you of my fears, for shunning you when all I wanted to do was haul you close, for not telling you before today that I love you so damn much. Indeed, have loved you from the first."

The words exploded in her heart, hurling out that emptiness which had dwelled within.

"Aaah," sighed the passengers before all fell quiet, witnesses to this eternal play of love.

"And I love you, Alex, so very deeply."

A handkerchief was whisked out by Mrs O'Driscoll, but even so another nudge hit Aideen's ribs. "If you want anything else from him, say it now. 'Tis doubtful you'll ever get another chance."

Aideen ordered her tumbling thoughts.

"Charlie, you nodcock, the line!" yelled the captain, and they all turned, mouths agape as the rope slipped away into the depths, a red-cheeked lad biting his lip.

"M'peepers were on the goings-on," he bewailed, as the breeze caught a half-unfurled sail and the boat lurched.

Rakecombe pivoted to the harbour gang but the gap between quay and boat grew.

"I'm sorry, Ya Grace," declared the captain. "Boat's turning with the tide."

"Nooo," Aideen wailed, leaning over the bow rail, arms

flung out, Mrs O'Driscoll keeping a firm hand on her red skirts.

Another rope was thrown from the quay but the beleaguered lad fumbled, and it fell listlessly into the harbour depths.

Rakecombe wrenched off his cloak, and shoving that and his cane at the chestnut-haired man, he then strode away. Aideen's heart plunged, her eyes sliding to the ever-widening breach of blue that separated them.

"Lord have mercy!" gasped Mrs O'Driscoll, and Aideen raised her head in time to see her husband charging full pelt along the quay towards the dawdling stern of the packet boat.

Her pulse thundered to his steps as he gained speed and threw himself from the edge, a slender black figure lunging through the air, fingers outstretched and face determined.

Shocked gasps and stuttering applause broke out even before the passengers knew the outcome.

Frantically straining to peer along the side, she heard no splash. Instead she could see Alex with a grip on the rail, swinging his long legs up, willing hands hauling him over.

A hubbub ensued at the stern, grumbles and cheers alike, and she craned her neck to see over the crowd.

Passengers began sweeping to the sides, and a child was grabbed and hauled into his mother's skirts. The duke seemed to have no trouble cutting a swathe, even without his cane, although a few pained gasps could be heard as he stomped on toes.

And then there he was, stood not five ducal strides from her.

No obstacles between them.

A nudge to her waist. "He's a fine piece o' Englishman, to

be sure," Mrs O'Driscoll whispered, before winking and shoving a few more folk aside to give them room.

Fine indeed.

A towering intense duke with a curl dangling over his forehead, a few days' stubble gracing his chin. Black thread ran through a black waistcoat she hadn't seen before. Gallant, upright, those verdant eyes glittering with passion as they caressed her.

She saw a man honourable yet haughty, caring yet ruthless.

She saw the complete man she loved most desperately.

"I have been alone for so very long, Aideen," he rasped. "And it has taken time for me to learn. But without you, I am a mere husk. Dry and barren, an unfeeling body without spirit or pleasure." He shook his head, taking two strides. "I trust you unconditionally, my duchess. With my own life and with yours. We've no need of rules between us."

Moisture stung Aideen's eyes.

Another purposeful step. "When you entered my life, I finally began to feel joy once more. Lost emotions coursed through me but I fought, Aideen, I fought so hard to subdue them. Yet you shattered my defences, invaded my senses with your care and your touch, and I will fight no longer. I will embrace that joy, hold it close and never let it go. Never let *you* go."

"Oh!" sighed Mrs O'Driscoll, dabbing her cheeks. "How romantic. My Mr O'Driscoll just said I made a fine colcannon."

Passengers hemmed in for a better view of the love-struck sinister duke.

He took the last two strides, and his calloused hand reached out to stroke her cheek, eyes pained. "When I heard your scream in that warehouse, I wished the earth to swallow me, to never release me, and that kept me silent. The fear. But I never disregarded you, Aideen. I couldn't as you are entrenched in my heart. I need you, my love. Be at my side always…please."

"I do not wish to be anywhere else, Alexander," she whispered.

Warmth lit his serious eyes. "Then let us stride forward together. With everything life has to offer and in whichever direction it takes us."

"Ahem," murmured the captain, "that would be Waterford then, if it's all dandy with the both of you? We're too far out to turn now, but no matter as 'tis a fine day for a crossing."

Her noble duke pulled her into his arms, secure and tight, whilst delighted Irish folk broke into cheers.

"Well, my unquenchable fire? Shall we?"

Aideen smiled, and Alexander lowered his head to kiss his duchess with ruthlessness, sincerity and love.

EPILOGUE

Three days later. The River Suir, Waterford, Ireland.

"May the curse of Mary Malone and her nine blind illegitimate children chase you so far over the Hills of Damnation that the Lord himself can't find you with a telescope," repeated the Duke of Rakecombe, peering up at his wife.

"Very good," she flattered, so he tugged a lock of hair until she was forced to bend down for a kiss.

The river gurgled its delight while he savoured the taste of early strawberries on his wife's lips and, as he lay with his head in her lap, he couldn't think of a better place to be than by this river, kissing his wife and learning curses.

As Rainham had instructed, he'd taken just a sennight to honeymoon with his duchess in Waterford, and not only had he met Aideen's father but also the infamous Uncle Seamus.

Her father had ranted about weak-willed English maggots, but a half hour in the study alone with him had seen a change of opinion. He was still the Duke of

Ruthlessness after all, and love, as Jack had proclaimed, didn't bring about miracles.

Then the much talked-of Seamus…

At this very moment, the jovial chap was bellowing to his dogs further along the river after they'd all enjoyed a picnic together. Her uncle was without doubt ingenious, an artisan, and he'd promised to craft a new cane for Rakecombe – an Irish wolfhound would grace the head this time, with onyx black eyes and a cherry tongue.

Aideen and he would return to London in a few days, as Napoleon gathered his strength and battle loomed.

Fraught times lay ahead, but Aideen would always be by his side, not separate but joined, for as long as forever would allow them.

The previous day, they'd discussed and agreed upon precautions for both their protection once they returned to the city. She'd removed a leaf from a tree with her red-enamelled pistol and nearly gutted him with her little knife. He'd apologised again for not trusting her, and thanked her for saving his life.

Talking late into the night, he'd offered to leave his work behind, but Aideen had tugged his hair and told him not to be ridiculous, that the country needed men like him more than ever with the coming danger.

Both of them had heard the unsaid words of sacrifice and love, care yet worry.

Long fingers brushed the curl from his forehead, halting his thoughts.

"Blasted thing," he said lazily.

"I adore it," she declared. "You appear…boyish."

"How dare you!" And before she had time to struggle, he reared and rolled her back, pressing his wife onto the woollen blanket with the weight of his body. "I shall have to ensure my ruthless mien returns for London."

"Oh good." She grinned, eyes hinting of dark chocolate on this bright day. "I miss my duke's cold stares and curt nods. They make me feel all peculiar."

He stroked her cheek, suddenly serious. "I can be that creature as well, Aideen. Priggish and aloof, but I will try not to–"

A kiss took his words, long and slow. "Don't you dare," she commanded. "It would be akin to me suppressing my curses. 'Tis a part of you and a part I rather love. I love all of you, Alexander. The cold, the hot, the passionate, the ruthless. They make you."

"My Aideen," he whispered, lowering his head.

"Do you think," she purred, as he plotted kisses along her bare shoulder, the sleeve having coincidently lowered with his teeth, "that I might at last know what your tattoo stands for?"

He smiled against her skin, deciding he would confide tonight about his alias's initial, but for now...

"Desperately in love? Dying for you?" he teased, but she shook her head, laughing.

He stole that laughter with a searing kiss and her body arched.

Mindful of their location, he gentled his touch. "I am both of those, my love," he murmured against her lips. "You are my wild River Suir, forever flowing with life and spirit, beguiling my mind with your melody, stealing my soul with your eyes, twining your grip around me. You quenched my ire and I was swept away with nary a chance to breathe."

She gazed up, lips parted and eyes moist.

Lust and love flared within and his head lowered to–

A cascade of freezing cold water landed on his back, a growl rumbling in his ear.

"Murchú! Gerroff the duke, ya great lump," shouted Seamus, "although from what I could hear, we've made an Irishman out of you in a matter of days with all that 'quenching' blarney."

Alexander hauled himself from his duchess, the Irish wolfhound puppy still attached to his back – the puppy that would be returning to England with them.

Smiling, he imagined the butler's face as this huge ball of fur hurtled and skidded around the marble hallways. The little blighter chewed his shirt and he grabbed hold of the drenched bundle, flumping it into Aideen's lap to many un-duchess-like shrieks.

"I do seem to have kissed my very own enchanting blarney stone quite thoroughly," Alex agreed, gazing at Aideen's rosy swollen lips.

She grinned and the part of him which was pitiless and ruthless grinned back, thinking of all the ways he would kiss her tonight.

"You do know," his wife replied, "that kissing the blarney stone is considered proof of perseverance, courage, and agility because, my duke…" She twirled a ringlet, raven eyes twinkling. "…it's so awkward to get at."

Seamus guffawed, and Alexander raised his duchess's fingers to his lips, basking in the love of her gaze whilst returning it with equal measure.

"And that is what makes my reward all the sweeter, *fy cariad aur.*" And Murchú yipped his puppy delight.

The End

ALSO BY EMILY WINDSOR

RULES OF THE ROGUE SERIES

An Earl in Wolf's Clothing (Book 1)

From the hallowed halls of London's Almack's to the unkempt taverns of Drury Lane, from whispered words in glittering theatres to seductive encounters at Vauxhall Gardens – an earl must pursue his love.
A determined lady. An even more determined gentleman.
Let the pursuit begin…

Merry Christmas, my Viscount (Book 2 - Novella)

Seduce a rogue? By Christmas Eve? What a troubling resolution for the most proper widow Mrs Lily Mereworth to be left with… How? And more importantly, who?
Ghost stories on a windy night, swordplay down the Great Portrait Gallery, a lady and a spymaster with no thought to love… Merry Christmas.

Let Sleeping Dukes Lie (Book 3)

"Strait-laced. Ruthless. Arrogant." – The Duke of Rakecombe has forever shunned love...and with good reason. "Forthright. Impudent. Capricious saucebox." – The fiery Miss Aideen Quinlan refuses to be shunned, unable to erase the memory of the duke's vehement kiss...
An unlikely couple, an unquenchable passion.
Resistance is futile.

Marquess to a Flame (Book 4)

The Marquess of Winterbourne has long been guided by his *Rules of the Rogue,* but as spy for the Crown, his next mission will break every single one. Sent to the wilds of Cornwall to beguile secrets from a lady, the last thing this rogue expects is to unearth his own buried heart.

NEW - GAMES OF GENTLEMEN SERIES

The Duke of Diamonds - Out Now

Casper Brook, the eighth Duke of Rothwell, has forever spurned frivolous pleasures, his restless emotions remaining buried beneath duty and command.
Yet when a titian-haired minx perches upon his ducal desk and claims to know the whereabouts of his one burning obsession, a game of wits and passion erupts...

CAPTIVATING DEBUTANTES SERIES

Captivated by the Viscount

ALSO BY EMILY WINDSOR

My Captive Earl

Her Noble Captive

ABOUT THE AUTHOR

Emily grew up in the north of England on a diet of historical romance and classical mythology.

Unfortunately, you couldn't study Georgian slang or the Regency London Season, so she did the next best thing and gained a degree in Classics and History instead. This 'led' to an eight-year stint in engineering.

Having left city life, she now lives in a dilapidated farmhouse in the country where her days are spent writing, fixing the leaky roof, battling the endless vegetation and finding pictures of well-tied cravats.

Happy Reading,
Love,
Emily
x

facebook.com/AuthorEmilyWindsor
pinterest.com/EmilyWindsorBks
bookbub.com/authors/emily-windsor
goodreads.com/EmilyWindsor
amazon.com/author/emilywindsor

Printed in Great Britain
by Amazon

49420738R00168